DRAWN TO YOU

VOLUMES 1-3

VANESSA BOOKE

Drawn to You: Volumes 1-3
Copyright 2015 Vanessa Booke

Editing by Rogena Mitchell-Jones Manuscript Service
For more information visit Rogenamitchell.com

FORMATTING BY SHOUTLINES DESIGN

This is a work of fiction. Names, characters, places, and incidents either are the product of the author's imagination or are used fictitiously, and any resemblance to actual persons, living or dead, brands, media, business establishments, events, or locales is entirely coincidental.

Without limiting the rights under copyright reserved above, no part of this publication may be reproduced, stored in or introduced into a retrieval system, or transmitted, in any form, or by any means (electronic, mechanical, photocopying, recording, or otherwise) without the prior written permission of both the copyright owner and the above publisher of this book. This is a work of fiction.

This ebook is licensed for your personal enjoyment only. This ebook may not be re-sold or given away to other people. If you would like to share this book with another person, please purchase an additional copy for each recipient. If you're reading this book and did not purchase it, or it was not purchased for your use only, then please return it and purchase your own copy. Thank you for respecting the hard work of this author.

DEDICATION

To my husband, thank you for helping to make my dreams come true —in more ways than one.

Happy 30th birthday, sweetheart.

"Sometimes I have the strangest feeling about you. Especially when you are near me as you are now. It feels as though I had a string tied here under my left rib where my heart is, tightly knotted to you in a similar fashion. And when you go to Ireland, with all that distance between us, I am afraid that this cord will be snapped, and I shall bleed inwardly."
— Charlotte Brontë, *Jane Eyre*

*"The great art of life is sensation,
to feel that we exist, even in pain."*
- Lord Byron

VOLUME ONE

PROLOGUE

Her hot breath blows in my ear as her skinny little fingers wrap around my hand to wake me. It's well past midnight, but I know whom the familiar touch belongs. Every night she sneaks into my bed and wraps her arms around my chest, snuggling deep beneath the covers. Her presence has become a nightly ritual leaving the smell of her lavender shampoo permanently etched into my sheets. My eyes flutter open just in time to see her angelic face inches from mine.

In the moonlight, Emily's blonde streaks shine & curl in golden locks that cascade down her shoulders like a golden waterfall. Her pink lips split into a mischievous smile that immediately makes me chuckle.

Over the past four years, I've gained a family by moving with my mother to the city. A family that includes a new sister and two older brothers named Nicholas and Alexander. My mom has been working as a housemaid for the StoneHaven family since I was in seventh grade. Although it was a big transition living here, I can't say that I regret it. I never realized how much I wanted to be part of something normal. Living in the same house as a New York millionaire should be intimidating, but Mr. StoneHaven has been nothing but kind to my mother and me.

It's a stark contrast to the relationship I had with my father. He was deported when I was six after a neighbor made an anonymous call to U.S. Immigration and Customs Enforcement. I wasn't sorry to see him go. He spent most of his days drinking. The rest of the time he spent verbally abusing my mother, but there's not a day that goes by that I don't think about what it would've been like if he had stayed.

"What are you doing here, Lily Pad?" I ask.

She giggles at the utterance of the nickname I've given her. I lift my head from my pillow to get a better view of her face through the darkness. Her fingers intertwine together as she balances back and forth on her heels. Her nervous gesture tugs at my heart. I have a feeling she's going to be a bit of a troublemaker when she's older. She slips her hand into mine staring at the ridges on my hand like a fortune teller looking into my future.

"I couldn't sleep."

She's only twelve, but in a few years, I know I'll have to help her brothers chase away other boys. Her innocence is endearing enough to make anyone wish they were her age again.

"Why not?" I ask, reaching over to ruffle her hair. She bites her lip right before the words came rushing out of her mouth.

"I heard my mom and dad fighting."

Emily's earnest little eyes look up at me through her blonde lashes. A warm sensation fills my chest as she waits with baited breath for me to say something.

"I'm sorry, Lily Pad."

I stroke her shoulder wincing at the sight of her eyes watering. She pushes her blonde bangs from her face. The intensity of her stare nearly takes my breath away. Unlike her brothers, Emily's eyes are a mixture of green and blue hues. I've tried painting them, but I can never quite get the color right. I've realized they're not replicable. They're one of a kind, much like her.

"Tristan, can I sleep next to you?"

I smile at her request. Despite the time I've been here, I don't think Emily's father or mother would appreciate their daughter sleeping in the same bed as the maid's son. I slip out of bed and gesture for Emily to slip underneath the covers.

"How about I read to you until you fall asleep?" I ask, clicking on the lamp near my nightstand.

"Okay," she says with a disappointed look.

VANESSA BOOKE

I walk to my bookshelf and scan the titles stacked against the wall. In this house, even the help reads. I guess that's what happens when your mother works for the owner of a publishing company. Fortunately for me, there's never a shortage of poetry to read.

"What are you in the mood for? Keats? Byron? Clifton? Melville?"

"Byron!"

Her excited face sends a smile across mine. I take a seat next to the bed and skim through the pages looking for the perfect poem.

"Here's a good one."

Emily leans against my pillow and rolls to the side to face me. Her eyes flutter sleepily as she tries her best to stay awake. I read through several of Byron's poems, but it isn't until I get to *She Walks in Beauty* that I have Emily's attention again.

"She walks in beauty, like the night... Of cloudless climes and starry skies; And all that's best of dark and bright... Meet in her aspect and her eyes; Thus mellowed to that tender light... Which heaven to gaudy day denies..."

"Tristan?"

I look up to find Emily staring at me with a tired gaze and a small grin.

"What's wrong, Lily Pad?"

"Do you think I'm beautiful?" she asks, drawing a circle on a spot next to her pillow.

I feel my heart in my throat as she stares at me waiting for my response. Emily's grown up so fast over the past year. Every time I take my eyes off her, it's like she's grown another inch. I love her like the little sister I never had, even if she isn't mine. The truth is there's nothing I wouldn't do for her.

"You're the most beautiful girl I've ever met," I say, leaning in to ruffle her hair once again.

Another smile sweeps across her face as she leans over and wraps her warm little arms around my neck. She hugs me tight, bringing me closer to her as she places her cheek against my chest. Her familiar smell of lavender invades my senses permanently affixing to my clothes. I don't think I'll ever get the smell out, but I guess it doesn't really matter because if I had a choice, I wouldn't do it anyway.

"Tristan?"

"Yes?"

"Will you kiss me?"

I can't help but laugh at her request. She reaches up and grabs a hold of my black hair. I feel a slight tug as she twirls a piece of it in her fingers, carefully studying it as if there's some secret message written in my DNA. She leans back against me, and before I have a chance to answer her question, her eyes flutter closed. It's only a few moments before I feel her chest moving against me. I reach underneath her and pull her small body from my bed. Despite how much Emily's grown this past year, she's lighter than she looks. She reaches around my neck and pulls herself closer to me as I carefully carry her back to her room. She doesn't wake again even after I roll her onto her side, covering and tucking the ends of the bed sheets beneath her.

"If you still want me to kiss you when you're my age, I will," I whisper to her through the darkness. "Goodnight, Lily Pad."

"Stefan, please don't do this."

I'm halfway down the hall from Emily's bedroom when I hear the broken plea echoing throughout the house. The eerily familiar voice propels me forward through the darkness of the hallway. A ray of light cascades down through the study reflecting shadows on the wood floor. Two rays to be exact. I quietly step closer following the voices coming from inside. As I cross the front of the doorway, I hear the voice call out again. The realization of who is in there hits me like a freight train. Mom? *What is she doing up so late?* I step closer, carefully positioning myself outside. The door sits cracked open just wide enough to see their blurry figures standing close together.

It takes me a moment to recognize the other voice as being

that of Stefan. The few times I've heard him talk it was only to bark orders at the help in the kitchen. To my surprise, my mother presses herself into his arms. The intimate gesture leaves me reeling in shock. *What the hell is going on?* I've never seen Emily's father anywhere near my mother. He's always kept his distance around the both of us. I'm halfway through the door when my mother's voice pierces through the air.

I watch in confusion as she sobs into Stefan's jacket quietly pounding her hands on his chest. Stefan grips her shoulders and slowly takes a step back in what I can only assume is an effort to keep her at arms distance.

"I'm sorry, Rosaline. If Evelyn finds out, she'll take everything from me," he says, brushing the back of his neck.

"So you're just going to throw us out like we're garbage?"

"You can stay until you find another position somewhere else. If you'd like, I can get you a position with another family."

"You asshole," she screams.

The thought hits me that maybe Emily wasn't hearing her mother and father fight, but rather my mother and her father. I can't be the only one hearing this. I turn and stare down the hall listening carefully for footsteps, but none come.

"Rosaline, stop."

"You told me you loved me. You said that you were going to leave your wife and that *we* would be a family."

"I have to think about what's best for my children," he says, annoyed.

"No, you're just thinking about what's best for you. You got your dick wet and now you're acting like none of this meant anything to you."

I clench my teeth at the bluntness of my mother's words. Growing up, I never once heard my mother say anything so crude.

"I do care for you, but I'm not leaving Evelyn. I can't tear this family apart."

"So that's it then?"

DRAWN TO YOU

"I can provide you with a year's severance pay. It should help you get back on your feet. If you need more, tell me."

"I can't believe this is actually happening."

I watch as my mother presses her hand to her mouth holding back another sob from escaping. A fire rages through me at Stefan's obvious indifference to my mother's tears. *How can he be so fucking cold?* I guess it shouldn't be surprising that someone so wealthy would think a quick fix is to just throw money at the situation.

"I'm sorry, I don't want to hurt you," he says, touching her shoulder lightly.

"It's too late."

"I want to help you."

"Keep your money, Stefan. I don't want anything else from you."

My mother's hand lands hard across his face with an intensity that even surprises me. Even more astonishing is Stefan's restraint and composure. He doesn't flinch at the heat of her hand. Instead, he merely straightens his jacket and walks over to fill himself another glass of brandy. Tears stream down my mother's cheeks as she turns away from him clenching her apron in her hands. I feel a pull in my chest at the sight of such a forlorn look on her face. I hold back the anger that's been slowly building as it erupts through my veins. *How long has this been going on?* I grit my teeth as Stefan stands a few feet away from her seemingly unaffected by her distress. It's hard to believe this is the same man that I've looked up to for the past year. This cold asshole isn't who I thought he was.

It isn't long before my mother forces herself to walk out of the room. Before I have a chance to leave, she catches me standing just outside the room. As if her tears weren't bad enough, the humiliation washing over her breaks my heart. The need to comfort her overwhelms me, but I know there isn't anything I can say that will make any of this right. I have no control over this situation and that scares the hell out of me.

"Did you hear all of that?" she asks.

I nod, unable to form words for the anger and disappointment that radiates through me. She slips her arm around me and I embrace her. Hot tears slip down her cheeks soaking my shoulder. I murmur I'm sorry against her long ebony hair.

"We need to pack our things and go," she says.

Go? I look around the halls of the limestone mansion that I've learned to call home. My dream of having a normal life evaporates into thin air in a matter of seconds. My mind wanders back to the blonde angel only a few doors down and the words that she whispered to me. *I hope you stay with us forever.* I guess forever was never meant to be.

> *she is my dark lady, my* MUSE.

CHAPTER 1

TRISTAN

FOUR YEARS LATER

I start the night like any other night at the Pleasure Chest, dragging one of my subs into a playroom. Although I like to keep my relationships brief, I promise each one that no experience is ever the same. The women who come to me to play don't necessarily live the BDSM lifestyle, but they relish carrying out their fantasies in the bedroom with me. Most of them are high-strung CEOs, stockbrokers, and even housewives looking to relax. I'm not one to argue if a paddle on their ass is how they like to let loose, but I'm more than happy to oblige them.

They always beg me to tie them up, gag them, or bring them to release with the heat of my tongue and the pressure of my hand. It doesn't matter what toy or prop they want me to use on them. I always accomplish the task at hand. The only requirement that I ask before we begin our time together is an agreed upon safe word and the opportunity to incorporate them into my art. It's utterly beautiful the way women fall to pieces in your arms at the peak of their orgasms and there's nothing in the world like watching someone lose all control.

I step outside of the Pleasure Chest smelling like latex and day old pussy. After a long night of playing, I'm ready for a long hot shower and a warm cigarette. A blast of cold air hits me as I lift my last soiled cigarette to my lips and flick the lighter. I inhale the warm burn letting it filter through me as the cold wind whips at my cheeks. Tonight was a lot more lucrative than I had expected. It seems the kinksters at the Pleasure Chest get a kick out of my paintings and as my friend Vivian predicted, a couple of Doms approached me about commissioning a private session with them and their subs. I couldn't ask for a better twenty-first birthday gift, especially when I only have fifty bucks to my name.

My cell phone buzzes and I flip it in time to see Vivian's name illuminating across the screen with a text:

Vivian: I got a gig Saturday night at The Pearl Hotel and the catering manager just called asking if I knew anyone who could serve. I mentioned your name. Text me back if you're in.

Serve? I could definitely use the money right now, but dealing with rich bastards is not in my repertoire. Although I would rather slum it on the streets, I'm not just looking after myself. I have my mother to keep an eye on and lately she hasn't been doing so well. I slide open the keypad on my phone and text Vivian back.

Me: I'll think about it.

My phone buzzes again in my pocket. She's probably pissed that I'm not immediately jumping all over this gig, but how can I? I don't even own a suit, let alone dress shoes.

Vivian: Asshole. You had better be there tonight.

VANESSA BOOKE

The pungent scent of booze, stale cigarettes, and weed trails behind me as I climb the stairs to the third-floor apartment complex where my mother and I live. On the way up, I pass a row of strung-out losers hanging at the top of the staircase. The two teens lift their heads just high enough to nod at me in recognition, but their gaze quickly falls back to the pipe in their hand. They haven't moved an inch since the last time I saw them, except maybe to refill their stash.

My eyes strain through the darkness of the living room as I walk through the front door of our six-hundred square foot apartment. No matter how many times I open the blinds, they always seem to find their way back to being closed. If people actually gave a shit around here, they'd probably wonder if we're vampires.

I pass a stack of collection notices scattered across the roach-infested floor. To my surprise, there's even a stack of scratchers sitting on top of the coffee table in a pile of ash. Mom must've bought these over at Jimmy's liquor. It doesn't matter how many times I tell the owner not to sell booze or lotto tickets to my mother, he does it anyway. *This is our life*—lingering between debt and wishful thinking.

After an hour of cleaning up the apartment, I finally manage to find my way into the bedroom. The room is just big enough to fit a queen mattress and a dresser, leaving little room to walk around. I spot my mother's frail body splattered across the bed. This isn't the first time I've found her passed out drunk, so it's no surprise to see her in this unconscious state. I walk over and gently shake her leg, but she doesn't move. After several seconds, I shake harder. *How much did she drink this time?* Panic quickly filters through me at the stillness of my mother's petite frame.

"Mom, wake up," I command.

"Tristan?"

"What are you doing still asleep?"

She doesn't answer me. Instead, she rolls her head to the other side of the pillow. The smell of dry vomit radiates off her clothing. Her long chestnut hair sits in a messy half bun. I lift her from the bed hoping to get her up and moving around with an actual shower, but her frail body hangs limp in my arms as I carry her into the bathroom. She probably doesn't even know the last time she showered. Just outside the door, I find a new empty bottle of Jack Daniels. The sight of it is an ugly reminder that the past is never really in the past. It doesn't matter how many months go by, she isn't getting better with time. After stripping her pajamas off her, I lay my mother in the tub beneath the warm shower spray. A soft moan escapes her as the water hits her face.

"Tristan."

She lifts her head just enough to look at me through glazed bloodshot eyes.

"Mom, what are you doing to yourself?"

"He hasn't written me back. He hasn't come to get me," she mumbles.

The *he* she so lovingly mentions is the man who's the reason for our current miserable existence. The same man who selfishly ruined our lives by kicking my mother and me out in the streets. It's been four years since we moved out of the StoneHaven's lavish house to the gritty dump we call home. Four years since I lost my best friend and the only family I've ever really known.

"He's not going to come here, Mom."

"He will," she says as she shifts in my arms. "He loves me."

"Mom, you have to let go. Whatever he told you was a lie. He wouldn't have done this if he loved you."

The broken look on my mother's face nearly shatters me. She turns her cheek and sobs hysterically into my shoulder. Her vice-like grip doesn't let up as I slowly run a damp sponge across her face. I turn the shower water to a warmer spray and kneel to wash the dried up vomit from her hair, carefully sponging away the evidence from her face. She shivers, whimpering like a small child. The woman who raised me, who used to be so strong, is now in pieces on our bathroom floor.

I leave my mother to soak in the tub while I rummage through the apartment for a pair of clean pajamas. To my dismay, I find a crumpled up news article sitting beneath the bed covers. The name in the headline immediately draws my attention. *StoneHaven Publishing to Host Book Launch at Pearl Hotel.* Great. This is the reason why my mother went on another drinking bender. Wait, isn't this the same place Vivian was asking me to serve with her?

I flip open my phone and find Vivian's previous text. To my surprise, the name of the hotel matches up. It only takes me a matter of seconds to realize that this is an opportunity to face Stefan that I probably won't ever have again. I'm sure he's never been to The Bronx and besides going to the Pleasure Chest, I've avoided coming to Manhattan at all costs.

Me: Viv, I'm free to cover the shift you needed.

In a matter of seconds, my phone vibrates with a new text from Vivian.

Vivian: See you then.

> "she is my dark lady, my MUSE."

CHAPTER 2

TRISTAN

Fucking rich bastards. A strange rush of anxiety filters through me as I spot Stefan smoking a cigar on the other side of The Pearl Hotel's ballroom. The sight of him standing there sends a wave of nausea through me. Despite the many years that have passed, only the crinkles around his eyes are evidence of stress. The same can't be said for my mother. Her years of drinking have taken a toll on her physically and mentally. She's not the same vibrant woman she used to be. Not even close.

    I cringe as Stefan's boisterous laughter fills the room. A crowd of guests gather near him, entranced by the sound of his voice. I swipe a glass of champagne from a nearby table watching as a cluster of suits surround the appetizers, nibbling at the assortment of overpriced cheese and organic fruit. My stomach rumbles at the thought of how much food is being wasted on Stefan's guests, but I doubt it means anything to him. From the looks of this hotel, he's accustomed to surrounding himself with the company of extravagant things. I guess nothing has changed. *Money over love. Money over family.*

    I've never felt so out of place as I do at this very moment.

DRAWN TO YOU

Even the over the top décor of the room is a stark contrast to the worn out dress shoes and slacks given to me by my mother. I promised Vivian I would help serve drinks to guests tonight, but I haven't mustered the strength to let Stefan out of my sight.

"Hey, are you okay?"

Vivian pops into view with a sterling tray—a tray of what I can only assume is some kind of over-priced sushi. Her curious eyes watch me as I shift on my heels. "You've been staring daggers at the corner over there for the past half hour," she says, nodding toward Stefan. "What's eating you?"

My past has never really been up for discussion when it comes to our friendship, but I feel compelled to tell her my sorted history anyway.

"That older man over there…."

Vivian's eyes light up as she spots Stefan in his charcoal suit standing amongst a flurry of VIP guests.

"The suit with the cigar?"

"Yeah."

"This is his party…"

"He used to sleep with my mother," I say, gritting my teeth at the sound of my confession.

"I'm assuming it didn't end well."

I shake my head, feeling one hell of a headache coming on. It kills me to know he's here drinking whiskey and smoking his Cuban cigars while my mother is at home detoxing from all of the shit she has in her system. Our apartment still smells like vomit and whiskey.

"No, it fucking didn't," I confess.

"What did he do?"

What eats away at me is not what Stefan did. Sending my mother out the door without a second thought is fucked up, but the final nail in that coffin was when he refused to acknowledge any of her letters. It didn't take long for her to shut down after each one came back returned and unopened. She stopped going outside after that and she didn't bother ever trying to find another job again.

"I'm going to go take a smoke break."

"Go," Vivian says with a small smile. "I'll cover you." Despite the massive amount of people at the party, Vivian seems undisturbed by the room full of wealthy tycoons and entrepreneurs. In fact, I think it's safe to say that she's annoyingly humming with excitement. *At least one of us is enjoying this party.*

"I'm going to go take this tray back to the kitchen."

"Tristan, don't lose your shit. The night is almost over, and then you won't have to see him anymore."

"Thanks, Viv."

"Seriously, just try not to get us both fired." She smiles. "Don't go dueling pistols at dawn or anything."

"Don't worry, I left my white gloves at home," I say.

> she is my dark lady, my MUSE.

CHAPTER 3

EMILY

These heels are killing me. Never mind the fact that my dress dips way too low, but I'm almost sure I'll break an ankle if I step the wrong way in these heels one more time. My evening dress flares out in turquoise waves as I move across floor toward the refreshment table near the lobby. Even the beaded hem comes alive as it sparkles each time the lighting from the chandelier hits it. As much as I love the it, I'll be happy when I can trade it for a pair shorts and a t-shirt. My father promised my brothers and me if we attended this evening's book launch, he'd give us the keys to our summer beach house for this weekend.

I pass the appetizer table, narrowly avoiding running into Mr. Stokes, aka Mr. *Strokes*, my father's accountant as he hovers over the assortment of food. He pulls his attention away from his plate long enough to assess me with a critical but curious gaze.

"Ms. Emily, you've grown so much. What a beautiful dress…"

I can almost see him salivating as his eyes slowly trace the dip of my dress with interest. He slides a hand in his pants pocket and I cringe at the thought that he might be touching himself through an open hole. It wouldn't be the first time I've caught him doing it in public. It's the main reason why Ceci came up with the nickname, *Mr. Strokes*. Now, every time I see him I have to remind myself not to say it aloud. I watch as his salt and pepper eyebrows furrow in disappointment as he spots the shawl surrounding my shoulders. I pull it tighter around my naked skin hoping that my obvious discomfort will deter him away. I'm not used to having men look at me the way he does, especially men who are three times my age.

"How is your brother Alexander doing running the business?"

"He loves it. I'm sure my father will be happy to retire earlier than he expected."

"Amazing. Alexander is going to make an incredible CEO."

It's true. Alex is the brains in the family. He somehow graduated law school early. A feat most people don't even accomplish and he did it all while working at StoneHaven Publishing.

"And your brother, Nicholas?"

"He is… Well, I'm not sure what he wants to do. He's still in school."

I've always found it funny that my two brothers look similar, but they couldn't be more different. Alex is level headed, down to earth, and at times, a little predictable. Nick is sort of a wild card. My parents have been trying to pull the reins on him for a while.

"Emily!"

I turn and spot Ceci scurrying across the ballroom floor with a wicked grin on her face. She's not even halfway over when her eyes lock on Mr. *Strokes*. She throws me a knowing look as she lifts an eyebrow at him.

"Ceci, you made it!"

"Emily, your brothers are looking for you," she says.

Time to make my escape.

"So what's on tonight's agenda?"

"Doing our best to avoid grabby hands and taking advantage of the chocolate fondue." I smile.

"Emily, you're always such a good girl," Ceci says beside me as we stare out into the crowd of guests. "Forget about behaving tonight. Be daring. Go blow some guy at the coat check-in."

I blush at the thought of going in the back of the hotel coatroom with just some random stranger. Not because I'm afraid. No, because the thought of doing it sends a thrilling sensation throughout my body—a feeling I can only assume will multiply such an experience.

"No," I blush.

"At least make out with someone."

"I'm all right."

"You're boring." Ceci huffs. "C'mon, you can practice on me."

"Go practice on my brother, Nicholas."

"Practice what on me?"

Nicholas's bright smile pops into view as he rounds the corner of the ballroom entrance. Trailing just behind him is my brother, Alex. A flurry of women descends to the dance floor at the sight of them. Even the older women nearby seem to trip over themselves. I've always been envious of the way people seem to be drawn to my brothers. No guy has ever looked at me the way women see them.

> she is my dark lady, my MUSE.

CHAPTER 4

TRISTAN

I almost convince myself that no matter how this evening ends, I'll leave here in one piece. I believe it with all of my soul until the moment she walks into the room. My breath constricts at the sight of a familiar blonde angel entering the room. The sight of her sends a strange shooting pain in my chest. I watch her as she crosses the ballroom floor like a figure from one of my paintings wearing a bright blush on her cheeks and her hair spun in a bun. *It can't be her.* It never crossed my mind to think that Emily would be here tonight. It's been more than four years since I've seen her and the last time, she was four years younger with a goofy smile permanently fixed to her face.

Her name floods my mind with memories of late night poetry, warm embraces, and that familiar smell of lavender. *My Lily Pad*—except she's not so little anymore. The figure gliding across the room is very much a woman. The turquoise dress she's wearing does little to hide the curves that accentuate her petite frame—curves that weren't there before. My emotions pull at me as her cheerful smile makes the room seem just a little bit brighter. I step forward hoping to steal a glimpse of her to take with me when I leave, but I stop myself at the appearance of Alexander and Nicholas beside her. The three illuminate the room with their mere presence. I'm tempted to follow them, but I stop myself. I'd hate to think that I came here to give Stefan a piece of my mind only to be thwarted by the family I once thought I deserved.

I slip away and make my way to the kitchen to drop-off my tray, stopping for a moment to search for a cigarette. I'm just about to light up when I feel something, or rather a *someone*, run straight into me. It isn't until I hear her yelp that I realize it's a woman. The impact of her small frame takes me by surprise as she sends us both tumbling to the marble floor. The sound of glass shattering spills across the room as the force knocks the tray from my hands. My heart constricts as crystal goes flying everywhere. If I didn't want to make a scene before, I'm sure as hell making one now.

A stinging sensation runs up the side of my back as we land with a loud thud. A crowd of gasps circulates through the hall as guests turn and inch closer to see the spectacle. I wipe the sliding mess of champagne off my face and look up to find bright aquamarine eyes staring down at me in shock.

Shit. Her.

To my surprise, she doesn't immediately untangle herself from my lap. Her stare grows increasingly intense as if she's trying to mentally extract information from me. Several seconds pass before she finally moves, or at least tries to move. I hear the sound of her dress swishing as she steadies her arms at the side of my head. She wiggles to free a part of her skirt trapped beneath me and I inwardly groan at the pressure of her rubbing against me. Fucking hell. My cock twitches leaving me with a growing erection.

"Stop doing that."

"What?"

Her startled eyes return to me with a look of confusion. I silently chide myself as my gaze wanders down her slender neckline to the top of her breast. The sight of her disheveled outfit taunts me as she sits slightly exposed. She isn't old enough to be running around this party by herself. In fact, if it were up to me, I'd say she's not old enough to be wearing a dress like that. I roll to my left freeing her dress and giving her just enough room to sit up. As if to avoid our awkward encounter, the crowd around us quickly returns to their polite conversation and drinks. I dust my slacks off, acutely aware that I've torn a hole in my pants at the knee. The truth hits me as I kneel down to pick up the shattered champagne glasses.

Fuck. Vivian is going to kill me.

I can only imagine how much it's going to be to replace these stupid glasses. It's not as if the hotel is just going to be like, *oh, you broke three hundred dollar glasses? That's okay.* And it's not like the fifty bucks I'm making tonight will cover even one of these glasses.

"I'm so sorry, my heels..." Her soft voice interrupts my thoughts as I gather the shards of glass together. I watch her as she brushes back a few loose strands of hair and leans over. "Let me help you," she offers.

There's something in her voice—a strand of despair that shakes my very core. I look over to find a bright blush staining her cheeks. My heart squeezes and I find myself drawn to her pink lips that are slipped between her teeth. I ignore the sudden need to reassure her that it's all right, to touch the skin just below the base of her neck, and the growing desire to pull her back down on top of me.

"You should be careful where you're going. You could've hurt yourself..." I say hoping to clear my head of tempting thoughts.

"You nearly killed me." I smirk.

"I'm sorry, I didn't look where I was going and then suddenly, there you were."

Her shy smile only seems to draw my attention back to the beauty of her face. My hands itch to touch her, to hold her to me, but instead, I busy my hands again picking up the final remnants of glass.

"Ow."

A stream of blood gushes from her finger and palm as she pulls a shard of glass from her skin. Without thinking, I grab her hand and wrap the hem of my jacket around it. She looks up at me with a small smile and a look of curiosity as I squeeze the fabric to her skin. A trail of blood trickles down her wrist evidence that the cut is deeper than I had hoped. I look into her eyes, wishfully hoping in the back of my mind that she somehow remembers me, and that I'm not just a figment of her imagination because she was always real to me.

"Thank you."

Several seconds pass and any hope of her recognizing me quickly dissipates.

"We can't stand here all night," I say. "Let's get something else to wrap this."

I pull her with me, and we silently head toward one of the employee bathrooms to look for a first aid kit. It isn't until the touch of her skin makes contact with mine that I realize she's touching me. A strange sensation fills me as I spot her hand in mine. I look back down at her, but she doesn't look up. I almost chuckle at the sight of her brushing back a strand of her hair. The nervous tick is all too familiar.

Try as I may, I can't ignore the feeling that her hand naturally fits mine—it's just a little too right.

"My name is Emily," she offers, with a blush.

My Lily Pad.

CHAPTER 5

EMILY

'Emily, you're always such a good girl.' Ceci's words replay in my mind as I stare up at the stranger walking so closely beside me. He ushers us through the crowd never letting my hand go, despite the cluster of people standing in our way. It's strange to say I feel a connection to someone I've just met, but I do with him. There's something about the way he touches me that sets my skin on fire. Although I know it can't be true, it feels familiar in a way.

His long dark hair hangs just shy of his collar as it sits pushed black in one long swoop of gel. From the length of it, I can guess that he isn't used to having it slicked back. It's easy to imagine him wearing it down like some heavy metal singer from the eighties with leather pants and a black tee. He would look good in leather pants. *Too good.*

Now I'm glad that Ceci decided not to follow me when I left for some fresh air. My best friend has a knack for seducing men and women. Some are even twice her age. Fortunately for me, she's on her best behavior tonight. *At least so far.* I look up to find the handsome waiter staring at me. His face looks incredibly familiar, but

DRAWN TO YOU

I can't put my finger on when I've seen him before. Perhaps I saw him waiting at another party.

"Do you work at the hotel?" I ask as I try to fill the silence.

"No, I'm just here for tonight."

I wince as he runs my finger underneath hot water and warmth spreads through my body as his leg brushes mine. The employee bathroom doesn't give us much space to move, especially when it isn't any bigger than a broom closet. I focus my attention on his hands hoping to calm my fluttering heart. I watch him as he meticulously wraps a small piece of gauze around my palm. His hand smoothly moves the cloth across my skin and the mere touch sends a shiver down my body.

He looks up as if noticing my reaction, and I feel the air slowly sucked out of the room. His finger brushes across the top of my hand with familiarity. Several seconds pass in silence, as the tension in the room grows thicker.

"So you never told me your name," I say.

Unfortunately, talking to guys is not on my skills list. Even Ceci would agree. A look of disappointment crosses his face as he contemplates my question. *Did he already tell me his name and I forgot?*

"It's Tristan."

Tristan? The name rolls over me like cold water filtering through my veins. It's been a long time since I've heard that name. *A very long time.* I bite back a gasp at the realization of who he is. *Tristan Knight. Our Tristan.* The last person that I ever thought I would see here. He looks different from what I remember. His once scrawny features are now replaced by thick muscles and a rugged jawline.

"Are you here with someone?" he asks, pulling me from my thoughts. The unusual question catches me off guard.

"Someone?"

"You look too young to be here on your own," he says, wrapping a piece of surgical tape around my finger. The touch of his hand sends a hot streak over my body and to my center.

"I'm sixteen," I reply.

He pauses for a moment and looks down at me. The gesture pulls my gaze to the suit that he's wearing. I didn't notice it at first, but there's something about the smoke color that brings out the green in his hazel eyes.

"Only sixteen?"

"Yes," I laugh. "How old are you?"

"Twenty-one," he smiles.

"I see."

"It's such a pity…" he begins to say.

"What?"

"That I can't kiss you."

"she is my dark lady, my muse."

CHAPTER 6

TRISTAN

The shocked look on Emily's face makes my lips itch to follow through with my jest. I don't know why I said it, but the thought of kissing her was the first thing that flew out of my mouth. As much as I would like to think that it isn't true, I'd be a fucking liar. In fact, I feel like a fucking pervert for even saying it. She's sixteen. Even the idea of other men looking at her that way would make me crazy. *Who am I kidding?* I'd punch the fucker that got near her. *Christ*. Seeing her makes me feel out of control.

I haven't spoken to her these past four years and now here I am, acting like a little school boy as I trip over my thoughts. *I need to focus.* I'm not here to reconcile my relationship with them. I'm here to confront Stefan about my mother and that's it. Perhaps I'd feel better if I punched him in the face. Maybe then I could move on.

"We should get back to the party," I suggest.

"Do you really not know who I am?"

A look of disappointment crosses her face as she brushes back a strand of her hair. To be honest, I wasn't even sure she remembered me. Maybe I was making those years with the

StoneHaven family a bigger deal than they were. After all, I was just part of the help. It didn't seem like it back then, but maybe I was kidding myself. Perhaps they spent time with me because they couldn't find anyone else to entertain them. I can't think of any other reason why they didn't come looking for me.

"Because I remember you," she says as she grabs my hand. "We missed you when you left. I couldn't believe it those first few days…"

Guilt racks its way into my chest as she purses her lips and carefully studies my face, looking for any hint of recognition. I need to get the hell out of here. *I can't do this.* Coming here was a mistake. I didn't think I would feel this way seeing her. Her beautiful smile is an ugly reminder of everything I lost. Now, the only thing I have to go home to is a dumpy apartment and a sick mother.

"I need to get back to my shift."

"Wait!"

I step around her and return to the party just in time to catch sight of Nicholas nudging Alexander's shoulder. I slow my step just to capture the image of them in my mind. I can't hear what they're saying, but they laugh together clinking their glasses of champagne. I wince at the realization that they're going on with their lives just fine without me while I'm barely holding myself together. Just like my mother. The thought leaves me breathlessly in pain. I scan the room for Vivian, but she's nowhere in sight. Fuck it. I'll apologize to her later.

Stefan's voice calls out to me as I'm halfway across the ballroom floor. The conversations of his guests die down to a murmur as he walks over to me. I keep my back to him hoping that I can still slip outside without causing a commotion, but I know it's too late.

"Tristan, stop."

I'm tempted to tell him to go fuck himself, but I hold myself back at the sight of Emily entering the room. Her cheeks turn red as she rushes over to me, her hand still wrapped in gauze. *Fuck it all to hell.* I turn to find a gray haired Stefan staring at me with wide eyes.

His gaze washes over me as he grinds the end of his cigar on a nearby ashtray and walks past a gawking crowd. I step back in reaction as he comes closer. Even my body is telling me to put space between us. Although it really doesn't matter the amount of space I put between us because it seems it will never be enough to forget him.

If I ever needed a cigarette, right now would be the perfect time.

"What are you doing here?" he asks.

I'm sure he never thought he'd see me again. I'm tempted to make a fool of myself and knock him in his teeth, but I can't seem to muster the strength with everyone watching. God, this is so fucked up. I force myself to remember the image of my mother lying passed out on the bed after I helped bathe her and the way she cried out for Stefan when I burned the newspaper article with his name.

"I was just leaving," I say through gritted teeth.

"Son, wait."

I'm not your son, you fucking shit. My fists clench at the way the word *son* rolls off his tongue. He reaches out to touch my shoulder, but I dodge his grasp. His face turns red in frustration as I stand there trying my best to look completely unaffected by the frown plastered to his face. I'm sure he hates being embarrassed in front of his guests. I spot Vivian maneuvering through the crowd of people still holding her silver tray. She's far enough away that I can't hear her, but I see her waving *stop* at me through the air. If I get in a fight with Stefan now, I'm sure she'll be fired for recommending me to do this gig.

"Is this how you treat someone who helped you?" Stefan asks, pulling my attention.

"Helped?" I scoff.

"Wait, what?" Alexander, Emily's eldest brother, steps through the crowd of onlookers and joins his father's side. "Dad, maybe we should take this outside."

I was never close to Alex, but it was probably the differences in age growing up. He was almost never home when he was away at college and when he was, he didn't even have much time to hang out with his own siblings.

"I think it's time for me to go."

"Tristan, wait," Emily squeaks. She fidgets with her dress staring past me as the words tumbled from her beautiful lips. "Stay. You've been so missed."

Nicholas's frown lightens as a small smile breaks across his face. He steps forward, hesitating just slightly before he pulls me into an embrace.

"Where have you been?" he asks. "High school wasn't the same without you." The surprising gesture sucks the tension that radiates beneath my skin as I return the embrace.

"You should ask your father."

"Dad said you and your mom moved out of state. Something about finding another job somewhere."

A feeling of nausea passes over me. Moved? That's the last thing I would call it. "Your dad lied," I answer bitterly.

"What?" Nicholas says.

"He's been lying to you," I say.

Nicholas turns back to Stefan with a confused look on his face.

"What is he talking about?"

I turn to leave, unwilling to watch the train wreck behind me. I need to get the fuck out of here. *Now.*

"Tristan, don't leave," Stefan calls out.

CHAPTER 7

EMILY

My father's voice sounds like it's on the verge of breaking as he tries to grab hold of Tristan. The scene in front of me is enough to send me over the edge. I feel hot tears sliding down my cheeks as the venomous words shot from Tristan's mouth. The hate that had spewed from him leaves me reeling in shock. Where is the loving and tender person that I used to know when I was little?

"Dad, let him go. He obviously doesn't want to talk to us," Alexander says.

Where has Tristan been all of this time? I keep asking myself the same question as I stare at his closed off expression. To my surprise, Alex steps forward and pulls my father to the side. He keeps his voice low, but I hear him talking about the crowd of guests watching us like zoo animals in cages. I'm sure any media at the event are salivating like hyenas over the scene we're making. I watch my father hand Tristan a crisp eggshell colored business card with gold lettering that reads *Stefan Isaac StoneHaven, CEO of StoneHaven Publishing*.

"If you don't have plans for the Fourth of July, I hope you'll consider joining us at our home," he says before turning and heading back to the crowd of gaping guests. I watch as my brother, Alexander, does his best to do damage control with the flutter of photographers nearby. Eventually, my reluctant father heads back toward his guests while acting as if nothing happened.

"I'm going to assume from your silence that you don't have any plans," Nicholas asks Tristan with a polite smile.

"Nick, I think your family's house is the last place I should be."

A look of despair washes over Tristan's face as he studies the sleek card in his hand. Despite his outburst, I can't help but feel like he wants to be here with us, or he wouldn't still be standing here.

"Perfect, then you'll join us for dinner. I'll have our driver pick you up next Friday at five p.m.," Nicholas says. "Just text me your address."

"You're not listening," Tristan says, looking up at him.

"Look, I don't know what's going on, but I'm sure we can fix this. I just want my best friend back."

"Please, come, Tristan," I beg.

Nicholas squeezes my shoulder to console me, but I feel the air leave my lungs as I watch Tristan leave. All of this time, I was beginning to think that I wouldn't ever see him again. After the first few years, it started to feel like I had made the entire memory of him up. Nicholas stopped talking about him after my father told him he left with his mother and that he wasn't coming back. I know Nicholas was angry that Tristan didn't bother telling him that he was leaving.

I just can't believe he was so close to us all this time.

"What do we do now?" I ask Nick.

"Tristan just has some shit to figure out."

Nicholas's words are meant to sound reassuring, but instead, I get the feeling that he isn't so sure himself that Tristan's coming back.

CHAPTER 8

TRISTAN

The Fourth of July is my favorite holiday. It's one of the few days where it isn't a complete pain in the ass to walk down the street in New York City. With over 5 million residents leaving to celebrate out of town, it's like having the Big Apple all to myself. For the past four years, I've spent each Fourth of July walking through Central Park and sketching the random visitors and bums that seem to find their way there. It's one of the few things I find entertaining and free.

This year might be the first Fourth of July I don't spend alone. The last holiday my mother and I actually celebrated was our first Christmas in our apartment. It was three months after we left the StoneHaven's and it was also the first Christmas I spent cleaning up after my mother.

At seventeen, you don't expect to have to become the adult in the relationship. It was already bad enough that I had to drop out of high school, get my GED, and start working. That's how I met my friend Vivian. She worked at a bar next to the Pleasure Chest. I used to pass it on the way home from the library in Manhattan. It was a great place for digging up fries from their trash. The first time Vivian caught me, she brought me out a burger and told me to come back later. When I came back the next night, she had a job for me as a bus boy.

My mother enters the kitchen holding the butt of an old cigarette that looks like it was found between the cushions of the couch. She rubs the matted spots of hair against her head and takes a seat at the kitchen breakfast bar to smoke. I wince at the sight of the dark bags under her eyes. They add at least ten years to her face. Maybe it's better that I don't leave her alone again tonight. A few days ago, I stayed out late to play at the Pleasure Chest and when I got home, the front door was wide open. My mother seems to be forgetting simple things like closing doors and windows. Thankfully, we don't really have anything to steal.

"Mom, would you like to go out today?" I ask hopefully.

"No."

"It'll be quiet. We can go to a museum…"

"I think I'll stay here."

"All right," I say, giving up. "I'll be back tonight. I'm just going to go out for a few hours."

She walks over and briefly kisses my cheek before quickly retreating to the bedroom. After a few moments, I hear the blinds in the room close and the sound of the bedsprings compressing together. *She must be going to sleep again.* I'm starting to doubt that mother will even notice I'm gone.

CHAPTER 9

TRISTAN

After a long cab ride over, I finally arrive at the all too familiar limestone mansion the StoneHaven family calls home. The size of the house is bigger than I remember. Black wrought iron gates surround the home sectioning it off from the outside world. When I was younger, I was told it was one of the original mansions on Fifth Avenue. I must admit the handful of houses beside it pale in comparison to its architectural magnitude. I'm sure even the most esteemed architectural engineer would agree.

I spot a row of flashy cars that line the street leading up to the house. I recognize each one from the car magazines they leave stowed in the bathrooms at the Pleasure Chest. I wouldn't be surprised if just one could pay our rent for several years.

As I arrive at the front door, the sun finally begins to set behind the vanilla pink summer sky that surrounds it in an amber glow. Despite the pent up anger I've felt these past years, I find my nerves getting the better of me as I pause to take in my reasons for coming here. Why am I nervous? I rub my hands against my pants as they begin to sweat.

DRAWN TO YOU

At the door, the sight of one of Stefan's maids greets me. My stomach spirals as she smiles and happily ushers me into the house. Dark thoughts filter their way through my mind as I watch her. I can't help but wonder if Stefan's stopped his old ways or if he's somehow involved with her, too.

We step into the foyer and then we pass the spiraling staircase as we head toward the dining room section of the house. The inside is just as I remember it with its marble floors and cherry wood furnishings.

"You're here," a voice calls out.

A petite woman with raven hair and green eyes walks up to me. She's holding a plate of cookies in her hands. Her thin lips curve into a smirk as she eyes my faded jeans and ripped up Depeche Mode t-shirt. There's a certain haughtiness about her that tells me she doesn't let people like me into her house. I've come to terms that much like my worn out clothes, I'm just another piece of filth that permanently litters this city to them.

"Hello."

"You must be…"

"Tristan."

A flicker of irritation crosses her face as I extend my hand. She doesn't even remember me or at least she sure as hell is pretending like she doesn't. She turns, completely ignoring my hand as she heads down the hall.

"Follow me," she says mostly to herself. "Stefan is waiting for you in the reading room."

For years, I imagined this moment, standing in a room alone with Stefan, and each time I picture my fist ramming into his face. Never did I imagine that I would be drinking a glass of his scotch in the same reading room that he told my mother to leave. The interior of the room hasn't changed much with the exception of the number of books overflowing from Stefan's shelves.

I watch as Stefan paces the room glancing up at me a couple of times between his sips of scotch.

"I want you to stay here with us," he finally says, placing his glass on a nearby table. "There are more than enough rooms in the house. You can stay as long as you want, and if you decide to stay, I'll pay for you to go back to school. You can even study art if you agree to at least minor in business."

The words come rushing out of Stefan's mouth so fast that my head feels like it's spinning. I feel a tight pull in my chest. He'll pay for me to go back to school? It never occurred to me to even try to go to college and study art. Although it would help my technique to study around other artists, I just can't see myself being another gray suit in New York with a degree that I allow to go to my head.

"Why are you doing this?" I ask.

"I want to help you."

I practically laugh in his face at his words. *Help me?* Never in my wildest dreams would I ever imagine someone wanting to help me in this city. There's a reason why you hear about decomposing bodies being found weeks later in apartments—you're practically non-existent here. What's one less person in a gritty world of money, sex, and lies? *Nothing*. The only thing he owes me is an explanation of why he screwed my mother over.

"If you think you're going to make up for what you did to my mother, forget it. I don't want anything from you."

"Let me help you."

"Why?" I ask.

He looks me over once more as if trying to find his reasoning within me. A somber look comes over him as he turns to pace the room once again. Several seconds pass because I hear his voice again, but this time, there's a sliver of regret mixed with it.

"Because I loved her. I know you don't think I did, but I made her leave for her sake."

His words cut me to my deepest core. He loved her, but he never went looking for her. He never even bothered to see if she was okay. Right now, she's sitting at home wondering why the hell he never loved her enough to fight for her. I don't know what compels me to tell him, but the words tumble from my mouth before I have a chance to stop them.

"You were all she ever talked about."

"I think of her often too."

"Why did you tell her to leave?" I push.

"Evelyn almost found out. Your mother left me a love letter in one of my pockets and my wife found it in the washer. We have an infidelity clause in our marriage contract. I'll lose everything if she finds out about your mother and me, including my children. They'll hate me if they find out."

"They deserve to know what kind of father they have."

Even as I say the words, I know they're not entirely true.

I watch as Stefan walks over to me and places a hand on my shoulder. My skin itches to push him off, but I don't. Before I know it, he pulls me into an embrace. The familiar smell of Cuban cigars fill my senses and I feel something crack in the wall I've built between us. As much as I want to pull away, I can't. My eyes begin to water with tears as I feel his embrace grow tighter around my shoulders. *I hate him. I fucking hate him.* I keep repeating the words inside my head, but when I open my eyes, I realize I'm returning his embrace.

"I regretted sending you both away the moment you left. I was just too much of a coward to do anything about it," he says.

"Why are you telling me this?"

I step back from his embrace needing to put as much distance as humanly possible between us.

"Because I'm trusting in the fact that you wouldn't want to ruin Emily or her brother's lives by saying something."

"So you brought me here to pay me off?" I ask.

"If you want money, I'll write you a check right now, but I'm offering you a chance to become part of this family. You were an important part of it once…"

"I have to think about it."

He nods with a hopeful look and a smile that daubs his face.

CHAPTER 10

TRISTAN

Tonight, I did the one thing I thought I would never do—I broke. In the four years that have gone by, not once have I cried over the shit storm my life brought. There were plenty of times where I felt myself being tested. When I wasn't looking for work, I was trying not to starve. Or I was trying not to drown in the surmounting amount of debt we had incurred over the years of taking my mother to the ER when she took to the bottle too hard.

These thoughts continually plague my mind as we gather for dinner in the dining hall. Somehow, I've found myself in yet another clusterfuck, except this time I'm not sure how I'm going to walk away in one piece. As I enter the room, Stefan leads me over to a chair fixed between Nicholas and Emily. Despite my growing desire to leave, I smother my fears and sit down. Surprisingly, Alexander is absent from the table leaving the five of us to dine alone.

"Tristan, are you okay?" Emily asks, placing her hand on my forearm.

I'm tempted to tell her the truth—that part of me isn't sure if I'll ever be okay. My life feels like it's constantly spiraling out of control and the only time it isn't is when I'm at the Pleasure Chest. My time there is a peaceful escape from reality. It's the only time I ever feel in control of what's going on around me.

As the excitement of dinner dies down, I find myself yet again thinking about the possibility of living here with Emily and Nicholas. My thoughts are quickly disrupted by the sound of Evelyn entering the room in red high heels. I smirk at the sight of the apron draped across her Vera Wang dress. It's an amusing sight given the fact that I doubt she's much of a cook other than baking. She places a tray of chocolate chip cookies on the table before taking a seat directly across from me. Her gaze flickers over me before quickly returning to her husband.

"These look great, Mom."

She swats Nicholas's hand away from the hot tray as he tries to snatch one.

"Eat your dinner first."

"This is my dinner," he says as he pops a fresh cookie into his mouth.

"You're going to burn yourself," Emily laughs.

I watch them, taking in their words and easy smiles. They're the kind of smiles on someone who has never known what it feels like to not know where your next meal is coming from. The contrast between them and me doesn't go unnoticed. A small part of me begins to wonder if I could actually fit back into their lives and become part of the family that I've desperately wanted over the years. It's ironic that although I'm an adult now, I've never felt more like a child.

Stefan clears his throat drawing everyone's attention back to the head of the oval table.

"I have something to announce," he says.

"Sweetheart, can't this wait until after dessert?" Evelyn asks, eyeing me with a curious but irritated gaze.

"No, it can't."

"Dad, please…" Nicholas says, shaking his head. "I really don't want to see you guys duke it out over the dinner table."

"I'm not asking your permission, so just listen."

All eyes turn to me with interest as Stefan walks over and places his hand on my shoulder. A strange feeling comes over me as he carries on about changes that come and go in their lives. My mind tunes out his voice as I force my mind to engrave the image of Nicholas and Emily into my memories. It isn't until I hear him say the words *stay with us* that I realize what he's said.

"You'll be happy to know that Tristan has decided to stay with us for a while."

Fuck. I told him I was thinking about it. A shocked gasp escapes Evelyn's throat as he raises his glass to make a toast. Something tells me that he didn't have a conversation with Emily's mother prior to reaching this decision.

"Welcome home," Stefan says holding his glass to mine.

"she is my dark lady, my MUSE."

CHAPTER 11

EMILY

It's well past midnight and no matter how many times I count the cracks in my bedroom ceiling, I can't seem to fall asleep. Tristan is moving in with us in the next few weeks, and the excitement of it all has me buzzing with energy. I called Ceci tonight to tell her the good news and she wouldn't stop teasing me about what Tristan said to me at the Pearl Hotel. I hadn't forgotten the flirtatious tone he had when he told me he was sorry he couldn't kiss me. Every time I think of it, it sends a strange flutter in the pit of my stomach.

It's the same feeling that scares me. Deep inside, I know I shouldn't have feelings for Tristan. It doesn't matter that I don't see him the way I see Nicholas and Alexander because he's still my family. At the least, I feel as if he's my adopted brother.

I keep telling myself that I'm just happy to have him back in my life. In a couple of days, everything will be back to normal and having him around won't feel like my whole world is imploding. Maybe then, I can laugh with Ceci about how silly I must be acting. *That must be it.*

I lie back against my sheets and close my eyes, willing myself to

DRAWN TO YOU

forget the way Tristan touched my hand. My fingers slip over my palm and I smile at the small ridges where the shattered glass broke skin. Something tells me that it's going to leave a permanent mark.

CHAPTER 12

TRISTAN

What the fuck am I doing? I've been asking myself that same question all afternoon. I feel like the shittiest son for leaving my mother in the care of someone else's hands, but I can't take it anymore.

The night I came home from Stefan's Fourth of July dinner, I decided she needed more than prayers to battle her addiction. My heart squeezes at the memory of her shambling to the taxicab like a zombie this morning. I feel guilt-ridden for leaving her alone, but my presence hasn't made things any better. In fact, I'm beginning to think, in a way, I was a crutch for her. A reason to not get up in the morning and try to start again. I've always been there to pick up the pieces and the messes that she's made, but I realized I never let my mom do anything for herself because I didn't think she was strong enough.

Sometimes, I still don't think she is. I can't help but wonder how much longer she has with all the damage she's done drinking. Four years of watching her self-destruct is more than enough to last me a lifetime. Sadly, it's only given her more time to get wrapped up in the past instead of moving forward. Seeing Stefan made me realize just how bitter I felt because of it. The world obviously isn't sunshine and lollipops between him and me, but I'm taking everything a day at a time.

The sound of my cell phone ringing pulls me from my thoughts as I head toward the boarding zone for my destination. I curse under my breath as my prepaid cell phone lights up with the telephone number of the Magnolia Rehabilitation Center. Fuck. Did something go wrong?

At first, my mother didn't go to the facility willingly. It wasn't until we were on the subway train that I told her where we were headed. She was pissed that I lured her out with promises of a new bottle of liquor, but I knew it wasn't going to be easy getting her to go.

My mother's soft voice calls to me over the distorted line as the reception on my phone goes in and out boarding the train.

"Tristan, I don't like it here. I want to go," she cries into the telephone.

I'm not sure how she's calling me when the facility strictly told me that personal calls were only allowed three times a week. I'm not going to bother thinking about the amount of money my mother is going to be in debt after this. In fact, I'm surprised the center offered the opportunity to schedule monthly payments. I left the only credit card I have on file with them, hoping that by racking up a few more commission pieces I'll be able to pay for her treatment.

"Mom, we agreed that you would give this a chance. For yourself."

"But I'm scared. My head hurts. Everything hurts."

"It'll be okay."

"Why can't I stay with you at the apartment?"

I don't tell her that I've taken the few things we had in the apartment with me and gave the building manager our thirty days' notice. One way or another, we're getting her out of that shit hole. This facility is the first step.

"You promise you won't leave me here alone?" she asks.

"I'll be back in two weeks."

Her voice cuts out before I have the chance to tell her about staying longer. The check-in staff working there said that she might need to stay there for sixty to ninety days before they transition her to a sober living apartment complex. It's hard to imagine being away from her for so long, but it's for the best. At least, I keep telling myself it is to stifle the guilt I feel in the back of my mind.

"she is my dark lady, my MUSE."

CHAPTER 13

EMILY

It's strange the way Tristan falls back into place among our lives. Like a missing puzzle piece that was just waiting to be found. Seeing him every day becomes a comforting rhythm, even when I don't always get to talk to him. In the mornings, I wake and he's there reading his books or painting outside in the garden. At night, studying him at the dinner table. Watching him carefully chew the colorful food on his plate. Each bite is savored and chewed as if it might be his last one. When I sleep, I find myself dreaming of him. And in my dreams, he touches my skin in soft circular motions. In my dreams, my body is his empty canvas waiting to be brought to life.

"Are you going to stare at me all day from over there?"

Tristan's firm voice calls out to me pulling me from my daydream. I blush as he pauses painting and glances up at me with curiosity. I've tried to savor the hours I spend with him and to store the memories for safekeeping. Every time I'm at school, I can't shake the anxiety that he's going to leave again. He told my father that his presence would only be temporary until he gets back on his feet, but so far he hasn't mentioned leaving.

"How was school?" he asks, ignoring my silence.

"It was fine."

I walk over to the outside of my mother's garden and sit beside the edge of the waterfall. Tristan sits transfixed by the colorful array of roses as he slowly dips his brush into a small cap of green paint. He traces a border of vines hand drawn onto the cover of his book almost giving them a 3D look.

"I hope that's not one of my father's," I smile. "Don't let him catch you because you'll never hear the end of it."

"This one's mine," he smirks and then continues tracing.

"What are you drawing?"

"Mostly florals. they're good practice."

He hands me the leather bound book and I slowly study the pastels painted into the leather. They're beautiful. I turn the book to study the spine, immediately recognizing the author's name. *Byron*. He kept the copy he used to read to me before bed? My heart warms at the sight of the withered sides. It looks like its seen better days.

"Is this the same copy?"

"Yes," he says. "I took it for memories."

I smile at his confession. It feels good to know that I'm not the only one that was affected. I started sleeping in his room after he left. I wanted to bottle up the smell of him and wrap it around me. After a few months, the smell of him was gone having disappeared entirely. Nicholas stopped talking about him. Alexander didn't mention his strange departure, and my father avoided mentioning him or his mother entirely. The only person who brought him up occasionally was my mother.

"Do you have many memories of us?"

"Mostly of you," he murmurs. "And a couple with Nick."

"You guys used to play in the attic upstairs all of the time. I remember Nick never wanted me to play with you guys."

"Because you stole all of the attention."

"Whose?"

"Mine."

I hate to sound so needy, but it's true. Every moment spent with him was time I treasured.

"Speaking of Nick, I'm going out to a party with him tonight, so we'll probably be back late. I know you mentioned needing my help for an art project, but do you mind if it waits until morning?"

I bite my lip, hoping to hide my disappointment. I mind, but it doesn't matter because I shouldn't. I slip the book of poems back into Tristan's hand and swing my backpack over my shoulder. I should probably study anyway. I'm sure I have a ton of math homework.

"No, of course not. Have fun."

The words fall flat from my mouth. As much as I would like them to sound genuine, I know they don't. A small smile breaks across his lips as he stares down at the book of poems.

"Why don't you hold onto Byron for me tonight?"

I smile. "Okay."

> "she is my dark lady, my MUSE."

CHAPTER 14

TRISTAN

Hot lips slide across the base of my neck as I reach for the car door. On my right shoulder, a tall brunette named Penelope leans into me. She's an English major, but from the way her fingers move down to my belt, I'm willing to bet that she's not the stereotypical shy bookworm. I catch a flash of her silk black thong as she hikes up her skirt and grinds against my crotch. She moans against me, and despite the awkwardness of someone else being in the car, I feel my cock harden.

"Okay, buddy, I think I'm going to move this upstairs," Nick says, pushing off the petite dancer he was sucking face with seconds ago. I chuckle at the memory of him pointing out how he was going to enjoy testing her flexibility. She didn't seem to have any hesitation leaving the party with us, but I guess it helps when you show up driving a hundred thousand dollar car like it's no sweat off your brow. I was tempted to ding Stefan's car up until the point where Nicholas said his father had recently given it to him.

I watch as Nicholas exits the car, wrapping his arm around the waist of the petite dancer. She giggles at his side throwing her long blonde hair over her shoulder. I'm filled with a strange, comforting calm watching him head toward the inside of the house. It's the first time in four years I feel like I actually belong somewhere. That my life actually matters to someone. *To them.*

"Hey, Christian, you're not paying attention to me," the brunette says as she pouts.

"It's Tristan."

The brunette who is dry humping my leg stops and slowly begins to unzip the top button of my pants. She looks up at me through long fake lashes and smiles. There's something about her voice, her face that annoys me. It's like she's trying too hard.

"Do you want me to blow you?" she asks enthusiastically rubbing my cock through my jeans.

"I swallow," she smiles.

"How about I gag you?"

"You're into that kinky stuff?"

That kinky stuff? I smile. "You have no idea."

Light footsteps echo on the floor as I head toward my room with the brunette from NYU. We're halfway inside when I hear a voice calling out to me. I turn half expecting it to be Evelyn checking up on us, but I'm surprised to see Emily standing a few feet away in a pink satin nightie. Her long blonde hair flows past her shoulders in golden waves. The vision of her in it stirs a strange feeling inside me. My eyes wander down to the bare skin peeking out from a slit in the fabric. Who the hell sells pajamas like this to high school girls? *Fuck.*

"Tristan, are you going to tie me up or not?" an impatient voice asks from behind me.

I turn back to find the brunette standing next to me as she eyes Emily. A wave of embarrassment washes over me as I realize how bad this looks. I can only imagine what must be going through Emily's mind as she stands there gaping at the college girl beside me. Her dress is revealing enough that her bottom practically hangs out of it and her tits are barely held in. She isn't anyone that I would be proud bringing home to my mother.

Emily's gaze wavers for a moment before she turns and begins to walk back up the stairs.

"Go to my room. It's the door on the right," I say over my shoulder to my guest.

"But…"

"Go."

It takes what seems like forever for her to quit her pouting and go back to my bedroom. I wait for her to disappear around the corner before rushing up the stairs after Emily. I nearly trip twice on the carpet runner as I spot her standing outside of her bedroom door. She stands there leaning against her door with her eyes closed. There's a defeated look on her face and I'm not exactly sure why.

"Hey," I whisper.

Her eyes pop open with a startled look. She steps closer peering into the darkness until she's only a few feet away.

"Hi."

I chuckle at her obvious discomfort with the scene just moments ago. She locks her fingers together, fidgeting with them. Fidgety fingers and lip biting have replaced her nervous tick of balancing on her feet back and forth. She looks up at me to say something, but I quickly cut her off as the words come out of my mouth.

"I'm sorry I couldn't help you with your art project today."

"Oh, uh, that's okay."

"Are you having nightmares again?"

She laughs. "I'm too old to be tucked in, Tristan."

I can't help but let my eyes trail over her. I know she's older now, and that's the problem. I can't look at her like the small little girl she used to be. That person is gone. The young woman standing in front of me is an entirely different problem that I'm not sure how to handle. And what scares me most is I'm not sure it's something I can control.

"I'll be downstairs if you need me," I offer.

"Okay, thanks."

I'm not sure why I do it. Maybe out of habit of kissing my mother on the cheek goodnight, but I step forward and gently press my lips against her cheek. I hear her breath hitch as I'm doing it, but I don't stop. Something inside propels me forward. Her warm skin brushes against the shadow of hair on my face and it takes every fiber of my being not to slide my lips across her mouth. This is a dangerous game I'm playing, and I don't know why I'm doing it, except for the pleasure of feeling her skin on my lips.

Emily's bright eyes stare up at me, as if waiting for me to do it again, to pick up where I left off. *Space. I need some fucking space.* I step back letting go of her warmth and rush to go down the stairs. I'm such an idiot. What the fuck am I doing?

"Tristan?"

Her voice draws me in like a moth to the flame. I turn to find her only a few inches from me. Her pink lips part, sending a hot streak of desire coursing through my blood. I bite back a groan as the thought of what they might look like wrapped around me creeps into my mind. I close my eyes as I fight the desire to see the look on her face when my cock is inside her lovely little mouth. Fuck, I'm almost sorry that there's a woman downstairs. *Shit.* I shouldn't even be thinking about Emily like this. Even if it weren't for the obvious fact that she's the little sister I never had, there's also an innocence about her that tells me there's a line here that shouldn't be crossed. *Ever.*

"Tristan?" she calls again.

"Yes, Emily?"

Her eyes search mine as if trying to decipher something inside them. I hope to God that she can't see the desire ripping its way through me.

"Do you still think I'm beautiful?"

Her words send a vibration throughout my body, setting my nerves on fire. I can still recall the memory of her asking me those same words four years ago. Back then, I didn't think twice about answering her. My response couldn't be misread for anything more than just brotherly adoration, but now I feel the words caught in my throat. I tell myself to turn and go back downstairs to the woman waiting for me in my bed, but I can't. My feet are firmly planted here taunting me to answer her. I know I'm going to regret telling her how I feel. Not because it isn't true, but because it's never been truer.

"You're still the most beautiful girl I've ever met."

She takes a step toward me sending my heart raging against my chest. *I can't do this.* I can't be attached to her this way. I don't want to break her because I know she could be the end of me and I'm already walking on eggshells around her. She flinches as I turn away from her. *Don't look back.* I keep my eyes forward as I make my way to my room. From the bottom of the stairs, I hear her calling out to me in a soft broken voice. I tell myself to ignore it, to drown out the sound of her voice the only way I know how.

"What took you so long?" the brunette in my bed whines.

"Nothing. Take off your clothes."

> she is my dark lady, my MUSE.

CHAPTER 15

EMILY

My eyes flutter open at the pressure of someone taking a seat on the edge of my bed. I sit up to find Tristan dressed in a dark suit staring at me with a broad grin. It takes me several seconds to get over the shock of seeing him wearing such an expensive suit. There's something about the way it hugs his muscles that sends my mind sputtering and my heart in a tizzy. It's the first time since he's been here that he isn't wearing his usual jeans and t-shirt. I guess Nicholas finally convinced him to go shopping for something new.

"Happy birthday, Lily Pad."

I smile at the way my nickname rolls off his lips in a playful tone. *I can't believe it's already my birthday.* If I could have any of my birthday wishes come true, it would definitely be to wake up to this every morning. The feeling of him sitting across from me could only be perfected by the feeling of his arms around me.

"I wanted to come up here before everyone else because I have a birthday present to give you. Two, actually."

"You didn't have to get me anything."

"I did."

DRAWN TO YOU

Tristan pulls out a small box from his pocket. As he opens it, I spot a silver chain with a charm hanging in the middle of it. Tears fill my eyes as I realize that the charm is a water lily sprouting from a lily pad.

"You've grown so much. I thought this was fitting."

"It's so thoughtful… does this mean you're going to start calling me Lily?"

Tristan chuckles. "I'll call you whatever you want… Here, let me put it on you."

I stand as Tristan steps behind me to place the necklace around my neck. I shiver as his fingers trace the base of my collarbone. I know he doesn't mean anything by it, but that's not the way it feels to me. To me it feels like more. His thumb stops and hovers just underneath my ear. Heat exudes from his fingers like hot stones pressed across my skin.

"You mentioned a second gift," I say.

His hot breath tickles my ear as he leans in and then twirls me to face him. It takes all of my strength not to stare at the way his hazel eyes pop against his tan skin. Every time I tell myself that Tristan is just a brother, I remember the way his hands feel against my skin and the way his eyes seems to linger ever so slightly over me.

"You're a greedy little thing, aren't you?" he says in a hushed voice. "Your second present comes later."

CHAPTER 16

EMILY

"Happy Birthday, baby sis!" Nicholas strides over toward me and scoops me up in his arms. He nearly squeezes the life out of me as he twirls me in a circle. I haven't seen him much lately because of Finals Week. He's always too busy going to parties, dating models, and getting in trouble with his RA at school for sneaking in girls. I'm not even sure why he stays there when he's home half the time. I blush as he plants a sloppy kiss on my forehead.

"Geez, Nick. Thanks for slobbering all over me."

He chuckles as I wipe the kiss off with the back of my hand.

"Happy Birthday." I recognize the voice before I see him. The smile on Tristan's lips reaches all the way to his eyes. It's the most alluring thing I've ever seen. Despite the persistent chilly morning we're having, I feel flustered at the sight of his tousled black hair, smooth tan skin, and blinding smile. My skin warms at the memory of him coming upstairs to see me before everyone else. He must've snuck back down here before lunchtime. I accidentally brush against Tristan and for a moment, I feel his fingertips grazing my elbow. As much as I don't want it to, the touch sends a pool of excitement shooting through me.

"You okay, Sis?" The concern in Nick's voice snaps me back from my thoughts.

"Yes, I'm all right." I melt as Tristan's eyes meet mine. His gaze never wavers.

"Good, you had me worried for a minute there. You sounded like you were having trouble breathing."

"I'm fine," I say more firmly as I stand, acutely aware of Tristan's eyes burning into my skin.

"I hope you're ready to party. Mom and Dad left for the weekend so we have the place all to ourselves," Nicholas says with a wicked grin.

I don't know how I'm going to survive today, but I'm happy that Ceci will be here later tonight to help celebrate my birthday. Or better yet, to keep me from making a complete fool of myself.

"Emily!" Ceci's high-pitched voice rings out across the foyer of the house as she enters with a large brown paper bag in her hand. I bite back a laugh as her too big high heels clack across the floor practically flying off her feet. A smile appears on Nicholas's face as he eyes Ceci's *I'm with the band* t-shirt, cut off shorts, and pop art leggings. If she weren't my best friend, I would question her sanity. I should be used to her far out sense of fashion, but there's just no getting used to it. It's like she gets dressed in the dark sometimes.

"Hey, stud muffin," Ceci says to Nick.

She throws him a wink as she jiggles her butt just enough to make him spit his orange juice across the counter. I burst into laughter as he tries to wipe the over spray from his Giorgio Armani Cardigan. He's not going to be happy when he realizes that he's going to have to send his cashmere sweater to be dry cleaned. I almost feel sorry for the person at the dry cleaner. I'm sure he's the most anal person when it comes to his clothing.

"Hey, Ceci. How are the mosquito bites?"

"Ew, Nick," I say.

Ceci pulls her blouse forward and stares down at her chest with a crooked smile.

"They're doing just fine."

"Ceci!"

"Don't worry, Emily. I'm not into mosquito bites," Nicholas grins.

It's strange to have my brother and my best friend under the same roof. Ceci is always acting even more bizarre than usual around him. I'm sure he loves that a little high school girl wants to screw his brains out—but, thankfully, he has enough sense to leave her alone—at least for the most part. It definitely doesn't stop him from teasing or giving her hell.

Ceci swoops her arms around me and we twirl together in a fit of laughter. I'm beyond glad that she actually made it down here. We have a lot of talking to do, especially with Tristan being here. Today is going to be amazing. I'm sure of it.

"Happy birthday, Em."

She pulls a bottle of Moscato wine from her purse and shakes it in front of me with a silly grin on her face. I grab the bottle and give her a quick hug before heading to the kitchen to hide it. Ceci trails closely behind me humming to herself as she takes a seat at the breakfast bar. She flips her chestnut hair and lets out a long whistle as Tristan enters the room in jeans and a tight black t-shirt. A strange sensation fills the pit of my stomach as Ceci fawns over him. I can't explain why, but anger seeps into my skin as she ogles him.

"Ceci," I whisper.

"Yeah?"

"Could you be more obvious? Stop undressing my stepbrother. It's so wrong."

Ceci turns to me as her cheeks burn in humiliation. Her hurt expression immediately makes me wish I could take my words back. But the damage is already done. She looks down at her nails and then back up at me before quietly brushing the corner of her watery eyes.

DRAWN TO YOU

"That was really mean," she whispers.

I watch her get up from her seat and hurry off to the bathroom. Even though I can't hear her, I know she's crying. *What's wrong with me?* I've never lashed out at my best friend. I'm used to her staring at guys and calling them man candy. Except when it comes to Tristan.

CHAPTER 17

TRISTAN

Across the room of StoneHaven's drawing room, I spot Nicholas's wolfish grin as he winks at me. There's a smug look of satisfaction as he slides his hand down the ass of the tall brunette next to him. They stand pressed against each other as they linger in the drawing room. *He has no shame.* I chuckle as he slowly pulls her strap to the side of her shoulder. I'm sure Emily is thankful that Stefan and Evelyn are out of town. Although I'm more than a little concerned to see Emily's friend Ceci bring tequila for her birthday. She's turning seventeen, not twenty-one.

"Hi," I hear a silky voice say behind me. "You must be Tristan."

I turn to find a familiar face and pair of tits staring up at me. It takes me a moment to place them, but as soon as I hear her name, I realize that she's the same woman I met at the party at NYU. The English major that I spent the night tying up and fucking.

"What brought you over?"

"Nicholas invited me. He thought you might want to see me," she says as she grabs the top part of my pants.

DRAWN TO YOU

Of course, he would send Penelope over. I should've known better than to think that this is all a coincidence. As much as I would like to say her unexpected presence is a welcomed one, it's not. I side step around her and grab a glass of champagne. It seems that in this house there's always an endless array of it.

"I'm thirsty," she says as her eyes trace over me. "But not for champagne."

Before I have time to react, I feel her small frame pressing up against me as she corners me between the wall and the table the champagne is sitting on.

"Penelope, this is my best friend's little sister's birthday. I'm not going to fuck you next to the fireplace mantel," I say.

She smiles at me with a look of hunger. It only takes her a few seconds to find her way to the front of my pants.

"So fuck me somewhere else."

Penelope follows me up the stairs as we head toward one of the guest bedrooms. I hear her practically squeal at the sight of the massive king size bed that sits in the middle of the room. If I didn't know any better, you'd think she's more excited to be on the bed than on my cock. Penelope saunters over never taking her eyes off me as she slowly undoes the top straps of her red dress. The fabric hangs tight against her figure leaving little to the imagination.

"Are you finding everything to your liking?" she asks, taking a seat on top of the bed. She pulls on the tie I put on for this evening and wraps it around her hand as she pulls my face toward her. My cock strains against my pants as she rubs her tits against my chest. I'm lost in the moment of her hips swiveling on top my lap when the smell of her perfume hits me. I don't know why I didn't notice it before. It's been a while since I've smelled it… lavender. Thoughts of Emily's soft skin and perfect mouth flood my thoughts.

"You're so hard," Penelope says, shoving her hand down my pants.

"What are you doing?"

My voice comes out raspier than I intend. I watch her lower herself onto her knees and slowly unzip my pants. She puckers her mouth in a seductive gesture. As much as I know this is wrong, I don't stop her. I can't. Because even though it's Penelope on her knees, she's not the person who I'm imagining.

> she is my dark lady, my MUSE.

CHAPTER 18

EMILY

It shouldn't bother me that Tristan is going upstairs with Penelope. Yet with each step they climb up, I feel something inside me slowly crumbling to pieces. My head and my heart are colliding before my eyes. I can't explain why I feel the way I do, but ever since the night Tristan left, I've dreamt of him coming back and being part of this family again. Now he's here, but there's something missing and I'm not sure how to fix it.

Despite the amount of time that Tristan has lived with us, it seems he's made it his mission to keep me at a distance. I feel like I've done something wrong, but I have no clue what it is. His relationship with Nicholas is the same as it was several years ago, yet he hasn't said much to me. I haven't forgotten the nights I used to sneak into his room or the way he would read to me until I fell back asleep. He was always someone I could run to even if it were just from my nightmares.

I watch as Penelope hangs on his arm gently pressing into his side. Her light laughter sends me over the edge. I can't deny that I feel a strange connection to Tristan. Sometimes I feel like there's a piece of me that left with him when he went away. I can't even recall the number of times I cried myself to sleep after my father told us him and his mother had left.

"Em, are you all right?"

I turn to find my friend Ceci staring at me intently. In her hand is a glass of champagne that I almost wish I were daring enough to drink myself. Her gaze shifts toward Tristan and Penelope and then back to me. I can almost see the wheels turning in her head as she takes in the scene. I don't know what to tell her and I don't know why it hurts to breathe after watching Tristan and Penelope go upstairs together. I overheard my brother mention her name, but I didn't think anything of it until I saw her hanging on him.

Ceci nudges me. "Is something bothering you?"

"No," I say with a forced smile. "I'm just feeling a little lightheaded. I think I'll go to bed early."

"Okay, so you want me to go?"

"You can stay," I offer.

"That's okay. I'll just call my parents to come pick me up. I'm sorry you're feeling sick. I guess this hasn't been a very good birthday."

"It's fine," I say.

Ceci embraces me and swiftly plants a kiss on my cheek before heading back to the kitchen. After waiting several minutes, I finally make my way upstairs, silently praying that I don't hear Tristan and Penelope fucking in one of the guest rooms. To my surprise, I catch Penelope in the hallway adjusting the bottom of her dress and patting her hair. *Perfect.* At least I'm glad I've already missed their fuck fest. She looks at me with a smirk as her eyes are gleaming with satisfaction.

"You must be Nick's sister."

"I am," I admit with annoyance. "And you must be the current flavor of the week." I smile at the memory of Ceci teaching me the phrase.

An annoyed look crosses Penelope's face as she walks over to me. She stops a few inches from me taking her time to scan the lavender dress that my mother gave me to wear tonight. Her eyes trail down my skin stopping just above my collarbone.

"It must be hard…"

"What?"

She looks up with another smirk.

"Living in the shadows of your older brothers."

"I love my brothers."

"I'm sure you do, but it must suck being the only one who didn't get their good looks. You're like a scrawny little boy."

Anger pulsates through me as I stare at the brunette with inflated tits. I've never been the type to stare endlessly into the mirror, but I know I'm not as ugly as she's making me feel right now. My hand itches to slap her across the face, but I stop myself at the sound of Tristan's voice.

"Penelope, what are you still doing here?"

I watch her turn toward Tristan with a pouty expression. She walks over to him wrapping an arm around his neck and slowly sliding the other down the front of his pants.

"I thought we were going to finish what we started," she says.

"Sorry, I'm done playing."

I bite back a smile at the torn look on her face and the huff that follows as she stomps her foot. I bet she wasn't expecting to hear that.

"And just so we're clear… don't *ever* talk to Emily that way."

Tristan brushes past Penelope as she reaches out to touch him. He stops briefly to intertwine his fingers with mine and I feel him tugging me with him as we head back down the staircase. I watch Penelope's mouth drop in surprise as Tristan hooks my hand through his arm.

"Why did you leave the party?" he asks, drawing my attention back to him.

"It's not much of a party… Why didn't you stay with Penelope?"

Tristan smiles. "I'm not really into women like her."

"Okay."

"When I'm with someone, I want them to be mine. Completely. I don't want to see the last guy they slept with when I look at them."

"So you want to be with a virgin?"

Tristan laughs. "I want someone who'll give themselves to me, entirely. I want my lips forever ingrained on their skin and in their mind. I want them to need only me because the reality is… I'll only need them."

My cheeks flame at Tristan's words and the thought of his lips on my skin. I brush my hair forward hoping to hide the red blush creeping its way up my cheeks.

"What are you thinking about, Lily Pad?"

"Nothing," I stutter.

"It sure doesn't seem like nothing," he says with a wink. "Don't worry. I won't be mad if you dream of me tonight.

"You're embarrassing me." I laugh.

"Are you ready for me to give you your other birthday present?"

"Yes," I smile.

"Okay, close your eyes."

A bubble of excitement rises up my chest as I obediently close them while waiting for Tristan's gift. I hear the rustling of his jacket as he steps closer. *Maybe he stuffed my gift in his coat pocket?* Several seconds pass followed by a thickening silence that seems to go on forever. I'm almost tempted to open my eyes, but the soft touch of Tristan's hand sliding around my neck stops me. The smell of his cologne engulfs my senses as he steps down and closes the space between us. Confusion trickles through my mind as he pulls me against his chest. His mouth is on mine before I realize what's happening. The taste of cinnamon and mint exudes from his lips as they press against mine. I bite back a moan as his grip tightens, leaving my skin aflame. The kiss between us only lasts for a few seconds, but it leaves me paralyzed in a euphoric state.

"I always keep my promises," he whispers.

My eyes are still closed when I hear him leave and head down the stairs. My body fights against me as I force myself to turn and head for my room. *What was that?* It isn't until I'm in my room again that I realize what he meant by always keeping his promises. *If you still want me to kiss you when you're my age, I will.* His words are tattooed in my mind. I don't think I'll ever forget tonight.

> she is my dark lady, my MUSE.

CHAPTER 19

EMILY

My morning thoughts are filled with the memory of Tristan's lips on mine. No matter how many times I bite my lip, I can't recreate the thrilling sensation that charged through me the moment he touched me. If it weren't for my stomach practically begging me to eat something, I'd be happy to stay in bed and relive the moment over and over. Famished or not, there's only one person who I'm looking forward to seeing today.

In the kitchen, I find Tristan standing with a glass of whiskey in his hand. The sight of his disgruntled appearance causes me to do a double take as I slowly take in the messy flop of black hair that seems to stand up from his head.

"Tristan, are you all right?"

"No, not really."

He looks up at me, but I do my best to avoid his gaze as I round the corner of the center island. My nerves have been on high alert since last night. The kiss between the two of us still lingers at the forefront of my thoughts. I can't help but wonder if Tristan spent last night thinking about what to say to me because I was definitely thinking about what to say to him.

"How are you feeling this morning?" he asks.

The reverberations of Tristan's husky voice fill the room sending shivers down my skin. I inhale and exhale slowly before turning to answer him.

"Fine."

It's the only word that doesn't manage to escape my mind as he stares at me with interest. My eyes shift to the bottle of wine sitting on top of the granite countertop that Ceci left behind. I'm tempted to take a drink of it. I've had wine a few times in front of my parents. Fortunately, wine and champagne are the two exceptions that they've allowed me at my age.

"I'm not sure if I believe you. You're not even looking at me as you answer."

I slowly make my way over toward the middle of the kitchen island and scour the cabinets for a wine opener. Tristan's heavy gaze follows me as I pop the cork and pour myself a glass of the imported Moscato. As I tip the glass to my lips, I hear irritation in Tristan's voice.

"You're not old enough to be drinking."

"What?"

Tristan's jaw flexes ever so slightly as I hold the glass to my lips. Why is he so upset today? Did I do something wrong?

"Ceci brought me the wine. I didn't think it was a big deal. Sometimes Nicholas lets me have wine or champagne."

"You're too young to start drinking so early."

"I'm not trying to get drunk," I say, stubbornly.

"There's some cranberry juice in the refrigerator. I think you'd enjoy that more."

"Why are you being so bossy today?"

My cheeks flame in frustration at the tone of his voice. I know I'm not twenty-one yet, but why is he acting like I'm a child. *I'm not.* I feel a strange static charge electrifying between us as he steps closer toward me, leaving mere inches between us.

"That's not how you show someone you care."

"You don't think I care?" he asks.

"No, I don't."

"You're wrong, Emily."

I close my eyes at the way my name rolls off of his lips. It's the first time in a while that he hasn't used my childhood nickname. Against my better judgment, I lean into him and the scent of Tristan's cologne consumes my senses. It's a unique mixture of the salty ocean breeze and firewood. He leans in close, so close that I'm not sure where my skin begins and his ends. Tristan's lips trail across my neck sending a strong pull at the center.

"You don't know just how wrong you are."

They're the only words that leave his lips before he sends us crashing inside the pantry. Tristan's hand grips my ponytail and his mouth crashes down on mine sucking every thread of air from my lungs. His touch sears my skin as it slowly unravels me. The sensation is enough to send my whole body into overdrive. I reach up to grab the back of his neck, but he turns me pushing me up against the pantry shelves. I feel his searing hot fingers pulling down my pants, and in the next moment, his erection is rubbing up bare against me.

"Tristan," I moan.

"Fuck."

The words coming rushing out of his mouth as he turns and leaves me panting inside the pantry. My head feels like it's floating above my shoulders as I step back trying to gather my balance. I run my hand over my swollen lips, excruciatingly aware of the blissful sensation between my legs.

> she is my dark lady, my MUSE.

CHAPTER 20

TRISTAN

It was a mistake. A mistake that I won't be repeating again. *Ever.* At least that's the promise I tell myself over and over again as I send a text to one of the subs from the Pleasure Chest. I've been avoiding inviting someone to come play in the same house as Emily, but after this morning, I'm not sure I can wait any longer. *Fuck.* There's no sense in denying that I'm scorched by the consuming need to kiss Emily again. To own those lips and silence her questioning eyes.

I know I'm playing with fire, but I can't get the urge to touch her out of my mind. Seconds earlier, when I felt her lips pressed against mine, my control snapped. The thing I value so highly completely incinerated before my eyes. There's no clear way to explain it, except that her moan unleashed something inside me. I wanted to fuck her. To show that insatiable mouth of hers where it belongs.

What the hell am I thinking? If anyone could see the shit that's going through my mind, they'd lock me up. This is the first time my fantasies are not something that I'm willing to make a reality. Not without consequences. Not without losing control. This morning and the other night should've never happened, but the sound that escaped Emily's greedy little mouth only made denying my desire harder. *It made me harder.* And the ugly truth of it all is that I started something I should've stopped weeks ago.

CHAPTER 21

EMILY

It's a needy moan that startles me awake. The soft sound of her voice vibrates through the air ventilation and into my room. My eyes flicker open and I stare into the darkness of my bedroom. *It's happening again. He's down there with another one.* I hold my breath as I strain to hear their voices. My heart races as their cries fill me with a lustful warmth, and I flush at the wicked thoughts that flood my mind. Thoughts of him touching me, thoughts of him spreading me open and taking me from behind. Thoughts of me being the naked woman entangled in his sheets.

A gasping voice calls out his name. *Tristan!* I hear his deep, throaty roar and the sound of her moan desperate for release. This isn't the first time I've heard him take a woman down to his room. There have been many nights I would lie here wondering what it must be like to be on the other side of that vent. I shouldn't be having sexual fantasies about Tristan. He's not my older brother by blood, but it doesn't make the situation in the pantry any easier to swallow. Even the kiss we shared on the stairs blurred the lines between us. I don't know how I should look at him anymore. Brother? Friend? Or something else entirely?

I turn over and try my best to go back to sleep, but their voices draw me in, and before I realize it, I'm panting with them. I grow wet at the touch of my nail gliding across my bud. *If he only knew how many times I've pictured him touching me.* I close my eyes and imagine his hand inside me, pressing up against me and rubbing me at a slow, torturous pace. I arch at the warm sensation that starts at my center and builds its way up. My nipples harden as I roll one of them through my fingers.

I'm so close. After several minutes pass, my hand grows tired. Frustration consumes me as the image of Tristan touching me dissipates. I lie there annoyed at the lack of release in my life. Most of my high school friends lost their virginity long ago, but I'm still stuck with mine. My best friend has reassured me that there's no need to rush into anything, but when everyone around you is doing it, it makes me wonder if she's just saying it because she feels bad.

After several minutes of tossing and turning and doing my best to drown out the sound with my pillow, I muster the courage to get out of bed and walk down the long set of stairs to Tristan's bedroom. I've always wondered why he chose to take one of the bedrooms downstairs. They're usually reserved for guests. From the bottom step, I spot a cascade of light seeping out from his bedroom door.

The scene before me sends a rush of heat straight to my center. I clench in arousal at the sight of Tristan's long, muscular frame kneeling between two lovely legs adorned around his shoulders. I've never seen anything like it. I can't see her face, but I hear the way her voice grows tight with each lick. Her body trembles as he kneels back and inserts two long fingers inside of her. I can feel myself dripping at the sound of his digits sliding in and out of her quickly.

I'm so lost in the haze of it all that I don't realize I've moaned aloud. Tristan stops and turns on his knee. His hazel eyes grow wide at the sight of me standing there as I watch the intimate session between two lovers. His lips part as if he's about to speak, but he says nothing. Embarrassed at being caught, I turn and flee from his watchful eyes. They burn into my mind, threatening to unravel me.

I'm halfway up the stairs when I feel someone grab at my heel. I turn and nearly tumble down, but warm hands are there to catch me. Despite the overwhelming darkness of the house, I know that it's Tristan. His fingers are slightly calloused from the constant pressure of the drawing pencil in his hand. I'd recognize those hands anywhere. His body hovers slightly over mine as he stares down at me. I can feel the cold steps of the stairs digging into my back.

For a moment, the only sound I hear is the ragged breath as it flows in and out of his shallow gulps. My breath hitches as I watch the reflection of the moonlight catch his face. His hair is ruffled into a mess and there's a strong shadow of facial hair spread across his jaw and cheekbones and around his lips. I subconsciously reach out and touch his face. His skin burns beneath my fingers. If it weren't for what I had just seen, I would be worried that he's getting sick.

Although the darkness of the house cloaks his frame, I know he's fully nude. In his haste to catch me, he must've forgotten to cover up. It isn't until I feel his erection pressing against my stomach that I sense a strange shift in the air between us. Without a word, Tristan positions himself between my legs. The world slows to a halt as his hand glides up my nightie. His warm fingers slide across me, leaving a trail of heat behind them. I tremble at the sensation. It's like nothing I've ever imagined. *It's better.* I feel him watching me as he pushes up the soft fabric of my nightgown and positions himself at the opening of my center. I writhe against him as he rubs his cock at my opening.

I moan, and in one quick movement, his fingers wrap around the front of my mouth. He stops for a moment, listening for the slightest movement upstairs. My frantic thoughts return to the memory of the woman whose legs were wrapped around his shoulders only moments earlier. *Where is she?*

Tristan loosens his hold on my mouth and leans in, letting out a harsh whisper against my ear. "You're so fucking wet."

It's the first and only words out of his mouth before I feel him thrust inside me. A sharp pressure hits me, and I immediately push back against him. This is what my friend Ceci had warned me about. Tristan slows to a stop as he sees discomfort etched across my face. I flush as concern and then disbelief fills his eyes.

"Fuck," he says, gritting his teeth. Without another word, Tristan pulls out, leaving me shivering against the stairs. The sudden shift in temperature from his warm body leaves me aching for him to envelop me once again.

"Emily, I didn't know…"

His words crash over me, and I'm left with a devastating feeling of regret. In one thoughtless decision, we've changed everything between us.

# VOLUME TWO

PROLOGUE

TRISTAN

I've ruined everything.

The thought filters through me as I climb the staircase with Emily in my arms. She shivers as we pass through the desolate hallway that leads to the bathroom adjacent to her bedroom. Emily's bright eyes watch me as I sit her down on the edge of the giant sunken bathtub. The bottom of Emily's nightie is stained red with blotches of blood. The sight of it gives me both pleasure and causes me pain. I turn to the bathtub and flip the faucet on letting the water rise to a tolerable temperature. Emily sits silently staring at me with a confused look on her face. I reach over and begin to pull up her nightie, but the bright flame that stains her cheeks stops me.

"A bath will help with any discomfort you might feel," I say, pushing back a stray strand of blonde from her face. "I'm going to go look for some aspirin while you get in. Just be careful. It might be too hot at first."

"Okay," she mumbles.

"I'll be back. Don't go anywhere."

I disappear down the stairs and into the kitchen, grateful that

DRAWN TO YOU

Nicholas hasn't woken up. I tear through the pantry in search of aspirin. I slip the bottle into my pocket and head back to my room to dress. It isn't until I'm halfway to my bed that I realize the sub I was playing with earlier is still in my room.

The young blonde's breathless voice calls out to me from the edge of my mattress as her hands are crossed and bound above her head. She tugs on the restraints to loosen them but they only squeeze tighter. A worried look crosses her face as I enter the room still reeling from what took place on the stairs. She tilts her head to get a better look at me, but I avoid her questioning gaze. I can't stand to look at her. Even worse is the fact I can't erase the image of Emily's startled face when she caught me with the sub.

"Is everything all right?" she asks hesitantly.

Fuck no. The smell of Emily on my skin guts me as I spot the wet marks on the sheets from my time with the sub. I untie her restraints and hand her the mini skirt she came in. She slowly slides off the bed pulling the sheet off my bed with her. I'm going to burn these sheets. I don't want any memory of tonight including the blonde in my bed. She kneels at my feet never taking her eyes off her knees. In the short amount of time together, she's learned me well.

"Master, did I do something to anger you?"

"You need to go."

"But we were just getting started..."

"I don't give a shit. You need to leave."

I watch her with irritation as she looks at me with a look of betrayal. I probably won't hear the end of it from everyone at the Pleasure Chest. They don't take kindly to those who screw over other members. I watch the blonde slip on the rest of her clothes and then scurry out of my room. I don't bother asking to call a cab for her. I know I'm a dick, but I don't care. I'm grateful when her pouty lips are out of my sight as she finally makes her way out the front door of the StoneHaven mansion.

A gutting rush of shame overwhelms me as I stare at my reflection in my bedroom mirror. There's no clean way out of the mess I've made tonight. The lines between Emily and I have been blurred, and I'm not sure we can ever go back. What the fuck was I thinking? I wasn't thinking. I let my emotions take control of me. I let go of the control I've desperately craved my entire life. How can I ever look Nicholas in the face again? Fuck, I'm going to lose them all over again.

Anger pulsates through me as my fist makes contact with one of my shelves, sending books flying everywhere. Despite the pain that radiates through my hand, it doesn't ease my guilt. The image of Emily's face as I push inside her sends my heart slamming into my chest. I took something from her I can never give back. There's no walking away from this in one piece. Surely, I'm eternally damned for this.

A light trail of steam flows out from inside the spacious bathroom. To my surprise, Emily is still in the bathtub where I left her. Her aquamarine eyes flutter open as I carefully close the bathroom door behind me. She watches me with a look of curiosity as I pace back and forth a few feet away. Try as I may, I can't look away from the way her naked curves peak up from beneath the water. She doesn't move or say anything as I lean down on the tile beside the sunken tub. Our eyes connect, and for a brief moment, I forget my guilt and the consuming need to fix what I've broken.

Leaning forward, I trace the curve of her breast with my fingertips. I feel myself harden at the sight of her nipples perking up. I reach over her for a nearby sponge and watch with a small trace of amusement as her eyes widen. She watches me as I slowly reach down into the water and run the sponge from her ankle to the center between her legs. Emily flinches, but she doesn't stop me as I put pressure against her. Her body arches against my palm, and it takes all of my restraint not to touch her any further. After running the sponge over the rest of her legs, I help her towel off.

She doesn't ask me to, but I turn to look at the wall as she dresses in my black Nine Inch Nails T-shirt. The black tee was a gift from my co-worker Vivian, but I haven't worn it once since she gave it to me. I turn at the feeling of Emily's hand on the back of my shoulder. The sight of her wearing my shirt sends a strange sensation through my chest. She's wearing my shirt. Somehow, it looks better on her.

If life were simpler, she would be mine.

And I would be hers.

EMILY

I wake several hours later to the sound of my alarm clock going off. It doesn't take me long to realize I'm back in my bedroom, alone. My memory is foggy, and despite the familiar surroundings, my room looks different. I reach down to lift my nightie over my head, but I quickly stop as I notice the fabric fits strangely big on me. It takes me several minutes to realize I'm wearing one of Tristan's shirts. *Tristan*. I shift in my bed, and a tender ache throbs from between my legs. The sensation increases as I sit up and lift my legs over the edge of the bed. I reach down, fingering the hem of the oversize shirt, and slowly pull it up. I blush at the realization that I'm not wearing any underwear. Tristan must've taken them off. Or perhaps I wasn't wearing any in the first place.

The smell of Tristan's cologne triggers a flood of memories. Memories of Tristan carrying me to the bathroom, when he turned as I undressed, and the gentle pressure of my loofa grazing the inside of my legs. My heart flutters at the memory of Tristan's gaze as he helped me bathe. I couldn't help but stare at him as he gently touched me. Neither of us said much, but it didn't take away from the need I felt for him to take me again. Even now, my body throbs at the thought of it.

I step off my bed and walk toward the freestanding mirror across the room curious to see if I look any different from last night. My hair is pulled back in a messy bun, and there are light circles under my eyes, but besides that, there isn't much different. I turn and lift my shirt again. As I stare at myself in the mirror, I spot a small bruise on my inner thigh. I reach down and run my finger over the bruise. Despite its dark color, it doesn't seem to hurt.

I've always hated how I bruise so easily, but this time, I don't mind. Butterflies fill my stomach at the thought of seeing Tristan again. How am I ever going to face him again without thinking about last night? Unable to contain my curiosity, I quickly pull on some jean shorts and head downstairs. The house is quiet, but I'm not surprised considering my parents are still out of town. Nicholas is probably still asleep, too.

"Emily?"

I turn toward the sound of a familiar voice and spot my older brother, Alexander, standing in the corridor with a cup in his hand. He's dressed in a fine blue suit with a matching baby blue tie. My cheeks warm as his eyes take in my frazzled appearance. Thank God he didn't see me earlier.

"Hi, Alex. I'm surprised to see you here."

"You are? I don't technically live here, but I try to stop by when I can."

The surprise in his voice catches me off guard. Alex hasn't been around Nicholas or me as much as we'd like him to be. As the heir to StoneHaven Publishing, most of his days are spent shadowing my father or reaching out to investors.

"It's nice to have you home." I smile.

His striking gray eyes wash over me before wandering over toward the front door of Tristan's bedroom.

"I thought I would stop by before going to see Nina."

Nina, Alex's college sweetheart and the woman he's been after for years. Except he only just realized he loves her. It's funny how sometimes you fall for the people who are right in front of you.

"Where were you headed off to?" he asks.

"I was just coming downstairs to make myself some cereal," I answer with a nervous smile.

He takes a sip from his mug before eyeing the oversized shirt I'm wearing. A rush of panic seizes my chest thinking he might know who the shirt actually belongs to. I watch as he sets his mug down and walks over toward me. A serious look paints his face as he places his hand on my shoulder.

"Emily, I know having Tristan live with us is exciting, but just remember, we don't really know him all that well anymore. I would hate for you to get attached to someone who will probably end up leaving in the next month or two."

"What do you mean? Why would you say that?"

A look of pity flashes across Alex's face.

"You can't really think he won't leave after he gets what he wants?"

I nearly choke on the thought that Alex knows about what happened between the two of us last night. How could he? Is it written all over my face? My mother used to warn me that if I had sex, somehow, she would know—as if losing your v-card is a status permanently tattooed to your forehead.

"Dad's already offered to pay for Tristan to go to college. I wouldn't be surprised if he sends him to Barcelona."

"Europe?" I squeak.

The small sense of relief fills me at the realization Alexander isn't talking about last night, and it's quickly replaced by concern. Tristan might leave? Again?

"Yes, Dad has some business partners out there who recommended a school. I was surprised he wasn't interested in sending him to France. Seems like the most logical choice considering we have the villa out there."

Alex steps back as he examines the lettering on the front of my T-shirt.

"By the way, whose shirt is this? You're a little young to listen to Nine Inch Nails."

The sound of the front door opening cuts Alex's interrogation short. I'm grateful for the small distraction as my mind spins at the new information. A burst of light spills through the front door as my mother and father come strolling in with several bags from what looks like a not so mini shopping spree. My mother's bright smile forces me to hide the deepening look of despair on mine. Her green eyes stare at me with curiosity as I lean against the staircase banister for support. She walks over toward me for an embrace, placing a small kiss on the top of my head.

"You look different..."

"It must be my lack of sleep," I say with a forced smile.

"Careful, sweetheart, that's how you ruin good skin."

I roll my eyes at my mother's strange obsession with trying to look twenty years younger at all times. She's always trying the latest beauty health trend. I'm surprised she hasn't discovered the rejuvenating secret of moose pee.

"I hope you had a wonderful birthday."

Wonderful is not even close to how I really feel about my birthday. Last night felt like a dream, but the tenderness I felt this morning is evidence that it was anything but that. The only thing I regret is the feeling I felt after Tristan pulled away from me. I'm not sure what scared him more—the fact that I was a virgin or that it was me.

> she is my dark lady, my MUSE.

CHAPTER 1

TRISTAN

TWO WEEKS LATER...

They say, when someone dies, they're never really gone. So why does it feel like every trace of my mother has been sucked out of this world?

Heavy rain pounds against the cement beneath my feet as I make way across the cemetery parking lot. The massive grounds in front of me reach farther than I can see, and the number of headstones lining the hills is daunting. I race through the muddy grass trying to escape the storm cloud that hovers above, but each step I take sends water splattering across the fabric of my pants.

I'm a fucking mess. No, I'm a traitor.

I'm a traitor who's wearing a borrowed five-hundred-dollar suit to his mother's funeral. His mother who died penniless and alone. *Who am I?* I woke this morning asking myself that same question over and over. A feeling of suffocation overwhelms me as I tear off the jacket of my suit and tie, flinging them to the ground. My lungs burn from running, but the feeling doesn't compare to the pain that rips through the rest of my chest as I get closer and closer to where her remains rest.

"There you are," says a voice calling out to me from behind.

I turn to find my old co-worker, Vivian, standing in front of me.

"What happened to you?" she asks. "Did you lose your jacket?"

"Something like that," I mutter.

I haven't spoken to Vivian in quite a while, and yet she's the only person I could think of to be here. The only person who would let me borrow money to cremate my mother. After calling the funeral director at a nearby funeral home, I quickly realized burying my mother would be out of the question. Where the hell was I supposed to get $7,000? While I'm starting to get more customers from the Pleasure Chest, the amount I make is nowhere near the money I needed. There wasn't a chance in hell I would ask Stefan for the money either. It's better that he doesn't know my mother has been alive all of this time. He doesn't get to have closure. My mother never did.

"Here," Vivian says, offering space for me to step beside her under the large umbrella.

Rain drips down the side of the umbrella-like water gushing from a spout. God, I hope she hasn't been here long. From her damp appearance, I can only guess she has. I take a step forward and approach the ever-daunting wall of names in front of the columbarium where they've placed the ashes of my mother. Vivian pushes back her black waves as she stares at the pattern of memorial plaques in front of her with a thoughtful expression.

"Thank you for coming," I say.

"I'm glad you finally called me. I was wondering if the city swallowed you up."

"Believe me, sometimes it feels like it."

She lays her hand on my shoulder and squeezes it lightly before returning her gaze to the wall in front of us. Rainwater washes over me, baptizing me in its cold sensation as I close my eyes and imagine what life would be like if the rain could really wash away our sins. If only we could all be forgiven so easily. I open my eyes as I feel a tap on my shoulder. To my surprise, I find Vivian staring at me with tears in her eyes. Since I've known Vivian, she's never shown a shred of weakness. If I didn't know any better, I would say she's the reason why people use the expression 'tough as nails.'

"I have something for your mother," she says.

My heart skips as I watch Vivian pull a small bouquet of roses from the wet plastic bag on her arm. Their beautiful pink hues match perfectly with the plaque for my mother's ashes. The flowers are delicately beautiful. A description once so aptly described my mother.

"I thought it would be nice to bring her some flowers."

"Thank you," I manage to say.

Despite the sea of names, it isn't hard to pick out my mother's memorial plaque. Hers seems to be the only one with a rose pink tint and gold lettering.

Rosaline Isabella Knight.

It's surreal to see my mother's name among the rest of the city's dead, and it takes every fiber of my being not to break down in tears at the sight of it. The bitterness I feel toward Stefan has consumed me since I learned of my mother's passing. It's all I've thought about. I know she committed suicide because she thought she had no one left, but I never expected her to feel that hopeless. It doesn't matter which way I spin this—Stefan will always be partly to blame. He took everything from me and from her. My eyes trace the hundreds of other plaques that sit abandoned beside hers. The surrounding flowers are dry and brittle. I'm almost certain they would come apart at the slightest touch, and for some reason, the thought of my mother's ashes sitting here next to them eats away at me.

It seems even in death, my mother's life has been reduced to just another name on a wall.

" she is my dark lady, my MUSE. "

CHAPTER 2

TRISTAN

The world around me is one chaotic blur of hospital waiting rooms and doctors in white coats. I should be used to this by now. My mother wasn't new to this, but it's not my mother who's lying in the bed across the room. And it isn't my mother who the doctors just said would never be waking up from a coma. It's Emily and Nicholas's brother, Alexander.

The sight of him lying on a hospital bed looking so broken and frail is unnerving. I've never really had a connection with Alex the way I did with Nicholas and Emily, but it doesn't make seeing this any easier. I pace the room feeling the need to reach out and comfort those around me.

"He has to wake up," Emily cries.

"He will!"

Nicholas storms past me and proceeds to slam his fist against the gray hospital room wall. It vibrates with the pressure of his hand and fills the room with a booming echo. The sound of Emily's broken voice calls to me from the other side of the room. Her frame sits curled in a ball on top of a chair as she rocks her body back and forth. It seems I'm destined to watch those around me suffer. I must be cursed.

"Please stop, Nick," Emily cries. "Tristan, make him stop."

Nicholas's gaze never leaves Alex's bedside as I stop to give him a quick squeeze on the shoulder. If I could help him somehow, I would, but the best thing I can do now is to comfort Emily. I walk over to her and wrap my arms around her shoulders. Her pale fingers curl around the ends of my hair just below my neck as she sobs into my chest in soft tremors that pull apart the very depth of my soul. The need to console her makes my very heart ache.

"Emily, look at me."

"No, I can't."

I lift her chin with my index finger, forcing her to meet my gaze. With a shaky breath, she finally gives in and looks up at me with watery eyes laced with pain. She blinks away tears from her eyes. *Damn it all to hell.* I wish I could draw every thread of tears from them and fill them back with stars.

"You're going to be okay," I say.

Her small frame presses against me sending electric waves of tension running through my veins. My cock throbs at the sensation and memory of two weeks earlier.

"Let's give Nicholas a minute," I say, lifting her into my arms. Emily's petite frame sags against me as I carry her across the room and outside.

"Tristan," she murmurs into my chest. "Tell me I'm dreaming. Tell me Alex is okay and that he's going to wake up."

I cradle her in my arms squeezing her against my chest. The sensation is hauntingly familiar. I held my mother this same way when I found her passed out on the floor. It hurts just thinking about her. I didn't make time to see her enough. *God, I miss her.* I wish she were here with me now, but I know that will never happen.

"I'm going to take you home," I say, squeezing Emily.

"No, I don't want to leave!"

I spot Stefan rushing down the hall toward me with a haunted look in his face. His broken gaze washes over me as he spots Emily sobbing in my arms. For a moment, I feel happy. Happy that Stefan finally understands what it is to lose the person you love most in this world. He's incredibly lucky he still has Nicholas and Emily, but I know Alex meant something greater to him. Alex meant his succession. It meant Stefan's name would live on. Now there's the possibility it will be forgotten over time. Much like my mother, he'll be reduced to just another name on a wall.

I force myself to purge the bitter thoughts from mind and focus on the blonde angel whose hands are wrapped around my shoulders.

"Tristan, could you please take Emily home?" Stefan asks.

The edge in his voice is undeniable.

"Yes."

I leave Stefan to mourn for his son. As much as I hate that he hurt my mother, I can't be the monster that takes pleasure in watching his world crumble around him.

I watch her lips curve into a smile as she falls asleep on the couch. The house around us is empty of all light with the exception of the television that's on. Despite the need I feel to tell her how much she means to me, I leave things as they are.

I slide my book of Lord Byron's poems underneath her hands for her to keep. It's the one thing I've kept from Stefan's library all of these years. The thought of leaving it behind for her to read is more comforting than any pleasure I'll get from re-reading it. Emily's eyes flutter open momentarily at my touch before quickly closing once again. I lean in, capturing her lips in a chaste kiss. The memory of it will stay with me always.

> she is my dark lady, my MUSE.

CHAPTER 3

TRISTAN

FOUR YEARS LATER

Two A.M.

It's the blaring echo of my cell phone that violently pulls me from my sleep. The sound resonates throughout my art studio with an intensity that could wake the dead. My eyes blink toward my nightstand as my hand fumbles in search of my cell phone. Who the hell is calling me now? Despite the cascading city lights that engulf the outside of my studio, the inside remains lost in darkness.

I find my phone barely hanging on at the edge of the nightstand. Curiosity gnaws at me as I swipe the screen and enter my passcode. There aren't many people who have my personal cell phone number. Most of my clients contact me by email. To my surprise, along with the missed call from a private number, there's a notification of a new voicemail. I hold the phone to my cheek and play the recording. A familiar voice floods the line.

Nicholas StoneHaven.

"Hey, I know you're probably busy or asleep, but I was hoping you'd come out and have a drink with me. I really need to talk to you, buddy. All right, call me."

My gaze lingers over my phone as I scroll through my contacts. Up until recently, keeping my distance from the StoneHaven family has been surprisingly easy with four years of school and then working on my art. I've never thrown myself into something the way I did with my paintings after the domino effect of destruction that followed my mother's death. It took all my strength not to seek out Emily when I found out about her mother selling Alex's death to the tabloids. I never liked Evelyn, but I didn't think she would sink that low for money.

I thought, with time and distance, I could forget about the way I felt for Nicholas and Emily, but the truth is, I can't. The bitterness I feel toward Stefan hasn't gone away, and I'm not sure if it ever will, but I refuse to hate Emily and Nicholas. I won't make them pawns. The anger I've carried since my mother's death has already disintegrated enough.

I replay Nicholas's message over again, and a wave of guilt washes over me at the sound of desperation in his voice. I should just delete the voicemail and pretend I didn't hear it. If he asks me about it later, I'll just tell him I never got the message. In the past four years, we've both kept in touch, but I've even kept him at arms length.

A text message flashes across the top of my phone in a bright green bubble.

Nick: Why haven't you called me back, asshole?

I smile. He really knows how to sweet talk someone. Another text message buzzes in just as I unlock the phone screen.

Nick: I'm just going to keep texting you until you come have a drink.

He's a persistent asshole. I'm fairly certain it should be considered a negative thing but, somehow, Nicholas makes it seem charming to women. I tap a text into my phone.

Me: Nice to hear from you too, Nick. Drinks tomorrow?

Nick: Too late. I started without you.

Me: Are you drunk?

Nick: Fffffuck yeah.

Me: Please don't tell me you're driving.

Nick: The hotel took my keys. Pick me up.

Me: You haven't changed, buddy.

Nick: It's been too long since we hung out. Shit. Paparazzi are here.

I stare at the text, and the memory of my mother's words before she died come rushing back to me.

"They'll ruin every good thing about you. Don't let them."

Against my better judgment, I text Nicholas back.

Me: What's the name of the hotel?

Nicholas: The Somerset.

Me: Stay put. I'm coming to get you.

I pull into the valet circle in front of the prestigious Somerset Hotel. It's not the hardest building to pick out, especially when it's practically made of gold. As I curve the corner, I spot Nicholas in a heated discussion with a small group of paparazzi. This is not good. Before I have a chance to hand the valet my keys, Nicholas swings at the cameraman in front of him. FUCK. The valet gasps as I park my car, throw my keys at him, and rush out of my car.

I push past the other hotel guests just in time to stop Nicholas from doing any further damage. It takes him several seconds to realize I'm holding him back from beating the shit out of the cameraman in front of him. The look of surprise on his face quickly fades into a look of relief. His grip tightens on my arm as he leans in and gives me a quick hug as a flutter of cameras flash behind us. Even if Nick doesn't say it, I knew he wasn't sure if I would come tonight. I grimace at the barely cloaked smell of whiskey on his clothes as it soaks into mine.

The paparazzo Nicholas hit slowly stands and cautiously inches back from the two of us. He massages the side of his face as the skin beneath his eye starts to swell. The rest of his skin is inked in angry red blotches.

"You owe me a fucking camera!" he says, spitting right in front of us.

Nicholas turns with a scowl. "You wish, asshole. I'm not paying for shit."

"Nick, let's go."

"Yeah, go home, rich boy. I can't wait to sell these to US Weekly. I bet they'll fetch big bucks."

The look of pure satisfaction on the paparazzo's face sends a rush of anger through me. What a dick. I guess I shouldn't be surprised the StoneHaven family is still a main target for the press, though. After their brother, Alex, died, the paparazzi became vicious. There wasn't a single press member that didn't want to scoop a story about the death of the heir to a multi-billion dollar publishing company. I can't count the number of articles I read on the subject. I wanted to burn down every newsstand that carried them.

CHAPTER 4

EMILY

"So where are we headed again?"

My roommate, Augie, looks over at me with an irritated expression on his face. He's pissed because we're late to a dorm party at NYU, and we've been driving around Manhattan trying to get a hold of my drunken brother.

"We're looking for the Somerset Hotel."

"Have I mentioned I'm going to kill Nicholas?"

"Take a number." I laugh. "I'm pretty sure my father will handle that one for you."

Augie rolls his eyes as he pulls a cigarette from the pocket of his T-shirt. He lights it up and hits the window before the puff of smoke can hit me in the face.

"Em, I was supposed to meet that sexy tuba player named Harvey. I think he was going to ask me out."

He is never going to let me live this down. If Augie misses his chance with the sexy tuba player, he's going to hate me for the rest of this school year. And that's not something I want when I have to sleep in the room across from his.

"I promise you we'll make it to the party. We just need to pick up my brother first."

I shake my head in frustration as I hold my phone to my ear and re-play my brother's voice message on my phone. *Sis, I need you to pick me up.* The habit of his is getting older by the second. Why didn't he just call a private taxi? And why didn't I just ignore his text. Any smarter, younger sibling would.

Damn, Nick. I love my brother but for once, I wish I could be the younger sibling in this situation. I should be out partying with my friends and getting drunk. Not him. Instead, we're spending Saturday night speeding across Manhattan. Maybe, I'm just looking for an excuse to get out of this party. The only reason why I'm going tonight is that Augie and my best friend, Ceci, convinced me to. Apparently, I act way too old for my own good. At least that's what they keep saying.

"I think I can see the hotel." I point to the towering gold building down the street.

"Are you sure? It's going to be a bitch trying to get over," Augie says, pushing his way to the left side of the road. "And why the hell didn't your brother just take a taxi? There're dozens of them here."

Ignoring Augie, I unlock my phone and tell my voice command to dial Nick's number. To my dismay, his cell goes straight to voicemail. Fuck. We better not have driven all the way down here just to have him not be here.

"Nick, pick up your phone! I'm here. Call me back."

I turn to Augie with a sorry expression.

"So you're going to have to park, and I'll run in to get my brother."

"Just remember, Emily... Harvey."

"I know, I know. I'll flag you down when I get back."

My dress flares as I speed-walk past the valet and head toward the front of the Somerset Hotel. A flash of cameras draws my attention toward TAP, the lush outside bar that frames the side of the hotel. There's a crowd of men in suits hanging near the front watching the beautiful women as they trickle in and out of the bar.

Not too far from them is a growing crowd of paparazzi. Perfect. I've almost gotten used to not having to deal with them, but they seem to hang around like vultures in this area of the city.

"Fuck you!"

I hear Nick before I see him. The anger in his voice sends a streak of anxiety through my chest, pushing me toward the crowd of paparazzi. Oh, God. He must be the reason why they're lurking around the outside of the bar. The crowd slightly parts just enough for me to catch sight of Nicholas taking a swing at the paparazzo in front of him. I cringe as the man stumbles back against the crowd. Incoming hotel guests stop to observe as profanity spews from his mouth. His face turns bright red as he confronts Nick. I can't hear what he's saying, but his mocking tone only makes my brother more hostile.

"Nicholas!" I yell, hoping to stop him from doing something incredibly stupid. A familiar figure pops into view as Nicholas steps forward to swing once again. I recognize Tristan within an earshot of hearing his voice. Before I have a chance to intervene, Tristan wraps his arms around Nicholas, immobilizing him as he pulls him away from the paparazzi. The cameras in front of us don't pause for even a moment as they flutter to capture the whole scene.

Shock overwhelms me at the sight of Tristan standing only a few feet away from me. He's so close I could almost touch him. It's almost too surreal to believe. What the hell is he doing here? I step back tempted to get lost in the crowd before he sees me, but it's too late. His eyes connect with mine the moment I start to step away.

"C'mon, Nick, let's get you home," Tristan says, wrapping his arm around my brother's shoulder.

As much as I want to hate Tristan, watching him protect Nicholas kindles a familiar feeling inside of me. My body betrays me. He doesn't call out to me, but I know he recognizes me from the disbelief that registers on his face. A streak of anger and desire filters through me as his gaze holds me. Tristan looks good. Too good. His designer suit melts against his body revealing muscular thighs and broad shoulders and an incredibly sexy Adam's apple. I watch it bob as Tristan swallows his words. A part of me is disappointed to see Tristan's hair cut short. I can't help but miss the length it used to be.

"I've missed you, asshole," my brother murmurs, pulling his attention back.

I'd be lying if I said I hadn't saved every news article I could find on the success of Tristan's paintings. It seemed like overnight he became a well-known sensation.

"Who are you?" A paparazzo asks stepping forward and snapping a picture of Tristan.

Before anyone has a chance to answer, a voice calls out from the crowd.

"That's Tristan Knight."

An excited murmur of voices surrounds us as the flashes continue. I'm not surprised New York loves Tristan. Who wouldn't love a story about a boy who grows up in the streets and then becomes a locally prized artist? Everyone loves a Cinderella story. So why can't I shake this bitter feeling? It seems the world has seen more of Tristan than I have, and they all seem to think he's this perfect being. But I know better. He's the same person who broke my heart into tiny little pieces and scattered them on his way out the door. Fuck him. Why the hell is he here?

Tristan steps forward blocking the view of the flashing paparazzo. The rawness of his voice sends a strange flutter through my chest.

"I'm a family friend and that's all you need to know."

Why is Tristan trying to be so sweet? Why is he acting like he didn't eject himself from our lives?

"Where have you been?" Nicholas asks, turning to Tristan. "Why didn't you come see us this past Easter?"

My brother's gaze searches Tristan's face for an answer. It's a question I've longed to ask for the past four years, except Tristan never really stopped talking to Nicholas. He just stopped seeing me. A flash of anger sparks from Nicholas's eyes, but more than that, there's hurt. An emotion matching the intensity of mine.

"I was planning to. I just needed to get some things in order..."

Tristan's gaze shifts to mine before returning to the walkway in front of him. "Let's go inside before the paparazzo does something else to piss you off."

The paparazzi follow us to the front of the hotel, but they're quickly contained as several of the hotel employees block them from entering the hotel. Sadly, it doesn't stop them from swarming the outside of the lobby doors as they click away on their cameras. I can't help but feel like a caged animal on display at the zoo as they stalk the outside of the hotel.

I grab Nicholas's coat and hook my arm through his. He sways as he drapes his jacket over his shoulder and tries his best not to stumble forward. The frazzled sight of him would almost be comical if I didn't know the reason for his latest drinking binge. My brother, Alexander. Of the two of us, I think Nick has taken Alex's death worse.

"Nick, why did you come to the Somerset?" I prod.

I know the answer, but I ask the question anyway. Today was Nina, my brother's finance's wedding. We couldn't expect her to stay single forever, but we were still surprised when we got her Save the Date cards several months earlier.

"I needed a drink," Nick says.

My brother avoids my gaze, but it doesn't deter me from my interrogation. Tristan's eyes are glued on me as I continue.

"Is it because—"

"I don't want to talk about it."

Nicholas breaks off and heads the opposite direction of where we were going. Frustration bubbles in my chest as he ignores me calling after him. Shit, Augie is going to be pissed. It's been more than fifteen minutes since I left the car.

"Nick, come back!" Tristan yells.

"Just let him go."

Nicholas ignores us as he stalks off toward the bathroom. I didn't even mention Alex's name, but he immediately knew what I was going to say. It stills feels like we lost my brother yesterday. I miss his stubborn silence and the goodness that he exuded.

"What's going on?"

"Nothing."

"That's not what it seems like."

"Alex's college sweetheart got married today. It wasn't in the papers, but we got an invitation to the wedding six months ago."

"Oh."

"You would've known that if you actually came to see us."

"Emily, please. Listen to me."

But I don't. I keep going, letting the words spill from my lips.

"Nick was doing so well, but every now again, he just seems to fall off the wagon. Last year, we went to the beach house and everything was fine until he went to Alex's room there. We haven't touched it since he passed."

"I'm sorry, Lily pad," Tristan says, reaching out to touch me.

"He needed you..."

I needed you.

CHAPTER 5

TRISTAN

The tension between Emily and I thickens as each minute passes. I wish I could fix what went wrong between Emily and me with a simple apology, but life is a little more complicated than that. And the past always seems to be looming over me. I want to forget what I did, but I'm the reason why their lives are so broken. I still wish I could forget the way Emily felt beneath me, or the way her aquamarine eyes heated watching me touch the submissive lying on the bed in front of me, but I haven't been able to. The innocent young girl I grew up with vanished that night. I should've let her go, but the moan that escaped her lips only made it harder. It made me harder. I'm sure she knew my intentions, but she didn't question me when I started touching her.

She refuses to look up at me for more than a few seconds, and I can't fucking stop thinking about her lips and the way her dress hugs those familiar curves. I watch her as she shifts from one leg to the other. It's a delicate balancing act that she carefully executes as she waits for Nick's return. I know she doesn't want to talk to me, but it doesn't stop me from trying.

"How's school?" I ask.

The question seems simple, but I should know better than to think anything is simple between us. Emily turns slightly toward me, but her eyes never stray from in front of her. She slowly slips her lip between her teeth. I know she's trying to keep quiet, holding back the anger inside. After several painful minutes, she finally gives in and turns toward me with her arms crossed. I know Body Language 101. Arms crossed are definitely not a good sign, but it doesn't deter me from trying to get her to talk.

"It's fine," she mumbles. "I actually took a year off, but now I'm ready to go back."

I don't ask her why because I already know the answer. She took a year off because, even after four years, Alex's death still didn't feel like it was over. At least not with the paparazzi hounding their family from day one.

"So what are you studying?"

"English."

I smile at the memory of staying up late and reading Emily poems.

"I'm sure that makes your father happy."

"He doesn't seem to care what I major in, as long as Nicholas takes over the company when he retires."

I'm not surprised Nicholas took Alex's place.

"Just do whatever makes you happy."

A small smile appears on her lips, but it quickly disappears.

"I'm sorry I wasn't there for you or Nicholas."

The words come rushing from my mouth before I have an opportunity to even think about what the hell I'm saying. I grit my teeth at the sight of a wince from her that almost goes unnoticed. I know I hurt her, and if I could take it all back, I would. At least if it meant she wouldn't react this way toward me.

"Alex said you would leave after you got what you needed from us. I guess I was just the cherry on top."

"It wasn't like that..."

"Emily!"

We both turn at the sound of a voice coming from behind us. A young man with brown hair and a wide smile slips between us and slides up next to Emily. She turns and pulls him into an intimate embrace. I try my best to restrain myself at the sight of it. A streak of jealousy washes over me as Emily smiles at the handsome stranger. What I wouldn't give to have that same reaction from me. It used to be that way before I went and fucked up everything good.

"I was looking all over for you, Em," he says. "I had to park two blocks down."

"Sorry, my brother was acting like a fool in front of the paparazzi."

Emily's gaze slips to mine and then turns back to the stranger beside her. Before she has a chance to introduce us, he steps forward and extends his hand to me.

"Hi, I'm Augustine Andrews."

"Tristan Knight. It's a pleasure to meet you," I say, gripping his hand. "How do you know Emily?"

I know my question is intrusive, but I don't care. I have to admit I never thought about the day that I would have to deal with Emily having someone else in her life.

"He's my boyfriend," Emily blurts.

My heart catapults as she intertwines her hand into Augustine's hand. I swallow the lump in my throat as I try my best to feign my happiness for the couple. Despite my bias against any man for Emily, and the fact that it kills me to admit—Augustine seems surprisingly nice.

"Yes, we've been together for almost a year now," he adds suddenly.

An awkward silence thickens between us as we wait for Nicholas to return to the hotel lobby.

"We should go," Emily says, piping up.

"Right, we were actually on our way to a party," Augustine says, shaking my hand. "It was nice meeting you."

"I'll get your brother home," I add.

Emily stops for a moment and looks at me as if she's going to thank me, but it isn't long before she quietly turns and follows Augustine out one of the side doors of the Somerset Hotel. I watch them run across the street and down the way, as an unsettling emotion carves its way into my chest.

    Perhaps, after all this time, she was able to forget me... I can't say the same.

CHAPTER 6

EMILY

I can feel Augie's eyes burning into the back of my skull as we head toward the party at NYU. Memories of Tristan taking me on the stairs back home flashes in front of me as we weave our way through traffic. I'll never forget the way Tristan felt inside of me or the pressure of his cock pressing against my stomach. I've seen my fair share of nude men since, but none of them could compare to him. Losing my virginity to Tristan was not how I imagined it would go, but here I am, reminiscing about the man who used me and then left.

"So... are you going to tell me why you introduced me as your boyfriend?" Augie asks.

"Probably not."

I try my best to avoid his inquisitive gaze as we drive further away from the Somerset Hotel. It just so happens, seeing Tristan again is the last thing I want to talk about. I can't believe I've been fawning after the memory of him for the past four years. Pathetic much? Feminists everywhere would be turning their noses at me in disgust.

"Is Tristan that guy who used to live with you guys?"

"Yeah."

"Hmmm... there's something you're not telling me."

"Nope."

Augie turns to me as we come to a full stop at a red light. Much like Ceci, he's relentless with his interrogations. I'm not in favor of lying to my friends, but this is one secret I've lived with for the past four years. If my brother or father ever found out, I'm not sure what they would do. Having your father as one of the most powerful men in the city isn't always a good thing. As much as I hate Tristan for leaving, I don't hate him enough to ruin his life.

"Yes! Fuck my ass harder."

The sound of my best friend's orgasm pierces the air of the empty hallway echoing all the way to the entrance of our stairwell. My cheeks flush at the sound of her incessant mewling. I'm almost certain that our elderly neighbor, Mrs. Abernathy, can hear her climaxing across the hallway.

"Well, I guess we know why Ceci wasn't at the party," Augie says with an eye roll.

"I'm sorry Harvey wasn't there."

From the sad look on Augie's face, I can tell he really does like Harvey. It's not just a crush anymore. I'm starting to think it's turning into something more serious.

"Me, too," he says.

Our apartment, although lavish, is surrounded by older residents and not the usual twentysomething's pad. The location is my father's way of keeping me out of trouble. The only cost of having it is that I keep my grades up, and I stay away from trouble. Trouble meaning guys. My best friend doesn't always make that an easy criteria to meet. She's supposed to be living with her parents still in a mansion on the Upper East Side, but she's almost always at our apartment.

We're halfway to our apartment door when I spot a pair of hot pink latex panties hanging from the doorknob.

"Lovely."

Augie's laugh echoes through the hallway.

"Why did we give her a key again?" I moan.

"She's like a stray kitten. We can't just leave her wandering outside in the hallway."

I smile at my childhood memory of Ceci with painted cat whiskers for Halloween. Her parents wouldn't let her hang out with anyone but me. They thought I was a good influence. If only they could see her now.

Aside from the trademark Barbie panties and Ceci's rowdy fucking, the bass pumping through the walls is a dead giveaway that she's in our apartment with her current flavor of the week. I'll never be able to listen to *Usher* without thinking of Ceci's sexcapades. Don't get me wrong. I adore my best friend because she has this loveable, in your face sort of attitude, but I can't stand it when she brings guys home. Twice I've found her fucking someone on our kitchen stove. A dirty condom in the stove burner is not a welcomed sight when I'm trying to make myself mac n' cheese, and I doubt Augie wants to explain to the fire department why it was there in the first place.

"Are you ready?" I ask, picking up Ceci's panties with my keys.

A wicked smile plays on Augie's lips.

"It would be the polite thing to let her finish..."

"Yes! Fuck. Me. Harder!"

A door slams behind us, and we turn to find Ms. Abernathy staring at us with critical glare plastered to her face. The sight of her serious expression makes her fuzzy mink coat almost comical. *Almost.* A loud boom echoed through the hall as I stood awkwardly trying to avoid her stare.

"Oh, yeah, right there!"

Shit, you'd think there was an earthquake happening in our apartment. Is Ceci trying to break the bed? Damn, I really hope she's on Augie's bed, not mine.

"That roommate of yours is always playing music at strange hours of the night—"

Thankfully, Ms. Abernathy doesn't know she isn't our roommate. I'm sure the housing co-op board would find some way to kick us out if they knew.

"I know. I'm so sorry, Ms. Abernathy. I promise I'll talk to Ceci," I offer.

"It's not lady like to have men over at all hours of the night. All that moaning makes it sound like there's a cat in heat," she says with a scowl.

"We will make sure she keeps it down," Augie says with a polite smile.

"Yes, just please keep it down. I can't take anymore loud noises."

A messy-haired Ceci opens our front door just as Ms. Abernathy walks back to her apartment.

"Hey, I thought you guys would still be at the party!"

A sly grin spreads across her face. There's a sparkle in her eye that I can't help but feel a little envious of.

"Uh huh. I'm sure you did," Augie says, walking past her.

Ceci's boy toy slips past us and out the door wearing nothing but a pair of boxer briefs as he carries his pants and shirt. I stifle a laugh as Augie's gaze lingers over the finely cut six-pack on the handsome stranger.

"Augie, you better close your mouth or a fly will get in there," I tease.

He blushes.

"Yes, mother."

Ceci throws on her jeans and walks over to the kitchen. I bite back a laugh as she rummages through the kitchen looking for food. I'm starting to think that we should've gone to a three-bedroom apartment instead of a two-bedroom.

"I'm going to go lay down," Augie says with an exasperated look.

"Sounds good," I say.

I watch Ceci silently pouring herself a bowl of cereal before plopping on the leather couch. She looks over at me with a smile.

"I know what you're going to say, Emily."

She stabs her spoon at the Cinnamon Toast Crunch cereal in her bowl.

"What am I going to say?" I ask.

"You're going to say that I'm always meeting different guys. That I need to be careful, but you know, I realized something the other night. I may put myself out there a lot, but at least I try. You stopped trying. You rarely go on dates anymore. It's like you've given up on being with anyone. I know when Alex died that was a lot for you, but you can't stop living."

I lost too much.

"I am living," I counter.

A stabbing pain hits me as Ceci rolls her eyes at me.

"No, you wake up, eat, go to school, come home, and repeat the same thing over and over."

"I went to the party at NYU. Maybe I didn't stay there all night, but at least I went."

"I'm surprised you went to the party, but remember, Augie and I had to beg you to go."

"It's not my scene. It's not me," I say.

"It used to be you," she says. "You've changed."

Maybe I have changed. Who doesn't change in four years? Alex's death changed me, Tristan's absence changed me, and both were out of my control. What am I supposed to do? Pretend like none of it ever happened? I can't.

"I think I'm going to go to bed, too. Good night, Ceci."

A sad smile appears on her face as I turn and leave. Behind me, I hear the TV switch on and the sound of laughter filling the screen. Despite how much I've tried to keep up with my friends and live my life, I can't fight the dreaded feeling that Ceci might be right. Maybe I'm just existing.

> she is my dark lady, my MUSE.

CHAPTER 7

TRISTAN

I slip a cigarette from my shirt pocket and light it as I lean against the wrought iron balcony of my studio apartment. The sun is just rising over the peak of the surrounding buildings, filling the room behind me with a celestial beam of sunshine. It's the perfect lighting to finish my canvas, but my mind isn't anywhere near the right state to return to my work. Despite the bottle of wine I had devoured last night, seeing Emily left me with an ache that I'm almost certain began at my soul.

I ache to feel her petite frame quivering beneath mine, to hear the way she gasped when I slid my cock inside her. Her sweetness ruined me the same way I ruined her. Those aquamarine eyes staring at me from against the staircase will forever be ingrained in my mind.

"Em, you're so wet."

It's taken all my strength not to break down and write her a letter detailing how sorry I am that I screwed up. I've thought about her every night since I left. I've longed to feel the warmth of her skin against my fingers again. It's better that I keep my distance. As much as I care for her, we fit in different worlds. At least that's what I keep telling myself.

A voice calls to me shattering my thoughts.

"Tristan, come back to bed." I look down at the naked dark-haired beauty that calls to me from my bed. I almost forgot she was here. Her coy smile completes her cat-like features as she crawls toward me on the bed. I know Francesca from the *Pleasure Chest*. Several of the art customers I have I met there. Although most of them are not intent on locking me into a relationship. The ones I've had over the years have not fared well, although the word relationship is putting it kindly.

"Francesca, you should probably go. I need to get some work done."

Her eyes taunt me to finish what I had started only moments earlier.

"You can paint whenever you want... I'll be here waiting."

"I told you this wasn't going to last forever."

A deep frown appears on her lips as she arches back against the bed and spreads her legs for me. I watch her as she slips her hand down across her sex. She's taunting me, but she should know better than to do it. Her dark tinted nipples pucker as I walk over to the bed. Her curious eyes watch me in fascination as I walk over.

"I have to admit I'm disappointed," she says. "I thought we had something special."

"We did. It's sitting in the corner."

My eyes slide over to the painting that Francesca commissioned me to paint of her. I move to get dressed, but the dark haired beauty stops me. She sits up sliding her hands across my shoulders as she pulls me into her embrace.

"Is it me?"

"No."

"Come to bed. Let me be your muse a little longer."

Despite the ache in my chest, I smirk at her persistence.

"Don't move," I command.

A look of excitement dances across her face. I watch her as she leans back and slides her leg across the sheets, giving me a better view of her wet pussy. Despite my command for her to lie still, she teases me by wiggling her hips ever so slightly.

"Didn't I tell you to lie still?"

"Yes, Sir," she says with a coy smile.

"Get on all fours."

I move closer as she gets on her hands and knees and spreads her legs inviting me to fuck her. I can smell her desire.

"Keep still."

I walk over to my bag sitting nearby and take a brush from it. Her eyes grow wide as I lean between her legs and wipe a trail of wetness from her lips. Despite her best attempt at keeping still, she moves as the bristle of the brush hits her skin. A soft moan escapes her. Her hips lean into my brush sending a smile to my lips.

"Unfortunately for you, you moved," I say.

Nails tear into my back as I flip Francesca and thrust into her. I close my eyes, and the first image I see is Emily's soft lips open and inviting. It doesn't take long for the dark haired beauty beneath me to unravel, sending me into a spiraling orgasm. She whimpers as I pull away and leave her wrapped in between the Egyptian sheets on my bed.

I bury my head in my hands as I will myself to stop thinking of Emily. It doesn't matter who the woman beneath me is—I always think of her. There's no escaping it. The moment I touched her, I damned myself for any other woman.

> she is my dark lady, my MUSE.

CHAPTER 8

EMILY

The Pleasure Chest

    The name is strange enough to conjure the image of kinky pirates and love knots by ruffian sailors. To be honest, it's not a club I've ever imagined myself going to. In fact, I wouldn't even be here if it weren't for Ceci. Her crazy ass is always getting herself into trouble and tonight is no different. She discovered an online dating app called Kinkstrest the other day, and I can tell it's already going to be trouble. The phone app is similar to Pinterest, but intermix BDSM dating. You pin pictures of the kinky stuff you're into and interested members message you. I warned Ceci about all of the crazies living in New York, but she didn't listen. She's been reading too many fictional romances about BDSM, and now she has these crazy ideas in her head.

    The part that bothers me is that I haven't heard from her in the past twenty-four hours, and Augie hasn't heard from her either. It wouldn't be so strange if she weren't always at our apartment. I even dared to call her parents looking for her. The last thing Ceci messaged me was that she would be at the Pleasure Chest with some guy named Torque. She never showed me a picture of him, but she described him as a hotter version of Chris Hemsworth.

Here I am, looking for a Thor look-a-like minus the mighty hammer. I should've called the police, but other than her vague description and a first name, I don't have much to go on. Besides, at this point, they wouldn't be looking for her. The building in front of me looks like a rundown packing factory. I hope to God this isn't the part where I get chopped up into little tiny pieces by leather face.

I approach the front entrance of the club and immediately feel somewhat relieved to see a normal looking man dressed in a suit standing in front of the door. He barely looks up at me before muttering at me.

"Membership ID?"

"ID?"

Shit. Ceci never mentioned anything about a membership ID. My eyes scan past him toward the entrance of the club. *I have to get inside.*

"I'm a guest of Torque's."

He scans his phone, which I can only assume holds the guest list to the club.

"Torque's a member here, but my list isn't showing any guest attached to him tonight."

If Ceci isn't Torque's, then where the hell is she? I really need to talk to this asshole. What if he hurt her? God, I hope her body isn't floating in the Hudson. Get a hold of yourself, Emily. You've watched way too many Law & Order: SVU episodes.

"Torque's expecting me. I'm surprised I'm not on the list," I lie. "I'm sure he'll be upset to find out you have me standing out here in the cold."

The man in all black finally looks up at me. His piercing eyes graze over me with a haughty disdain. I'm sure this isn't the first time he's heard something like this. I'd feel sorry for him, but I don't have time for it. I need to find my best friend.

"Enjoy your night," he mutters, sliding the black metal door open.

My heart skips a beat as a strange smirk creeps up his face. What am I getting myself into?

The inside of the Pleasure Chest is rich with color as I step inside. Portraits paint the walls of the industrial hallway leading up to what looks like a coat check in. I spot a tall redhead in a pink PVC dress and crystal clear platforms standing behind the front desk. Bright hot pink lipstick covers her lips giving her pale skin a luminous appearance. She smiles and calls me over with her index finger.

"Welcome to the Pleasure Chest."

"Thank you," I smile nervously.

Her eyes rake over my body with interest. I've never had a woman look at me the way she does. She smiles at the sight of my black mini skirt and teal lace top. The outfit is something I borrowed from Ceci's overnight bag. I distinctly remember my best friend going on and on about latex and skin-tight clothing. This will probably be the one and only time I ever come to a BDSM club, so why not go all out?

She slides over a clipboard with a non-disclosure agreement and a consent form. Her eyes sparkle with mischief as I take my time reading the documents. Having a CEO as a father has taught me always to be wary of things I sign. This isn't the first time I've seen a non-disclosure agreement, but it's the first time I've seen a consent form. I sign the document and slide the clipboard back over to the redhead.

I'm struck with surprise as she hands me a white mask and instructs me to put it on. I look up at her with a wary expression. Is this just for decor? Her eyes watch me with curiosity as I place the mask on.

"It must be your first time here," she giggles.

"Yes."

I bite back a smile at the double entendre. I'm sure if Ceci could see me now she would be laughing at me. *Damn, her.* I hope she's okay.

"Most of our members prefer to wear masks to conceal their

identity. The mask is optional so feel free to take it off inside if you need or want to," she says with a polite smile.

Despite the unknown ahead of me, the redhead's warmth toward me puts my nerves at ease.

"Is there anything else I need?" I ask.

"I'll need to take your phone if you have one on you."

"My phone?"

"Yes, we prefer that our members not have to worry about their activities being leaked to the press."

For that I'm grateful. I can only imagine my father's face if the press found out about my attendance at a BDSM club. I hand my phone and purse over to the redhead and watch her as she places it in a black cupboard behind her.

"It'll be here when you get back."

"Okay, thank you."

The redhead leads me to a red door on the other side of the room, which I can only guess is the real entrance to the club. I shiver as a cold draft hits me when she opens it.

"If you need anything, my name is Felicity. Feel free to come back if you would like to book a room. There are several I think you would like," she winks.

"I will," I stutter.

"Have fun."

Fun? She makes it sound like I'm stepping into a ball pit at McDonalds. I step through the door opening and take a turn down a red painted hallway. Toward the end of it I come face to face with a row of rooms. Several have windows covered with red curtains and others have clear glass. I reel back at the sight of a woman wearing thick black boots and a skin-tight police outfit. The spike on the heel of her boot sits pointed at the man's privates as he lays bound and gagged on the floor.

Holy shit. A shit-eating grin spreads across her face as he writhes on the floor. The more pressure she puts on him, the more he seems to enjoy it. I move on to the next room hoping to find my best friend, but the further I go into the club, the more hopeless I feel. If Ceci isn't dead when I find her, she sure as hell might be before we get home.

I quietly pass a beautiful brunette being led on a chain by a gorgeous man in a gray suit. I'm immediately drawn to the stern look that reflects in his dark blue eyes. The only shred of clothing on the brunette is the hosiery on her legs and the collar around her neck attached to a chain. It's hard to imagine letting any man parade me around like the way he's doing with her. Then again, he might be handsome enough to tempt me.

I'm a few steps past them when I hear the gush of excited voices. My heart skips as I gravitate toward the sound and past a set of curtains. I arrive at a center room where a dozen or so couples surround an illuminated stage. What's going on here? A show?

My eyes scan the crowd of club members as I look for any sight of Ceci nearby. It isn't until I'm all the way in the room that I spot *him* standing in front of a black cross on stage with a whip in his hand. The black mask surrounding his eyes is thick, but it isn't enough to keep me from knowing the face hidden beneath it.

My eyes rise up to the broad chest slightly hidden beneath the leather vest he wears. The matching black jeans he's wearing ride low on his hips revealing a pleasurable sight of hair trailing down from his navel. My gaze is glued to his movements as he scans the crowd in front of him.

It can't be him. Can it?

I nearly knock into someone as I blindly step closer to the stage. The closer I get to him the more I'm sure it's him. *Holy shit. Tristan Knight is at a BDSM club?* My heart squeezes at the strange, but arousing realization. What the hell? Tristan stalks the stage like a wild animal hunting its prey.

"Any volunteers?" he asks.

My body compels me forward as curiosity overwhelms me. Before anyone else has a chance, I raise my hand and walk toward him. His gaze immediately falls to me as the crowd around me parts. To my surprise, he doesn't say anything to me. At least, not at first. Tristan reaches out to me as he helps me climb the tall steps of the stage. A warmth spreads across my skin from the touch of his fingertips wrapped around my wrist.

It isn't until Tristan's touching me that I feel a strange shift in the air. He hesitates pushing me against the black cross, but eventually, gives in. His gaze washes over me as I wait with anticipation for him to recognize me. To say my name, but sadly, he doesn't. In fact, he doesn't say anything at all.

Instead, he focuses on the cross behind me.

"Are you sure you want to do this?" he asks, leaning in.

No.

"Yes."

A small smile escapes his lips.

"Take off your shirt."

CHAPTER 9

EMILY

I've never been the type to enjoy being in the spotlight, but this is a completely new way of being on display. I'm grateful for the mask given to me by the beautiful redhead at check-in. It provides a small amount of relief to the anxiety that filters its way through me as I stand half naked on stage. As hard as I try not to let them, my nerves get the better of me as I watch Tristan's face as his eyes slowly trace over my hot pink bra.

Eventually, he turns me and gently places my hands in the restraints at the top of the cross so I'm facing away from the crowd. I jerk each time his hands run across my body as he checks my positioning. The feeling of the rough edge of his skin sends my head reeling with memories of the past.

"Are you ready?" he asks, standing behind me. "If at any time you want me to stop, just say RED."

I silently nod. I have the feeling I'm not sure if I'll want him to stop when he's finished. A bright flame warms my cheeks as I feel Tristan step back to assess his masterpiece. Despite my inability to see him, I can feel his gaze on me. I tug on my restraints, but they don't budge. I couldn't escape even if I wanted to.

"I'm going to give you thirteen lashes on your back, butt, and thighs," Tristan says next to my ear.

He says the words so matter of fact that a streak of fear runs through me. *Why thirteen lashes?* Most people seem to associate the number with bad luck.

"Remember to call out RED if you want me to stop."

The fact that Tristan is repeating what he's already said makes me believe this is probably going to hurt. *Is this what Tristan's been doing*—whipping women at some BDSM club? Although I can feel the hungry, watchful eyes of the other club members on me, my anxiety quickly fades. My attention is swallowed up by the sensation of Tristan pacing around me. I wish I could say that over the years, I've gotten over him, but it would be a lie.

The sound of the whip resonates through the air as it goes flying with a swivel of Tristan's wrist. A loud snap fills my ears as the pressure of the lash hits my unmarked skin. Delicious warmth spreads across my thigh as the sharp sting licks me. My limbs tense as I wait for the inevitable strike to follow. I feel my skin heat at the impression left by the lash. The next one that follows only deepens the sting of the first. The room around me is quiet with the exception of the occasional moan or throaty groan of approval.

My sex tightens at the realization that there are over a dozen people watching us right now. Somehow, I thought I would feel embarrassed coming up here, but there's something liberating about being watched. It's as if my skin is a blank canvas and Tristan's whip is the brush. The finished product is the pleasure of witnessing my unraveling.

My skin starts to tingle as the endorphins in my body release with each lash. I bask in the feeling of Tristan's hands behind each stroke. My body feels like putty permanently molded to the cross by the time he's done. I try to move, but my limbs refuse to comply.

I feel Tristan's breath wash over me as he steps behind me once again and loosens the restraints from my hands and ankles. I collapse against him as he holds me, petting the side of my face. His thumb snakes underneath my mask and pulls it forward. Our eyes collide as his gaze melts into mine. The intensity behind his eyes, both delight and scare me.

"I could never quite forget those eyes," he murmurs. "Come with me."

I watch as he takes off his leather vest and pulls on a clean black T-shirt. His motions are hypnotizing as my eyes get a full view of his perfectly sculpted abs. After dressing, Tristan grabs a hot towel from a nearby heating container and hands it to me. I happily take the towel and rub off the sweat on my face and chest. Tristan takes a seat beside me and lightly dabs my back down with another towel. This one is cool and damp against my skin. I bite back a moan at the pleasurable sensation.

"What are you doing here?" Tristan asks, calmly.

I turn to find his fingers tracing over the red marks on my skin. A small smile plays on his lips as he looks up at me with interest.

"I came here looking for Ceci."

"Ceci? I've never seen her around here."

"Do you come here often?" I ask.

"Yes."

"Do you whip other women here often?" I blurt.

It takes him a moment to answer my question, but eventually, he does.

"Yes."

I'd be lying if I said that last 'yes' didn't hurt. My eyes trail down Tristan's body. What woman wouldn't want to be whipped by him?

"I have to go," I say, standing abruptly.

"What do you mean? Where are you going?"

I can't spend a moment longer around Tristan. My stomach flips at the realization that this is a mistake. I shouldn't be here. I shouldn't do this to myself. My cheeks flame in embarrassment as I grab my shirt and exit the VIP room.

The redhead at the front desk named Felicity greets me again with an open smile, but it quickly falters as she sees the look of distress on my face.

"Are you all right?" she asks rounding the corner.

"Yes, I just need to leave."

"Are you sure? We take member complaints very seriously."

"I'm sure."

Her sympathetic smile makes me like her even more. I can't imagine meeting her outside the club and not picturing her in her pink PVC dress. It seems to fit so well with her personality. She turns to the black cupboard behind her and pulls out my purse and phone. She quickly hands me the items, but her hands don't immediately let go.

"I hope to see you again," she says.

I smile, grateful to have made a friend in such an unfamiliar place.

My phone vibrates as I exit the Pleasure Chest. Ironically, the text is from Ceci.

Ceci: I didn't end up meeting the guy. I went to the club and dropped my cell in the toilet. :(

I laugh, despite everything I just went through to find my best friend. Somehow, I should've known she would lead me on a strange adventure, although I never expected to see Tristan here. On the cab ride home, I find myself trying to recollect the paintings that gathered along the walls of the Pleasure Chest. I hadn't noticed at first the strangely familiar art style, but now I'm almost certain they were painted by Tristan.

CHAPTER 10

TRISTAN

"Did the young, blonde woman leave already?"

A knowing smile spreads across Felicity's face as she watches me from the check-in. I should've gone after Emily instead of just letting her leave. I'm surprised she even got in. Non-members usually never make it past check-in. Not without a hefty fee.

"She left," she says, looking disappointed.

"It's probably better that she did."

"Oh, Tristan. Now I'm really curious."

Felicity's eyes light up with intrigue. Over the many years that I've come to the Pleasure Chest, I've learned to like Felicity more and more. I first met her through Vivian when they started dating. I didn't think my old friend would ever settle down, but the two have been inseparable since.

"I'm not in the mood to tell old stories," I say, turning back down the hall.

"Is she your muse?"

"What?"

"Your muse," she asks.

"I don't know what you're talking about."

Felicity walks over to one of the portraits hanging on the wall inside the club. She pulls it down with ease and walks it over to me. My heart palpitates as she slides her finger across the portrait to the woman's eyes staring back at me.

"Whenever you draw eyes, they're always hers. It doesn't matter if she's blonde, brunette, or a redhead, you always draw them aquamarine."

"Maybe I just like the color," I lie.

She laughs as she walks back over to the wall and rehangs the painting.

"Maybe."

I watch as Felicity grabs my wallet and keys from the black cupboard behind her. She slides them over to me with an amused look on her face, as if she's just discovered the reason behind Mona Lisa's smile.

"Or maybe she's your muse."

CHAPTER 11

EMILY

A pair of painted aquamarine eyes greets me as I enter my apartment after a long afternoon of classes. I stumble back in shock at the lifelike portrait sitting partially gift wrapped on top of my living room couch. The blue and green hues that bleed across the canvas immediately draw me, pulling me toward it. What the hell? Where did this come from? I know the answer even as I ask myself the question. It's been a week since I left the Pleasure Chest feeling like an idiot.

"It's beautiful, right?" Ceci asks, appearing from the kitchen with a bag of popcorn. "I was getting ready to watch a movie when the door rang. The guy who delivered it said it was for you."

A mischievous smile plays on her lips as she walks over to the painting and tears off the rest of the wrapping paper covering it. I stand back in shock at the majestic colors of a galaxy of stars that crown the outside of the eyes. Ceci pulls a card from the back of the canvas and hands it to me. She winks and heads back to the kitchen.

"Maybe it's an early birthday gift?" she asks. "Do you want me to read it to you?"

"Uh, no," I say, snatching the card from Ceci's hands.

DRAWN TO YOU

"Ohhh, or is it from a lover?"

I roll my eyes as she wiggles her eyebrows at me.

"Fine, I'll leave you to read your naughty card."

Ceci disappears from the living room as she makes her way toward my bedroom. My chest squeezes as I open the card and spot the beginning of Byron's poem.

Emily,

"She walks in beauty, like the night, of cloudless climes and starry skies, and all that's best of dark and bright, meet in her aspect and her eyes."

I hope you enjoy the painting. I made it to remind you of what I see every time I look at you.

- T.K.

There's only one person that I know with those initials. *Tristan Knight.* Why is he doing this now? Why did he wait four years to come back into my life? I wish I could tell him how much it hurt when he left. It was one of the most vulnerable moments I've ever experienced, and then he was gone. Why did it have to be him? It would've hurt less if it had been anyone else, but it was him.

The color of the painting draws my attention back to it. I can't keep this. I definitely can't keep this. *Can I?* No, I need to give it back. To my surprise, Tristan's address sits on the back of the card. It's almost as if he's daring me to come find him. Whether I want to admit it aloud or not, the idea of seeing him again is temptation enough.

I'll go and give him the painting back and then come home.

CHAPTER 12

EMILY

Anxiety takes over as we get closer and closer to Tristan's apartment. The confidence I once had drains quickly from me as we enter the Meatpacking District. I'm tempted to have the driver turn back, but it took a hell of a long time getting down here through rush hour traffic. *Why am I so nervous?* Memories of Tristan's whip hitting my skin jolts me. The marks on my skin have faded, but the sensation hasn't. What's wrong with me? I can't help but want to relive the moment over and over again.

The painting Tristan sent me sits taunting me from the opposite side of the car. Something about seeing it left my emotions in a whirlwind. Most people don't think about how much time it takes to paint something. I've heard Tristan talk about starting and finishing pieces. They never happened over night. In fact, he often said some took months to finish. My heart squeezes at the notion that for several months, I was all he thought about. *It's been years for me.*

It's stupid to want to keep the painting, but a small part of me does. It would just be a painful reminder of the adoration I once stupidly felt for him, but it's not just that. It's a reminder of the happiness I once felt being around him.

"We're here," Tom's voice says over the car stereo.

The Towne Car slows to a stop as we hug the corner of Washington and West 14th Street. Tom's face pops into view as the partition that divides us slowly rolls down. Despite his lack of questions, I can see a look of worry on his face. I'm sure at least half of that worry is because he's wondering if he's going to be fired for dropping me off without an address to know where to pick me up.

"Are you sure you wouldn't like me to drop you off closer, Ms. Emily?"

I roll my window down and take in the layout of the streets that surround us. The streets are buzzing with tourists and local bar hoppers.

"No, thank you, Tom. Here is fine."

"Should I wait for you?"

I exhale the shaky breath I've been holding in. I should have Tom wait for me, but something tells me this isn't going to be a five-minute conversation.

"Tom, I'll call you if I need a ride back."

"Very good."

Before Tom has a chance to open my door, I slip outside and head down the street carrying Tristan's painting with me. After Nicholas's fiasco at the Somerset Hotel, it's better if I don't draw attention to myself. I turn to wave Tom goodbye, but he's already slipped back into the swarm of traffic heading down the street.

According to my phone, Tristan's apartment is a five-minute walk from where I am. It's getting later and the sun is already starting to set. I walk past a group of guys who stop to stare after me as they chat with their friends. I cross my fingers silently hoping they don't recognize me. After all these years, I'm still not used to the attention people give me. It's never the attention I want. Between those who look at me sympathetically, and others who want to use me, I can't stand it. Being the daughter of one of the city's richest men isn't something you ever get used to. You never really know who's your real friend or foe.

The Meatpacking District is probably the last place I ever

imagined Tristan living. It's a neighborhood that's constantly busy with tourists. Despite how boring the name sounds, it's actually quite noisy. I'm almost to the other corner of the street when I spot the building where Tristan's apartment is. To my surprise, it isn't a lavish loft style apartment. In fact, it takes on the old look of the packing warehouses that used to line these streets. Complete with its gritty exterior is a solid steel door that's rolled down. My eyes are immediately drawn to the tagged up industrial door that sits adjacent to it.

This can't be right. I look down at my phone, but the blue circle on my navigation map points to the building directly in front of me. I set Tristan's painting down and after a few moments of fixing myself, I reluctantly knock on the gray door and listen for the sound of footsteps. The door reverberates on the other side, but no one comes. Maybe this is an abandoned building. My heart sinks at the thought that somehow the address is wrong. I set my mind on coming here. I told myself this was my chance to tell Tristan how I felt watching him leave us.

I should just go. Maybe I can still catch Tom. With this traffic, he's probably not even halfway down the street yet. I turn, but as soon as I do, I hear the click of a lock unlatching. A small slab on the door slides open and Tristan's gaze peers at me through the opening. His hazel eyes widen in surprise as I step closer.

"Emily?"

Despite my hurt and my anger, something in his voice pulls at me as he says my name. From the look on Tristan's face, he definitely wasn't expecting me to show up at his doorstep.

"Hold on," he says as he closes the latch and then opens the door.

He steps forward wearing tight jeans covered in paint. The top of them ride low on his hips accentuating the dip of his obliques. Fuck. His chest heaves as if he's been running and sweat trickles down his bare chest. A light brush of black hair paints his chest. My eyes rake up his body, taking in each cut and curve of his muscles. I hate him for looking so good. Not a lot has changed since the last time I saw him this way. There's just more. More muscle, more definition, and more to lose yourself in. I squeeze my knees together, blushing at the thought of seeing him fully nude again. Damn you, body. I shouldn't be reacting to him like this, but how can I not? All the things I wanted to say to him fly straight out of my brain the moment he opens his mouth.

"What are you doing here?"

Speak. But my body refuses to comply. My heart races as his eyebrows quirk up at my silence. His gaze scorches me. There's an intensity behind it that I wasn't expecting.

"Are you hurt?" he asks, stepping forward and pulling me into his apartment.

I feel his hands roaming over me and the feeling is far better than I remember. Why am I not stopping him from touching me? Tell him to stop. Even as I try to form the words, my brain feels fuzzy from his touch.

"I came to talk to you," I finally blurt.

"Oh, okay."

His hands stop touching me, and I immediately feel the disconnect between us as he steps back. I shouldn't want him to touch me. Not because he's my brother's best friend, but because he hurt me. He used me and then he left. My chest swells as I try to divide the emotions I'm feeling and the words I need to say. I'm stopped by the sound of a loud clank that echoes from behind him. What the hell was that? The thought of him being here with someone slowly creeps its way into my mind. Why wouldn't he be here with someone? Oh, God. Is that why he answered the door sweaty and out of breath?

"I should just go," I say, turning for the door.

"Wait. You wanted to talk."

"Not when there's someone else here with you."

I cringe inside as my words make me sound like a jealous little schoolgirl and not the confident woman I wanted Tristan to finally see.

CHAPTER 13

EMILY

A sexy smile lights up Tristan's face as he grabs my hand and pulls me down the hallway.

"Come with me."

He says the words like I have a choice, but I know I have little choice from the grip of his hand on mine. The shift in Tristan's tone makes me nervous. I can only take so many surprises from him. Seeing him at the Pleasure Chest was shocking enough. I'm still not sure how I feel about him being part of a BDSM club.

Before Tristan can usher me further into his apartment, I manage to grab his painting as the industrial door closes behind us. Leery of what I'm about to see in front of me, I opt to study my surroundings. The inside of Tristan's apartment is bare, except for his paintings that hang along the walls. As we travel further toward the back of the building, the themes of his paintings change from innocent views of the cityscape to portraits of nude women in sexual positions.

As we get closer to the back of the studio, I spot several bursts of light coming from several steel lamps that hang from the ceiling.

DRAWN TO YOU

In the center of their display lays a brunette chained to a red velvet antique couch. My eyes do a double take at the sight of one of Tristan's muses, who is very much real. A thick collar encrusted with diamonds surrounds her neck and between her legs lays a silver-like chain.

I nearly choke in embarrassment at the sight of her. This is definitely not what I was expecting.

The collar around her neck seems as if it would be painful, but the surprising twinkle in her eyes tells me differently. She smiles but says absolutely nothing. *I've seen her before.* It takes me a moment to realize she's the beauty from the Pleasure Chest. I saw her briefly before as I walked down the red painted hallway. The man with her was equally as mesmerizing, but this time, he's not here with her.

"This is Selena," Tristan says, watching me.

I turn to him in confusion. Is he sleeping with her, too? Why would he invite me inside to show me the woman he's having sex with? Is he purposely trying to hurt me—or perhaps, he doesn't think I care. I don't. Do I?

"She's here with her Master," Tristan says, catching my chin with his hand. "I'm painting her for him. It will be part of their personal collection."

Oh. Wait. Master? As in, she's a slave? A part of me almost wishes I were her.

"I should go."

"Wait."

I turn into a wall of steel muscle. Or at least that's the way it feels when I run into a handsome stranger on my way out of Tristan's apartment. I'm surprised to see the familiar brown-haired man standing in a gray suit blocking the front door. He looks down at me with a polite, but amused smile. I'm taken back by the scent of his cologne. No, not cologne. He smells like what sex would be like if it came in a bottle.

"Sebastian, this is a family friend. Emily, this is Sebastian, Selena's Master."

"It's a pleasure to meet you," he says.

I extend my hand, but he doesn't touch me. He simply smiles and looks to Tristan. A silent conversation passes between them before his gaze returns to me, and he extends his hand. I shake it, fully aware of the strong grip of his fingers.

"I see you've met my Selena."

"Your Selena?" I ask.

"Mine," he says with hungry eyes. "Let me officially introduce you."

I follow him, acutely aware of Tristan's gaze on my back. The stranger named Sebastian walks over to the beautiful brunette and pulls her chain. She moans as the chain slips between the lips of her center. She bows her head as he slowly helps her off the couch. My jaw nearly drops to the floor as she crawls on her hands and knees toward me. Sebastian never lets go of her chain.

I throw a look of confusion at Tristan, but he stands in the background silently watching me. His gaze never falters.

Selena crawls toward me, and I feel her breath inches from my skin. I look down at the naked angel forced on her hands and knees. A part of me almost feels sorry for her, but I can't help but think she would get up if she didn't like this position. It seems like an oxymoron, but I can't help but think it must feel somewhat freeing to be chained. I had a similar sensation when Tristan whipped me.

"She doesn't bite," Sebastian chuckles. "Not unless I tell her to."

I blush at the implied sexual innuendo. Unsure of what to do, I lean forward and place my hand on Selena's shoulder. Her skin is soft and before I can pull away, I feel her lips on the inside of my wrist. Perhaps her kisses are her way of saying hello.

"I like the way you taste," Selena whispers against my wrist.

I sense Tristan close in behind me as I pull back in surprise at Selena's words. It doesn't take me long to recognize the couple once they're beside one another. I remember seeing them for a brief moment as I ventured into the Pleasure Chest.

"I think we're done for today, Sebastian. We can continue next week if that's all right with you," Tristan says breaking the silence.

DRAWN TO YOU

Sebastian pulls Selena back by her chain. She pouts at the distance put between us. I'm grateful for the space to breathe as my head spins. Does Selena like women, too? My cheeks flush.

"Let me check my calendar, and I'll get back to you," Sebastian says with a smile.

"Perfect," Tristan says.

"Come."

I watch Sebastian lead the chained brunette down the hall. It isn't until they're almost to the door that I see him unchain her and hand her a yellow dress to wear. He leans in and kisses her with a possessive hold. I'm so entranced by the sight before me that I hardly hear Tristan calling my name. Although Sebastian and Selena's relationship is far different from any that I've ever seen, there's a tantalizing expression of love and adoration between them. I can't explain why, but my heart aches to have something similar.

CHAPTER 14

TRISTAN

My cock swells at the sight of Emily's curious gaze. She watches with amazement as Selena and Sebastian leave my studio. I force myself to stop imagining taking her on the red velvet couch Selena was just on. Seeing Emily at my front door was a pleasant surprise, but I honestly wasn't sure how she would react to my painting. Part of me wanted to give it to her myself, but I couldn't bring myself to. Now, she's here, and all I want to do is create another piece with her naked skin as my canvas.

"So he's paying you to paint her?" Emily turns, her cheeks still glittered with warmth. I can only guess what's going through her mind right now. I can't help but want it to be just as dirty as what's going through mine. Fuck. There I go again.

I smile. "Yes. Several of my clients are into BDSM."

"Oh."

"So, you said you wanted to talk to me," I say.

"Uh, yeah. I did," she says, pushing back a stray blonde hair as she clears her throat. "I mean I do."

Emily walks over to the other side of the room where her

purse lays. I watch her pull a canvas from the other side of the wall and flip it over. It's the art piece I painted for her, but why is it here? She picks it up and walks it toward me. My eyes wash over her searching for a clue of what she's about to say next.

"I came here to give this back to you."

I hear her words, but the anger that pulsates through my veins wrecks me.

"It was a gift," I say, angrily.

"I know, but if you think this makes up for... it doesn't."

So that's why she's here? I shouldn't be surprised. I deserve it, but I foolishly thought that I could change things. That somehow I could get her to forgive me for leaving. It pains me to say that she's right. I've avoided Emily for the past four years, all the while keeping in touch with Nicholas. I knew how it would seem to her, but I needed her to believe I didn't want her. Now, I'm not sure what I want her to believe. As much as I care for Emily, having feelings for her isn't easy. I can't just mess with my best friend's little sister because I'm losing more than just her if it doesn't work out.

"You can leave it here. I'll take care of it," I say, offering no other explanation.

Emily's voice cuts me as I turn to walk away. I can't take the pain of having her hate me. It was easier when I didn't see her.

"So that's it?"

"What?" I ask.

"You're just going to walk away."

I look up to find Emily's eyes watering with tears.

"You're perfectly fine if I hate you?" she asks.

"Is that what you came here for? To see if I cared?"

"Yes."

I cared enough to leave her alone. Any other asshole would've taken advantage of her and ruined her for all other men. I made a promise to myself that I wouldn't do that to her. I told myself that she'd get over me. That I would get over her.

"Caring has never been the problem."

"Then why the hell did you leave?"

She steps toward me, and I feel my control slowly slipping through my fingers like grains of sand. I could lose myself in those eyes. I could forget every shitty thing I've done and that her family's done to me, but I won't.

"Go."

"What?"

Her bright eyes widen in shock.

"Go home, Lily Pad. Go home and forget about me. Go back to your nice boyfriend who worships the ground you walk on. I'm sure he makes soft, slow love to you instead of fucking you raw."

"He is nice and the complete opposite of you!"

I laugh despite the pain that overwhelms me.

"If you think I'm going to be your knight in shining armor, sweetheart, think again. I'm not your prince charming. Far from it. Now, go."

As soon as the words leave me, I instantly regret them. The look on Emily's face is enough to shatter even the coldest bastard.

"You're right," she says as her voice breaks. "You're not the Tristan I once knew."

It takes all of my strength not to pull her into my arms and tell her that I'm a coward. That I'm lying through my teeth. The scent of her lavender shampoo fills my senses as she pushes past me. I close my eyes, refusing to watch her leave. She storms out of my studio in tears. I take the painting I made for her and break the canvas over my knee. The wood tears through the canvas, but it isn't enough. I take a box cutter and shred the rest throwing it in a nearby trashcan.

I am so sorry, Emily.

> "she is my dark lady, my MUSE."

CHAPTER 15

EMILY

Happy Birthday.

Except today doesn't feel happy. Not one bit. I promised myself that I wouldn't cry today, and if it weren't for the frozen margarita that my roommate Augie just made, I probably would be. It's been exactly two weeks since I spoke to Tristan at his studio. I know I shouldn't be expecting any apology from him. He made it quite clear he didn't want me near him, but the thought of having to live with the way our conversation ended eats away at me. I saw a different side of him that night.

"Hey, are you still moping about you know who?" Augie asks, pouring himself a glass of the strawberry drink.

I look up to find his inquisitive gaze glued on me. He rounds the corner of the breakfast bar to face me.

"You asked me to make margaritas at ten o'clock in the morning. Of course, I'm going to be worried about you."

"I'm fine."

I grab my margarita and head for the couch. I think I'll spend my birthday drinking fruity drinks and watching Girls on HBO. Then maybe I'll order a pizza to eat all by myself. Yup, that actually sounds pretty great. To top it all off, I'll make myself a chocolate cookie with some ice cream. The best thing invented by man ever.

"Do we need to have a friend-tervention?" Augie calls from the kitchen.

"No, I'm not telling Ceci about this."

"Why would you assume I meant Ceci?"

I roll my eyes as I click on the television for another distraction.

"Because you two are like peanut butter and jelly."

"We're nutty and sweet?"

"Mostly nutty," I say, taking another gulp of my drink.

Augie takes a seat beside me and leans his head on my shoulder. I know he's going to either ask me for a favor or tell me bad news. He is never the touchy-feely type, except in those two cases.

"So... I sort of did something bad."

"Don't tell me you spent our rent money on strippers again."

Now it's Augie's turn to laugh.

"No, I'm saving myself for Harvey, remember?"

"Are you guys talking?"

"This is not about me," Augie says.

"Right. So what did you do?"

"Um, well, I sort of told your brother that you wanted to go to the beach for your birthday weekend."

I glare at Augie with the best I'm-going-to-roast-your-ass on a spit look. Why the hell would he tell Nick that? And when did he even talk to him? I swear I can't trust anyone these days.

"Okay, well I think I'm just going to spend my birthday here."

Augie looks around the room at our pathetically sad apartment. Despite the pricey rent we spend each month, our apartment isn't the most happening spot in New York. We traded a gorgeous cityscape, parties every night, and gorgeous men from GQ just outside of our doorstep for free rent. My father was more than happy to help although I'm starting to learn that money always comes with a price.

My brother is the perfect example. Nicholas is destined to be my father's puppet.

"So, is there anything else you told him that I should know?"

"No..." he says with a nervous look.

"What did you do?"

"I might've mentioned that you wanted Tristan to come, too."

Fuck.

"I could strangle you right now."

"No," Augie laughs.

"I could and no one would know about it for at least two weeks."

"Ceci would know."

"What are you talking about? She would be right along with you."

"You love us too much to get rid of us. Admit it."

Augie scoots over on the couch and wraps his arms around my shoulder. I squeal as he lays the most over the top kiss on my cheek. The feeling of excitement that exudes from him is contagious. Maybe a weekend away from the city is exactly what I need. It's been too long since we've been to the family beach house. With Ceci and Augie with me, this weekend couldn't go wrong. Could it?

"There's only one problem," Augie says.

"What?"

"Doesn't he still think I'm your boyfriend?"

I don't even try to stifle the laugh that rips through me. It's better that Tristan thinks I have a boyfriend. I wouldn't have it any other way.

"she is my dark lady, my MUSE."

CHAPTER 16

TRISTAN

I'm not sure what possessed me to tell Nicholas that I would come this weekend to their South Hampton beach house, but I agreed nevertheless. It actually might be nice to hang out with Nick and go fishing, maybe even take out one of the boats I know his dad owns.

The sound of a whistle and a familiar voice calls out to me as I exit out the front of my apartment. I spot a familiar sleek white BMW as it slides into view. The window slides down as Nicholas's face pops into view. He's still wearing one of his signature suits. I noticed from the paparazzi photos that he started wearing them more often after Alex died.

"Hey, you look like a familiar asshole that I know."

I chuckle. "I'm glad to see you too, Nick."

"Your apartment isn't the easiest thing to find."

"I know. That's why I picked it. Is that why you took so long?"

"Sorry, I got caught up with something."

A satisfied smile crosses Nicholas's face as he unlocks the passenger door and I slide in. At a closer look, I can see Nicholas's tie is askew.

"From the looks of your tie, it looks like you got caught up in someone," I laugh.

"Very funny," he smirks.

"So what are your plans for today?"

"My plan is to whisk you away for Emily's birthday weekend. Everything else is up in the air."

A sinking feeling fills my chest. Emily's birthday weekend? I should've known that today would involve her. Her birthday was on Thursday, but I couldn't reach out to her after the way I left things when she came to my apartment.

"Are you sure it's a good idea that I come, Nick?"

"Why not?"

I shrug off his questioning gaze.

"She's twenty-two. She probably doesn't want her brother and his friend pestering her."

"It will be fine. She loves having me around."

The problem is I'm not so sure she loves having me around.

CHAPTER 17

EMILY

Blue foamy waves crash down on the sand in front of our beach towels sending a spray of water at Ceci, Augie, and me. I soak in the sunshine as I lay back on my towel and stare at all the hundreds of New Yorkers who've also come here to escape city life for the weekend. Augie laughs as each time I pull my sunglasses down, my eyes are assaulted by the sight of naked elderly men. Over the past four years, I've heard this side of the beach has become more liberal, but I wasn't expecting to find a colony of nudists intermixed with the rest of the beach goers.

"There's a lot of eye candy at this beach," Ceci says. "If you're into older guys. Much older."

"You mean saggy balls don't turn you on?" Augie asks.

I stifle a laugh as a disgusted look crosses Ceci's face. She came here thinking there would be tons of hot guys on the beach. I almost feel sorry for her. Almost.

"Are we ever going to get in the water?" Augie asks.

I'd love to be swimming right now, but instead, I'm sitting on the beach with a towel wrapped around me as I have a mini freak out.

DRAWN TO YOU

It's hard to relax knowing Tristan will be here soon. I brought the sexiest outfits I could find in my drawer and now I'm feeling stupid. Tristan doesn't want me. I shouldn't want him, and on top of that, he thinks Augie's my boyfriend.

"I think we should all just follow in that guy's footsteps and get naked," Augie says.

Without thinking, my attention is pulled to the one hot looking guy standing within a few feet. I try my best to keep my eyes trained on his face, but his abs are far too tempting not to let my gaze linger. The three of us stare at the sexy specimen, taking in all of his wonderful glory.

"I don't mind getting naked," Ceci says, untying the top of her bikini.

"Ceci, no," I argue.

"Tristan and Nicholas are coming." Augie laughs.

"Even better."

My heart beats in a chaotic rhythm as I spot Nicholas's white BMW parking just outside of our beach house. This weekend was supposed to be a relaxing getaway from the shitty reunion I had several days ago. Damn Augie for telling Nick to invite the one person I really don't want to see right now and damn Ceci for getting naked. In a matter of minutes, I'll be forced to come face to face with Tristan yet again. It doesn't seem fortuitous to be meeting like this.

My nerves are showing as they exit the car and immediately head our way. I spot a large ice cooler in Nick's hands. He probably brought beer. I turn back to my friends and catch Ceci lying back on her towel with her top off. She scoffs as I grab my towel and throw it on her chest. Augie laughs in the background obviously amused with the scene in front of him.

"Hey, sis," Nick says, sitting down between Ceci and me. "Are you enjoying your birthday weekend so far?"

"Yes, of course."

I'm almost thankful that Nicholas sitting next to me forces Tristan on the other side of us. That is until I realize he's sitting next to Ceci. Tristan's gaze briefly catches mine before he begins a quiet conversation with my best friend. I can't help but feel a slight tinge of jealousy as the two laugh together. The private smiles they share fill me with frustration.

"I'm going to go swimming."

Eyes fall on me as I get up and unwrap my towel from me.

"Yes, finally!" Augie says.

The black bikini I brought hugs my body tightly as I walk toward the water. Augie doesn't wait for me to get in the water; he simply pulls me in with him. Cold saltwater hits me, and I cough as some of it gets in my mouth. The water is cold, but our bodies quickly get used to the temperature as we tread through the water.

"Yuck, this is so gross," I say, avoiding the dead seaweed that floats by me.

"He's staring at you," Augie says, nodding to Tristan back on the beach.

I look to the beach and spot Tristan standing next to Ceci and Nicholas. To my surprise, Ceci's top is back on. For a brief moment, Tristan's gaze lingers over toward us in the water.

"He's too busy flirting with Ceci."

"Oooh, do I detect some jealousy?"

"Fuck you," I laugh, splashing Augie.

Augie pulls me into his arms and pushes me underwater. When I rise back up, my eyes search for Tristan. This time, I see him standing close to the water and Ceci's with him. I turn to Augie trying to ignore the gnawing feeling in the pit of my stomach at the sight of them together. Augie looks down at me with a sympathetic smile.

"It's okay to let yourself like him."

"I don't."

"That's why you lied and said I was your boyfriend?"

I swim away from Augie toward the beach, but he quietly follows behind me. Sadness fills my heart as I watch Tristan walking along the beach laughing with Ceci about something. I wish I could be that carefree around the person who took my virginity. Took is the wrong word. I freely gave it to him. It's my body that betrayed me. I shiver, but I'm not sure if it's at the memory or the temperature of the water.

I turn back to Augie as a volcano of emotions threatens to explode.

"I lied because Tristan was the guy who ruined me for all other guys. I don't think I ever loved anyone as much as him. He was the first guy I had sex with. It was so brief, I'm not even sure you could call it sex. Then he left after my brother died. He kept in touch with Nicholas, but he completely removed himself from my life."

The surprised look on Augie's face makes me want to both laugh and cry. He pulls me into his arms and gives me a tight squeeze.

"I have a feeling that you're most upset about him leaving than the actual sex part."

"Maybe," I admit.

"I know it's hard putting yourself out there sometimes."

"Not for you."

Augie laughs and rolls his eyes. "Speaking of, would you hate me if I left tonight?"

"No... Why?"

"I got a text from Harvey. He wants to go out tomorrow night."

I smile. "That's great!"

"It is. I should probably go get my stuff together."

"I'll help you pack," I say, grateful for the distraction.

As we head back to shore toward the beach house, I see two bimbos with giant tits hanging around Nicholas and Tristan. I thought my bikini was tight, but theirs look like they were taped on. *Don't look at Tristan. Don't look.* It's better if I just ignore my feelings for him. My self-control works for a while, but at the last minute, I look back. *Fuck.* A sting of jealousy hits me as I spot Ceci pressing herself against Tristan as they walk the beach.

I stare blankly into the kitchen taking in the words of my

conversation with Augie earlier today. The house is quiet despite the party atmosphere that lingered earlier. I step out into the living room to find Ceci sprawled across the white suede couch still passed out from swimming earlier. My brother is nowhere in sight, but I can only assume he went home with one of the models Tristan and he ended up talking to. I grab a spare blanket and cover Ceci as she shivers in her sleep. It's already late in the evening, but I still can't sleep.

The sounds of waves crashing outside draw me to the window as if calling my name. I grab one of the bottles of leftover beer from the kitchen and step through the sliding glass door. I find myself walking further and further from the beach house. Outside, the moon floats high above me reflecting on the tips of the waves breaking on the sand. My eyes are drawn to the black abyss that reaches as far as the naked eye can see. As hard as I stare, I can barely make out the lines where the sand ends and the ocean begins. I shouldn't venture too far, but I can't help but feel relieved as the tension from my shoulders releases with each step I take. The farther I walk down the sandy trail, the easier I find it is to breathe.

A gust of wind whips at me as I spot the perfect place to sit and stare up at the stars. I sit back and drink my beer as I listen to the melodic sound of the nature around me. It's not long after I finish the beer I found that I feel myself drifting into sleep. *I should head back.* I quickly give up, as my limbs feel too heavy to move. The feeling of the ocean sand brushing up against me suspends me in its gritty warmth. Despite the cold that creeps up my skin, the sand beneath me is strangely comforting. I rub my eyes as I spot a shadow moving in the distance. I try to focus on the shadow, but my eyelids droop. I force them open, but after a while, it's pointless.

It feels like I've been sleeping an eternity when I feel something warm grab ahold of me and lift me mid-air. The strong pressure against my side envelopes me in warmth. The feeling is strange yet addicting. I move my body closer against it hoping to draw it out.

"You're so cold, Lily Pad."

DRAWN TO YOU

My eyes flutter open just long enough to see the ends of Tristan's hair whipping around in the ocean breeze. His intense gaze is trained on my face as he brushes back my hair from my eyes. My head spins, but I'm not sure if it's from the beer or the sensation of his touch.

"Tristannn?" I slur.

"Yes, sweetheart?"

The sweetness of his voice catches me off-guard. My mind tries to process the words I want to say, but the only question that tumbles from my mouth is the one I've been wondering about for four years.

"Why did you leave me?"

He doesn't reply. For a moment, I start to believe I'm dreaming, but it isn't until I feel the soft fabric of my bed sheets that I realize he's carried me all the way to my bedroom. Strong fingers grasp my shoes and slip them off. I try to pull off my jeans, but he beats me to it. His hands leave a trail of warmth as he pulls them over my hips, down and off my feet.

"There's fucking sand everywhere."

I shiver at the nakedness that I feel as my skin sits exposed to the coolness of the room.

"Let's get you warm."

A soft blanket slides across me as he pulls it underneath my chin. I look up to find Tristan looking down at me through the darkness as he tucks the ends at my sides.

"You could've died from hypothermia. Nicholas is too preoccupied to notice you're gone and Ceci is passed out."

"I'm fine," I say, rolling to my side. "I would've been fine."

"It's freezing outside! If something happened to you..."

"Tristan, are you staying or going?" I ask, annoyed.

"What?"

"You can either stay and keep me warm or go and leave me alone. Pick one."

His silence sends a sharp pang through my chest. Of course, he's going to go. Before I can pull my blanket over my head, I feel

Tristan's frame on top of the mattress. His warm hand slips under my chin as he forces me to turn and meet his gaze. A slow heat spreads among us as his skin meets mine.

"You don't know what you're asking me," he says with a dark gaze.

"I know what I'm asking. I'm just not sure you can behave."

He chuckles. "So you're not asking me to touch you?"

"No, I'm asking you to lie beside me. Is that too much?"

It's not enough, but I don't care. I want him to stay.

"Fine, but I'm keeping my jeans on."

"Whatever," I say, turning my back toward him.

The bed dips as his frame stretches across the bed and the thud of his shoes on the wood floor. I smile to myself as he turns to me. A sound of frustration rumbles from him as he lies back against his pillow. I gently shift my hips as I press my bottom against him letting out a fake snore. To my surprise, the motion doesn't go unnoticed. Tristan leans into me and encircles his hand around my waist pulling me against him. I gasp as his hot breath blows against my ear.

"Careful, pet. You're poking a bear."

"Am I?" I ask, shifting my bottom against him again.

"I think you had little too much to drink tonight."

I press my bottom into him again. This time, his lips carefully trace the edge of my ear sending a rush of excitement through me.

"You like living on the edge, don't you?" He chuckles.

"Yes," I gasp.

"Goodnight, Lily," he whispers, kissing my cheek.

What? I huff in frustration as he turns and buries his face into the pillow beside me. After several minutes, the tempo of his breathing slows. Did he really fall asleep? Anger filters through me as I fling my pillow at his head. To my dismay, it does almost nothing. He lifts his head for a moment, adjusts his position, and then slips my pillow under his chest. Perfect. Now I have no pillow.

It doesn't take long for my drunken anger to fade as sleep overtakes me.

DRAWN TO YOU

    Tristan's gone by the time I open my eyes again and with him, he takes the comforting heat of his skin.

CHAPTER 18

TRISTAN

The following morning I find myself wandering outside in a state of unrest. The sun peaks over the horizon as I head back toward the beach house. After hours of walking on the sand, I'm finally exhausted enough to get some sleep. Keeping my hands off of Emily last night was no easy task. I could've touched her, but where would that leave her with her relationship. As happy as it would make me to feel her once again, I'm not going to ruin her happiness.

As I step up a set of stairs leading to the house, I find Nicholas sitting on the veranda of the beach house drinking a bottle of Heineken. His ruffled waves of blond make a stark contrast to the perfectly combed look that I saw the other night. Nick looks up from his bottle momentarily with a small smile on his lips before chugging back the rest. His expression gradually morphs into a scowl as he stares across the white sandy beach. I know there's something on his mind. He's probably the least quiet person that I know. In fact, I'm surprised he isn't talking to the Baywatch Babes down the way.

"So you're out here drinking by yourself?"

"Not anymore," he says, passing me an unopened bottle.

"Is everyone still sleeping?"

I take a seat next to Nicholas, stretching out my legs. He smirks at me as I pop open the beer with my palm.

"They're awake, and I think they're on their way to another nudist section of the beach today. It's supposed to be very exclusive."

"What?" I ask.

"Yeah. I would've been more than happy to go, but I would claw my eyes out if I saw Em nude. It was bad enough hearing Ceci talk about going topless the other day."

Emily nude. The memory of her soft skin beneath me sends my cock stirring. Nicholas would kill me if he knew I couldn't say I feel the same. I haven't been able to get her out my head. It's hard not to think about how much I wanted to fuck her last night.

"I'm surprised you didn't say anything to your sister about going," I say, hoping Nicholas doesn't pick up on the strain in my voice.

"We were around a bunch of nudists the other day."

"Yes, but your sister wasn't taking off her clothes then and Augie was with them. You know there are going to be creepy men there right?"

A somber expression crosses his face. I watch as Nicholas puts down his beer and then stands up. I watch him as he places his hand on the wooden railing that wraps around the veranda. His hands bunch into fists as he rocks back and forth on them.

"You'd make a better brother to her than I would any day."

"Don't ever fucking say that."

Nicholas turns to me confused. His eyes search my face for some kind of clue, but I give nothing away. God only knows how I would've been a horrible brother. I couldn't even keep my hands off of someone who was supposed to be family. Guilt filters through my chest reeking havoc on my insides. I took her virtue like a fucking thief in the night, and the depressing part is I loved the feeling of doing it.

"So what are the plans for tonight?"

Nicholas's face brightens as he lets out a hearty laugh.

"Ceci and Emily are going out dancing. I'm not sure if we're invited."

I smile. Dancing is something I am surprisingly good at. I have my mother to blame for that. When I was younger, she was always dancing around the house. It's one of the few great memories I have left of her.

"What do you say to crashing in on their plans?" he asks.

"Hmm—I have a feeling someone might be pissed."

Nicholas laughs and throws his arm over my shoulder as he pulls me toward his car. A mischievous look lights up his face sending my mind whirling with possibilities.

"But, what kind of brother would I be if I didn't give my sister a hard time?" Nicholas says.

I laugh. Tonight should be interesting.

> she is my dark lady, my MUSE.

CHAPTER 19

EMILY

The memory of Tristan's hands on my hips plagues me as we enter the bar called Oasis.

Ceci and I make our way past the sea of people on the dance floor as we search for Tristan and my brother. Surprisingly, the two of them decided to join us tonight. The bar is just as flooded as the dance floor, making it almost unbearable to walk, let alone dance. If Augie were here, I would kick his ass. I can't believe he ditched us for a date with Harvey. What happened to chicks before dicks?

"Emily!"

I see Nicholas as he pushes his way through the crowd. To my surprise, Tristan follows closely behind him. In spite of last night, he greets me with a normal warm smile. Unsurprisingly, he still manages to keep his distance from me, avoiding my touch at every opportunity. As hard as that sounds with a club full of bodies, he makes it seem easy.

"It looks like we weren't the only ones with the same idea," Nicholas yells over the club music.

I catch Ceci adjusting her boobs as she pulls down her shirt.

DRAWN TO YOU

She tugs her pink tank so that it's barely holding her chest in. I could kick myself for letting her borrow the shimmery top.

Nicholas laughs. "What are you doing, Ceci?"

"Getting us drinks," she says determinedly.

"I don't know how appealing mosquito bites are," Nicholas taunts.

Ceci teases her hair with her fingers and then heads toward the bar as if she's going in for an audition of a lifetime. Tristan's chuckle draws my attention. A pang of jealousy hits me as I watch him stare after Ceci. The thought of Tristan enjoying the sight of Ceci's chest is enough to make me want to vomit.

"My boobs are bigger than you remember," Ceci says.

Something about the way Tristan is looking at Ceci annoys the hell out of me. How dare he check out my friend right in front of me? What the hell?

"Libations are on their way, boys," Ceci says.

"I'm coming, Ceci," I pipe in.

"Perfect. Four boobs are better than two." We break off from the guys and head toward the bar, positioning ourselves closest to the front of the tabletop.

Nicholas rolls his eyes. "I gotta see this."

"Don't pester them, Nick. They're trying to get us drinks." Tristan smiles.

Despite the flurry of women in the room, the bartender doesn't seem to notice the way they throw themselves at him. I would think most guys would love the attention. I stare at the brightly colored tattoos that run up his arm compiling into a sleeve. He seems young with his spiky black hair, but from the few peppery stray hairs on his sideburn, I'm fairly certain he's older than I am. It isn't until his gaze catches mine that he moves over toward us. A perfect smile breaks across his face as he wipes the counter in front of us and leans in to take our drink order.

"What can I get you beautiful ladies?"

Ceci elbows me, acutely aware of the way the bartender is

staring. My best friend might be wearing her shirt low, but he hasn't taken his eyes off me.

"Can we have two gin and tonics and two—"

"Shots of Patron," Ceci finishes.

I shoot her a knowing look as I'm reminded of the last time I had tequila. The unfortunate night ended up with me face down over the toilet at one of my father's work events. It wasn't too long after my mother left and I was feeling more emotions than I ever wanted to feel. I swore I would never touch tequila again.

"It'll be fine," she whispers.

"Anything else," he says as his gaze washes over me.

"You can give my friend your number."

I blush in embarrassment. "Oh, Ceci, he doesn't want to give me his number. Just let the guy do his job without being harassed." To my surprise, he takes one of the coasters, writes his number, and then slides it to me.

"I'm Tyler and I'm off at eleven."

"Oh, okay." I smile.

I've quickly learned over the years that any guy who wants to meet after work is usually a booty call. While this probably isn't any different, Tyler is definitely a welcomed distraction from having to deal with Tristan. I lean forward flashing him a knowing smile. Maybe tonight won't be so bad after all.

> she is my dark lady, my MUSE.

CHAPTER 20

TRISTAN

I have no right to be fucking jealous, but I am. I watch with anger filtering through my veins as the bartender with the tattooed sleeves flirts with Emily. The sight is torturous. I'm tempted to walk over and tell the guy to fuck off, but I stop myself.

Breathe. Fuck. Just breathe.

Emily stands directly in my line of sight as if taunting me. After the past few weeks, I wouldn't blame her. I have acted like an asshole. I teeter between wanting to wrap her lovely legs around me and trying to get as far away from her as I possibly can. I'm starting to think it doesn't matter. Either way, the mere sight of her tortures me. She is my Dark Lady, my muse.

"You all right, buddy?" Nicholas asks, eyeing me curiously.

"I'm fine."

"It's strange, right?"

"What is?" I ask caught off guard.

A sliver of anxiety crawls its way into my throat as Nicholas looks at me with a curious gaze. I've often wondered if he could see right through my act. I'm not even sure what I could say to Nicholas if he ever found out about me sleeping with his little sister.

"It's strange seeing guys flirt with Emily. I sure as hell don't want to see anyone messing with my sister. I still see her as the sweet little brat who always wanted to hang out with us."

"Yeah," I swallow my lie.

What Nicholas doesn't know won't hurt him, right? Fuck, he would murder me if he knew the sordid past between us.

I force myself to look away, but it isn't long before my eyes trail back to Emily. A pang hits me in the chest as I watch the bartender slip Emily a piece of paper. I can only assume it has his number on it. If he thinks he's leaving with her tonight, he's dead wrong. There's no way I'm letting that happen. I may not be able to have Emily, but this guy isn't getting anywhere near her. Plus, she has a boyfriend, but not a very good one because he isn't even here.

"I guess you must not like Augie?" I ask.

Nicholas turns to me with a surprised look before bursting into laughter.

"Augustine? The guy you met the other night?"

I watch Nicholas wipe away the tears from his eyes.

"Am I missing something?" I ask annoyed.

"Let's just say that Augie is more likely to hit on me or you."

"What?"

That little brat. She played me for a fool. My fingers itch to bend her over my knee and spank the living hell out of her for lying to me. She's far too smart for her own good.

"Why would you ever think that?" Nicholas pries.

"No reason," I chuckle, shaking my head. "It's a misunderstanding."

"So what's going on with your art?" Nicholas asks, pulling my thoughts back.

"Business is good. I have several repeat customers, and I'm booked throughout this next year. I'm actually donating one of my paintings for a silent auction at a Black Tie event this month. I'm hoping it will bring me some publicity."

I'm grateful for the change in topic and the distraction of small talk. For the past four years, my art has been my one consolation and my meal ticket. I've been lucky enough to find clients through word of mouth from the Pleasure Chest. Sebastian and Selena are just one of several whom I've met over the years, and they've been more than kind to me.

"Wow. A self-made millionaire. Dad should put you in charge of StoneHaven Company."

"Nick, why would you say that?" I ask.

"It's nothing," he says with a small smile. "So, you're donating your art? You should be opening your own gallery."

It bugs me that he's changing the subject, but I know in time, he'll talk to me.

"One day," I smile.

"I'm sure my father would help you. He asks about you a lot."

Nicholas's words both surprise and annoy me. Asking Stefan for money is the last thing I would ever do. I didn't ask him for money to cremate my mother, so why would I ask for money now? I despise the idea of owing someone anything.

"Or I could give you the money," Nicholas says as if reading my thoughts.

I smile as Nick throws his arm around my shoulder.

"You know you're like a brother to me," he says.

I look at him at the sound of his tone growing serious.

"I know, but sometimes you need to make your own way in the world. Even if it means struggling a little more."

He flashes me a wicked grin. "Just know that you always have someone here to pull you out of the water if things get too rough."

"Thanks, buddy."

"I'm glad you made it out this weekend."

Emily's sweet laughter catches my attention as I survey the club goers around us. She presses her petite frame on the bar top in front of her, giving the tool behind the bar a better look at her chest. Something about the way she does it makes it all the more painful to watch. It's like she can feel me watching her.

"Me, too. Although I'm not sure if it was the best idea coming."

"Are you kidding me? It was a great idea. Plus, I know Emily wanted you here. She loves you."

She loves you.

I never thought those words would affect me the way they do. I watch Emily walking back toward us with a flushed smile. My chest aches at the bittersweet sight of it. I've never felt more hate for anyone than I do for that bartender. I envy his ability to make her smile and the freedom he has to take advantage of being with her. The time I spent with Emily when we were younger now seems so far away. That kind of happiness seems so far out of my grasp that I know it will never happen again.

But maybe it should be enough just being around her. Watching her be happy. That could be enough.

CHAPTER 21

EMILY

I try my best to hide the flush on my cheeks behind my hair. It feels strange and exhilarating to flirt with a stranger knowing that Tristan's watching. A scowl crosses Tristan's face as we return with our drinks. I'm not surprised by his silence, but the way his eyes penetrate me sends a shiver down my body. I watch as Nicholas leaves us to dance with a young woman he spots across the room wearing a dark red cocktail dress.

"Tristan, dance with me," Ceci says, snuggling up beside him.

I choke on my drink surprised at Ceci's words. Does Ceci like Tristan? It wouldn't be the first time she's paid attention to him. I try to fight the overwhelming desire to look at Tristan, but fail miserably. Our eyes collide for a brief moment before I hear him answer Ceci.

"Actually, I promised the birthday girl a dance."

Ceci's smile falters for a second before returning to a full grin.

"Of course, don't mind me. I'm going to go find someone to play with."

Ceci saunters off before disappearing into the crowd of bodies.

"Why didn't you just dance with her?" I blurt.

Tristan reaches out to touch me, but I quickly move out of his grasp as I pretend to see someone familiar. My rejection doesn't go unnoticed. In fact, it only seems to make Tristan more persistent.

"Dance with me?" Tristan asks.

I ignore his chest brushing up against me as I try to shift away. After several seconds, his hand grips the top of my hip, stopping me. The sensation throws me off balance, but his hold tightens steadying me. I look up to find his intense hazel eyes peering down. There's a strange look in them that I can't quite figure out. What does he want now? The weight of his hand resting against my hip immobilizes me as his fingers sear through the fabric of my jeans. The touch sends a tingling sensation across my hipbone and down my pelvis. I feel myself grow wet at the thought of his hand slipping further down my front. It wouldn't be the first time I've thought about it.

"I think it's better if you don't touch me," I say breathlessly.

He chuckles. "Don't worry, I promise we'll just dance."

Tristan leads me toward the dance floor with a small smile playing across his lips. He places my hand on his arm and the other he holds in his palm. My body resists as he pulls me in closer. The alarms going off in my head warn me to pull back and to make some excuse so that I can leave. Any excuse.

"Let go," he whispers.

'What?'

"Let. Go."

"Let go of what?"

I look up at him confused at his subliminal message. I can't let my emotions get the better of me. I can't let him in again.

"You're resisting me. I can feel it..."

"Dancing takes a certain amount of trust."

"Yes, it does," he says, pulling me against him.

I laugh nervously. "So I'm just expected to surrender and trust that you know what you're doing?"

"Letting me take the lead doesn't mean you're powerless. There's power in submission. Don't ever forget that."

My cheeks warm at Tristan's words. Somehow, I don't think we're talking about dancing anymore.

A new song starts, and I feel Tristan leading me across the dance floor. It takes my body a while to adjust to his pace, but I feel myself slowly relaxing. Despite how much my mind resists him, it doesn't take long for me to stop focusing on my body and to start focusing on his. Tristan is an amazing dancer. I shouldn't be surprised because he seems to excel at almost everything, but it also makes me feel like I don't know enough about him. Tristan is still a mystery. A puzzle waiting to be solved.

"I'm sorry about what I said at my apartment."

"What?" I ask almost tripping on my on foot.

Tristan's hand catches my waist, stopping me from stumbling forward into another couple dancing nearby. My heart leaps into my throat as he sweeps me against him. My nipples pucker at the feeling. Somehow, there are not enough clothes between us to hide my desire. Tristan twirls me and then pulls me into him.

"I acted like an idiot," Tristan says, leaning the side of his face against mine.

The intimacy of the moment startles me out of my starry-eyed trance. My gaze wanders toward my brother. Does he see this? I spot him across the room dancing with the brunette in the corner. Well, dancing wouldn't be an appropriate word. It's more like dry humping.

"Did you hear me?"

I turn back to find Tristan waiting for my reply. He reaches up and caresses my cheek. I lean into the touch closing my eyes and savoring the brief moment of bliss. I still haven't told Tristan that I don't actually have a boyfriend. Part of me wants to be honest with him, but the other part of me wants him to believe I've moved on. I'm sure he has.

"Why were you flirting with the bartender," he asks.

"I'm not allowed to flirt with handsome men?"

Tristan smiles, but a flicker of annoyance grazes his lips.

"What about Augie?"

"Augustine?"

"Your little boyfriend. I'm not so sure he would like you parading your tits across the bar top," he says, mocking me.

I blush at Tristan's accusation and the realization that he somehow knows that Augie isn't really my boyfriend. There's no sense in denying it.

"Ass."

Before I realize what I'm saying, the word escapes my mouth. A low rumble erupts from Tristan's chest. It takes me a few minutes to realize he's actually laughing.

"What?"

"You're not the little girl who used to sneak into my bedroom at night anymore."

His words send a blush to my cheeks. I know he's referring to the nights he stayed up to read Lord Byron to me, but I can't help but think of the night on the stairs.

"You're right. I'm not a little girl anymore."

Tristan's gaze meets mine. The predatory look on his face sends a shockwave through me. A strange static charge goes off between us as his hand wraps around the back of my neck. I feel his thumb lazily skimming the side of my throat.

"No, you most certainly are not."

Without thinking, I lean into his caress. The world seems to stop as the voices of the world fade into muffled chatter. I close my eyes, subconsciously leaning into Tristan. The heat of his hand grows more intense as each second passes. I hear the DJ change songs, but Tristan never changes pace. I feel his hand tugging mine and before I know it, we're headed to the hallway adjacent to the bathrooms.

He stops for a moment before pulling me into the women's bathroom and locking the door behind us.

"What are you doing to me?" he asks, cornering me against the cold tile wall.

"Nothing."

The word tumbles breathlessly from my mouth. Tristan's gaze trails down the dip of my shirt. The room suddenly seems too small for the two of us.

"Every time I look at you..."

"What? Every time you look at me what?" I demand.

"Every time I look at you, I can't help but remember what you felt like wrapped around me. The thought of never knowing that feeling again destroys me. If I could cuff you to my bed and throw away the key, I would. I would never let you go."

I'm not sure if his words are supposed to sound threatening, but a shiver of excitement runs through me. I would willingly let him as long as he touched me.

"Come here."

Tristan pulls me to him as he winds his hand through my ponytail. His lips collide with mine sending us both knocking into the wall. A mixture of pleasure and pain rockets through me as he tugs me closer by my hair.

"Fuck, I need you right now."

"Yes," I gasp as he breaks our connection.

"Wait," he rasps.

"What?" I ask confused.

"I can't do this."

Anger ignites inside me at the sudden disconnect between us.

"Stop looking at me like that. It only makes this harder," he says.

A rush of confidence circulates through me as I step forward, closing the space between us.

"I want this."

A surprised look crosses Tristan's face as I begin unzipping his pants. His hand stops me from going any further. The sudden shift in Tristan's mood throws me off guard as he steps back putting an ocean between us. The static charge that I once felt at his touch dissipates as he lets me go.

"I'm sorry, I shouldn't have started this," he says.

A look of pain crosses his face as I feel him moving away from me. The loss of contact leaves me feeling strangely cold. I watch Tristan slip out of the bathroom leaving me alone. It doesn't take long for Ceci to find me, and when she does, it takes all of my strength not to come clean about my history with Tristan.

When I finally manage to clean my face up from crying, I find Tyler, the hot bartender, just walking out from his shift. Despite the anger that I feel, I force myself to smile and pull him on the dance floor with me. It isn't long before I see Tristan leave and Nicholas on his way out the door with a blonde on his arm. I wish I could say good riddance, but Tristan's the only person I want to be dancing with.

CHAPTER 22

EMILY

"You're back late," a voice calls from the living room couch.

The figure sitting on the other side of the room transfixes me. Despite the dimmed lights, I recognize the familiar silhouette.

"Why are you still up?"

A shiver vibrates through me as I step closer to Tristan's silhouette.

"I waited up for you, Lily Pad."

The words flow from his mouth in a sensual staccato. As much as I love hearing him call me Emily, I can't help but miss the way he used to say my nickname. I flip on the living room light, and the sight of his smile immediately takes me back. It fills my body with a familiar ache. It's the same feeling that I have felt each time I relive the moment his body entered mine.

His eyes follow me as I step closer. What is he doing sitting in the dark? Tristan shifts as he toys with an empty glass in his hand. He watches me with a dark expression. It isn't until I'm only a few feet away that I notice his hazel eyes are flooded with a look of pain.

"What's wrong?" I croak.

DRAWN TO YOU

His mood is strangely similar to the night of my birthday when he yelled at me in the kitchen for drinking champagne. I look down at the glass in his hand again. Has he been drinking? Tristan leans forward, and I catch sight of the way his black tee tightens around his chest and torso. My heart flutters at the way the fabric stretches across his skin, highlighting the cut of his muscles. I shouldn't want him, but I do. The thought of sex used to bother me, but now it only excites me.

"Did you sleep with the bartender," Tristan asks, sliding his empty glass on the coffee table.

His question stops me. His words both anger and confuse me. After telling Tyler that I wouldn't go home with him, I told Ceci I was heading back to the beach house. Thankfully, there was a cab available to take me back. Despite my need to forget about Tristan touching me, I couldn't fight the exhaustion that overwhelmed me after he left.

"Well?"

A serious look encompasses Tristan's face as he walks over to me. Something about the way he moves reminds me of a lion stalking his prey.

"You think you have the right to ask me that?" I counter.

He steps toward me, but my palms stop him from coming any closer. My heart ricochets against my chest as he grabs my wrist and pulls it to his lips.

"Ever since I saw Selena kiss you here," he says pointing to my wrist. "I've wanted to mark you."

My fingers ache to touch Tristan. Foolishly, I give into the temptation of feeling his face. I reach up with my palm and caress his cheek. Ceci told me that when you fall in love with someone, you couldn't imagine anything that would make you happier than to see them happy. That's how I used to feel about Tristan. I would've done anything for him. Sadly, I never had the chance.

"I'm going to go to bed," I say, feeling my exhaustion take a hold of me.

"Go then," he snaps.

I blink my way through the tears that threaten to pour out of me.

"Fuck you."

I'm halfway to my room when I feel Tristan grab me and push me against the wall. His hands scorch my skin as he holds me in place.

"You're my plaything, nothing more," he says with an icy gaze.

His words sound surprisingly hollow.

"If that were true, you would've fucked me already."

A look of shock covers his face as he reels backward. His gaze darkens before he quickly finds his composure.

"You don't think I'd fuck that little mouth of yours?"

"Try me," I laugh.

"Why would I want your bartender's leftovers?" he asks angrily.

His words are like a kick in the chest. It takes all of my strength not to break down. Tears slips from my eyes as I try to hide my face in embarrassment. Tristan's face falls at the sight of my tears. He steps forward to console me, but I keep my distance.

"Fuck, Lily Pad, I'm sorry."

"Get away from me!"

Tristan forces me to look up at him as he captures my chin. The look of raw lust on his face is enough to melt me where I stand. Despite the pain that radiates through my chest, I feel my anger dim and my desire take over. Tristan's thumb wipes a tear that trickles down my cheek.

"I'm sorry I wasn't there for you. You needed me, and I couldn't stand being around you. It was too painful."

"I missed you so much," my voice breaks. "Nicholas had you, but you distanced yourself from me. The only person I had besides Ceci was you, and you left without even a goodbye."

"Tell me how to fix this."

"You can't.

"I would do anything for you," he says.

It's the one thing he can't do that crushes me. I can't make Tristan love me the way I love him.

DRAWN TO YOU

"Is it bad that I can't stop thinking about touching you?" he asks.

His confession fills me with bliss. If he only knew how much I want him to touch me. To kiss me. To be able to show him how he makes me feel.

"Touch me," I dare him.

Tristan's face snaps up at me with a look of shock. It's as if I told him I'm the Loch Ness monster. My breath catches as his heated gaze slowly sweeps over every inch of me. My heart palpitates as he takes several steps toward me. I feel his palm slide up my shoulder and then to my cheek. His fingers tilt my chin up as he leans in and grinds his pelvis into me. Tristan reaches down and slowly lays his hand flat against me over my dress.

"Is this what you want, little one?"

"Yes," I gasp as his fingers press into me.

The feeling is enough to send my head spinning and my heart into cardiac arrest. The sound of my ragged breath only seems to entice Tristan to go further. To touch harder.

"I'll take any taste of you I can get."

My body hums at his confession. The slightest touch of his hand releases an unexpected moan from inside me. I bite back in embarrassment, but Tristan quickly makes me forget it as his hand grazes my cheek.

"Don't be embarrassed," he says in a strained voice. "I love the way your body responds to me."

I feel his thumb tracing the side of my lip in soft circles. He parts my lips and my tongue greedily licks his skin.

"Has anyone else ever touched you this way?"

Plenty of men have touched me, but not like this. Not the way he's touching me.

"No," I admit.

"Good."

Tristan moves his hand up my side, across my hip, and to my breast. His fingers roam up to my neck, and before I know it, I can feel them guiding me forward toward his bedroom. He closes the door behind us, locking it. I'm not sure where Ceci is, but I'm really glad Nicholas went home with the blonde on his arm.

"Take off your clothes," Tristan demands.

A shiver of anxiety slices through me at the change in Tristan's tone. I'm hesitant at first, but after several seconds, I feel him take charge as he slides off the dress I'm wearing. I tremble as a draft of cold air hits my skin. The sensation only makes me more aware of the awkwardness that I feel. Tristan's eyes heat at the sight of my pink lace panties. I wasn't sure about wearing them tonight, but now I'm glad I did.

"I like the look of these. Do you wear them all the time?"

"No, just sometimes."

"From now on, you'll only wear them for me."

My cheeks heat and my breath goes ragged at his demand. Excitement pulses through me at the idea of sharing something with only him.

"Okay," I mouth.

A ghost of a smile plays on Tristan's lips as I wet mine. It isn't long before he captures my mouth in one long, tantalizing kiss. His tongue grazes across my lips, and my nipples harden in response.

"Now, get on the bed," he says, tearing away.

I watch him as he pulls out a condom from his wallet. For a moment, my thoughts are paralyzed by the suffocating realization that he must always carry one with him. I can't even bring myself to think about the women Tristan's been with, but I'd be lying if it didn't make me feel self-conscious. I've only been with a few guys since him.

"she is my dark lady, my MUSE."

CHAPTER 23

TRISTAN

This isn't real. I keep telling myself that as Emily's chest rises and falls. The rhythmic motion leaves me hypnotized. Her breathing thickens as I lead her to the bed. To a voyeur, it may seem like I hold her in the palm of my hand and that I have all of the control in this situation, but appearances are deceiving. This little minx has me begging for more. Control seems like an ever-evasive thing with her. My feelings for her are everything they shouldn't be—deep, uncontrollable, and real.

"Are you sure you want this, pet?" I ask rolling on the condom.

I'm giving her a way out. A way to be free of me and from the feelings I have for her. But I won't let her leave here without hearing her say it.

"I always keep my promises," I say, leaning forward on the bed to kiss her.

"I know—that's the problem."

"This is your last chance..."

She doesn't stop me. Instead, she leans in. I smile at the impending disaster waiting for me on the other side of this kiss. Helen of Troy was the face that launched a thousand ships, but even her beauty could never tempt me the way Emily does. Soft lips meet mine as Emily stumbles forward catching herself on my arms. Her body molds against mine as I deepen the kiss, forcing her to relinquish control.

The soft moan that erupts from her only encourages me to touch her further. I wrap my hand around her hair and pull her head back to give me better access to her throat. I've dreamt of kissing her here. She shivers as I slide my lips from her ear to the dip in her collarbone. Ecstasy. It's the only word that describes the taste of her skin. A sigh reverberates through her as I let go. It isn't long before I feel her touching me back.

"Get on all fours," I command.

Emily's innocent gaze sends my desire over the edge. She obliges me mulling over my words. I prop her up against me, surveying the beauty of her unmarked skin. It begs to be touched. To be fucked. I circle my palm across her backside warming the skin. Getting it ready for me. My heart races as she turns and looks at me over her shoulder. Slow and steady.

"I'm going to teach you a lesson for lying to me earlier."

"I didn't lie," she argues.

"Bullshit. You told me Augustine was your boyfriend."

Her eyes grow wide and a blush stains her cheeks as she looks away.

"Why did you lie?"

She refuses to answer me.

"I'm waiting, pet."

"I wanted to make you jealous."

"You like watching me come unhinged, you little brat?"

I find myself itching to smack her bottom as she bites back a smile. I let my hand freely come down across her bottom in one quick smack. It isn't the feeling of her skin heating or the way her body jerks that makes my cock hard. It's the small moan that escapes from her as she writhes against me. The sound is heavenly. I spot her smile as she lifts her hand to brush back a golden strand of hair from her face. She loves it. I knew she would.

"Are you ready for more?"

"I guess," she taunts.

I roll her body underneath mine, pinning her arms above her head.

"Don't move your hands."

"What if I do?" she challenges.

I chuckle.

"Who'd know behind those innocent eyes is a trouble maker in disguise."

She jerks as I nip her ear with my teeth. Her eyes close in ecstasy as I run my lips across her neck and between her breasts. A moan escapes her lips as I bite the fabric of her bra with my teeth. I nearly tear the fabric as I pull it off Emily. I could devour her whole. Claim her as mine. I quickly stop my mind from wandering too far down that road.

"Are you ready for me, pet?" I ask, sliding my hand over her pelvis.

Nails tearing into my back follow her small gasp.

"If you leave marks, I'm going to return the favor," I warn.

She doesn't listen, or maybe she does, but she doesn't seem to care because her nails dig deeper into my skin. I lean my mouth forward capturing her right nipple in my mouth and slide my fingers inside of her. I can feel her pulse pounding as I slowly stroke her.

"More," she says, smashing her mouth against mine.

"What, sweetheart? I can't hear you."

"More. Please, Tristan."

I turn Emily on her stomach and press her chest onto the bed. Her legs shake in anticipation as her ass tilts in the air. I nudge her legs open and stroke her with my cock. Her lips glisten in the darkness and her sweet little rosebud sits swollen between them. My hands trace her skin from behind. I could paint our lives together, but no amount of skill could reflect the beauty of being with her.

"I love the way you feel," I say, rubbing my cock at her entrance. As her hips buck into me, I know I can only tease us both so long before I unravel in front of her.

"Please," she begs.

"Tell me you're mine."

I slide my lips across her back and up the side of her shoulder.

"I'm yours."

"Tell me what you want."

"Fuck," she moans as I press the tip of my cock inside of her.

"You want this?"

I feel her clench around me as I slowly press further into her. She's just as tight as I remember.

"Yes," she cries.

Emily's voice cries out as I slam into her from behind. I try to hold back as I feel myself peak at the sensation of her wrapped around me. Her moans echo throughout the room as I force myself to thrust faster. The harder I go, the more she seems to love it. My fingers intertwine into the bottom of her locks as I lightly tug on them. Her soft voice cries out to me begging me not to stop, and I happily oblige. A tremor radiates throughout her body as she orgasms beneath me. That's all it takes to send me unraveling. A soft moan breaks free from her lips as I pull out and bring her up against me. Satisfaction fills me at the sound of her ragged breath.

As she turns to look at me, the light feeling inside me is quickly replaced with a darker one.

Where the fuck do we go from here?

VOLUME THREE

CHAPTER 1

EMILY

Spending my birthday weekend in Tristan's arms was not how I imagined this trip would go.

His warm hands slide across my stomach as he molds my back against his chest. I lean into the sensation letting my body take in the warmth of his touch. My insides instantly heat as his hand roams over my hip and lightly squeezes it. Only hours ago our bodies were colliding in a rhythmic motion that left me reeling and in a breathless state.

Now, Tristan's touch is a clear reminder the lines between us have blurred once again. The ache across my bottom is yet another piece of evidence that last night wasn't a dream. I smile at the memory of Tristan's hand coming down hard on me. I'd be lying if I said I didn't relish the thought of sharing that experience with him again. *What's wrong with me? Now I like being spanked?*

"Good morning, pet."

I look back to find Tristan staring at me intently. His hazel eyes assess me with curiosity. I'm not sure how it's possible, but he looks even more handsome with bed hair. Black strands fall back just above his ear giving him a rather rogue appearance.

"Good morning," I say, slowly gathering the covers around me to shield my nakedness from the man behind me. The situation is foreign to me. Not that I'm ever used to being naked around anyone. The few times I have been never ended well. Tristan slowly slips from the bed and stands to dress. Despite the intimacy we shared last night, I can't help but feel embarrassed at the sight of his cock standing erect. I blush as he turns and catches my gaze. A ghost of a smile graces his lips as he walks toward me. His movement is almost predatory.

"I've seen that curious look before. Several years ago," he says.

I know exactly what he's referring to. I begin to pull a satin nightie on, but before I have a chance to finish dressing, Tristan yanks me up against him. I nearly moan at the sensation of his erection pressing into my backside. His breath tickles my neck as his hands slide up to my shoulders.

"Last night should've never happened."

My heart leaps into my throat as his words vex me. The only thing that softens the blow is Tristan's fingers. They trace the skin just above my collarbone as he slowly draws circles across it.

"But I'm glad it did," he reluctantly admits.

The raspy gruff of Tristan's voice sends shivers down my skin as he places one hot kiss on my shoulder. Relief floods through me at his confession. I've wanted this, whatever this is, for so many years. I would be naive to think everything is going to fall together now. I gasp as Tristan grabs me and captures my ear between his teeth. A shockwave of pleasure spills over me as I feel his hot breath against my skin. I'm not sure how much longer I can take him touching me without turning around and attacking him. He reaches down and traces over the fabric of my nightie.

"I might leave early today to go back to the city," he says, letting me go.

"So soon?" I blurt. I can't hide my disappointment even if I wanted to. Is this his way of making a clean break from last night?

"Sebastian Wolfe wants to meet so he can choose a few of my

paintings for the fundraiser he's hosting."

Sebastian? I blush at the memory of the mysterious Dom I briefly met at The Pleasure Chest and Tristan's apartment. Something tells me the paintings he'll be observing aren't the usual kind that you find at a fundraiser.

"I hope your meeting goes well," I say, trying my best not to sound disappointed.

Tristan smiles before quickly finishing dressing.

"I'm going to go back to my room and shower," he says.

Shit. I hadn't thought of anyone being home until this very moment. The room Tristan and I are in feels detached from the rest of the world around us. Sometime during the night, we moved from his room to mine. Thankfully, mine is positioned on the other side of the hallway from where my brother sleeps. Oh, God. If Nicholas finds out about what happened last night…I'm not even sure what he would do.

"You should go before my brother finds you here," I say.

A chuckle escapes Tristan's lips.

"Don't worry, pet. No one will keep me from you."

I look over to find Tristan's heated gaze watching me with intensity as I dress.

"In fact, I think I'll shower with you," he says.

My heart catapults in my throat as he walks over toward me and captures my lips. The kiss is tortuously slow at first, but it increases each moment with a renewed intensity. I feel his hands running through my hair and then down my ass. It isn't long before we're both crashing back onto the bed. My head spins with thoughts of Tristan taking me once again.

"I need you," he says, breaking the kiss.

I bite back a moan as his lips graze down my neck.

"I need you, too."

Tristan's erection digs into my stomach as he grinds his hips, leaving me breathless and gasping for him. I've never been so turned on without even taking off my clothes.

"Fuck, I want to spank you again and bury my cock inside

you."

Despite the deep tenor of Tristan's voice, I don't blush at his words. Instead, I swivel my hips into his as he grinds his erection against me again. Last night was the first time anyone has ever spanked me, and I can't help but hope it won't be the last. It's strange to admit, but I loved the explosive sensation that rippled through me when Tristan did it. I'm not even sure why that is, but it doesn't stop me from wanting more. I slide up my nightie at the feeling of his erection rubbing against my thigh. He moans in approval.

"Why are you so fucking beautiful?"

Tristan's words both shock and amaze me. I watch with anticipation as he takes charge and pushes me back against his bed. My heart swells as he looks down at me with a blinding smile. The sight of it renders me speechless, and it only widens at my silence. There's a wild look about Tristan as his hair sits ruffled back on his head. His light bronze skin blends perfectly with his hazel eyes.

"I wish we were back at my studio," he says with a growl. "I have some chains that you would look lovely in."

Whoa, chains?

Tristan smiles as if reading my racing thoughts. I wish we could stay here. I'm afraid the moment we walk out of this room, everything will change. Reality sinks in even further as each minute passes. Unfortunately, we can't stay in here forever.

"What are you thinking about?" Tristan asks, pulling back.

I hesitate at first to answer him, but after several seconds, I give myself permission to touch him. His eyes widen as I reach out and trace my hand from his neck, over his chest, and down to his abs. Me being here with him feels so surreal. It's difficult to even wrap my head around the idea. Tristan's ragged breathing turns heavier.

"I keep thinking about how much I wish you would've never left."

Tristan stops touching me and pulls back. He sits on his heels and watches me from the edge of the bed. The pensive look on his face immediately makes me regret bringing up the topic. It takes him several seconds before he finally answers me.

"I can't take the past back, but I can tell you there wasn't a day I didn't think about you."

I want to believe his words. I want to know they're true, but I was the only one he pushed away.

"Why did you stay away from me?" I blurt. "Nick still had you, but you completely cut me off."

A sea of emotions washes over Tristan's face.

"I couldn't have you…"

"What's different now? I ask.

His face suddenly grows serious.

"There's a lot you don't know about."

My chest aches as Tristan reaches out and brushes back a blonde strand of my hair. He's all I've ever wanted. I tried to forget him over the years, but trying to forget him only made me think about him more. You exhaust more energy attempting to forget someone than letting it occur naturally. I've only managed to etch him further into my heart.

"So tell me…" I plead.

A loud rapping on the door interrupts us. My gaze goes flying to it as I stumble backward on the bed.

"Morning, sunshine!"

Ceci's bright voice calls to me through the door. My heart skips a beat as the doorknob jiggles. Did we lock it? A streak of panic goes off like a flare gun as we both scramble to gather our clothes. *Oh, God.* I nearly fall off of the bed as I scramble for my clothes. Tristan wrangles on a pair of black jeans and a tight black t-shirt. After a few seconds, he helps me slip my nightie back on.

"Emily, why is your door locked?" Ceci calls.

"I'm getting dressed," I blurt.

I turn my gaze to Tristan as he watches me frantically pace the room.

"What are we going to do? If Ceci finds out, she'll tell Nicholas," I say.

"I'll go out the window," he chuckles.

I hurry to get Tristan out of my room, practically pushing him out the bedroom window. The irritated look on his face is almost comical, but I'm willing to bet he'll find a way to make me pay for it later. A grin appears on his face before he leans toward me and smashes his lips against mine. He's gone by the time I open my eyes, but the butterflies that fill my stomach linger.

VOLUME THREE

CHAPTER 1

EMILY

Spending my birthday weekend in Tristan's arms was not how I imagined this trip would go.

His warm hands slide across my stomach as he molds my back against his chest. I lean into the sensation letting my body take in the warmth of his touch. My insides instantly heat as his hand roams over my hip and lightly squeezes it. Only hours ago our bodies were colliding in a rhythmic motion that left me reeling and in a breathless state.

Now, Tristan's touch is a clear reminder the lines between us have blurred once again. The ache across my bottom is yet another piece of evidence that last night wasn't a dream. I smile at the memory of Tristan's hand coming down hard on me. I'd be lying if I said I didn't relish the thought of sharing that experience with him again. *What's wrong with me? Now I like being spanked?*

"Good morning, pet."

I look back to find Tristan staring at me intently. His hazel eyes assess me with curiosity. I'm not sure how it's possible, but he looks even more handsome with bed hair. Black strands fall back just above his ear giving him a rather rogue appearance.

"Good morning," I say, slowly gathering the covers around me to shield my nakedness from the man behind me. The situation is foreign to me. Not that I'm ever used to being naked around anyone. The few times I have been never ended well. Tristan slowly slips from the bed and stands to dress. Despite the intimacy we shared last night, I can't help but feel embarrassed at the sight of his cock standing erect. I blush as he turns and catches my gaze. A ghost of a smile graces his lips as he walks toward me. His movement is almost predatory.

"I've seen that curious look before. Several years ago," he says.

I know exactly what he's referring to. I begin to pull a satin nightie on, but before I have a chance to finish dressing, Tristan yanks me up against him. I nearly moan at the sensation of his erection pressing into my backside. His breath tickles my neck as his hands slide up to my shoulders.

"Last night should've never happened."

My heart leaps into my throat as his words vex me. The only thing that softens the blow is Tristan's fingers. They trace the skin just above my collarbone as he slowly draws circles across it.

"But I'm glad it did," he reluctantly admits.

The raspy gruff of Tristan's voice sends shivers down my skin as he places one hot kiss on my shoulder. Relief floods through me at his confession. I've wanted this, whatever this is, for so many years. I would be naive to think everything is going to fall together now. I gasp as Tristan grabs me and captures my ear between his teeth. A shockwave of pleasure spills over me as I feel his hot breath against my skin. I'm not sure how much longer I can take him touching me without turning around and attacking him. He reaches down and traces over the fabric of my nightie.

"I might leave early today to go back to the city," he says, letting me go.

"So soon?" I blurt. I can't hide my disappointment even if I wanted to. Is this his way of making a clean break from last night?

"Sebastian Wolfe wants to meet so he can choose a few of my paintings for the fundraiser he's hosting."

Sebastian? I blush at the memory of the mysterious Dom I briefly met at The Pleasure Chest and Tristan's apartment. Something tells me the paintings he'll be observing aren't the usual kind that you find at a fundraiser.

"I hope your meeting goes well," I say, trying my best not to sound disappointed.

Tristan smiles before quickly finishing dressing.

"I'm going to go back to my room and shower," he says.

Shit. I hadn't thought of anyone being home until this very moment. The room Tristan and I are in feels detached from the rest of the world around us. Sometime during the night, we moved from his room to mine. Thankfully, mine is positioned on the other side of the hallway from where my brother sleeps. Oh, God. If Nicholas finds out about what happened last night...I'm not even sure what he would do.

"You should go before my brother finds you here," I say.

A chuckle escapes Tristan's lips.

"Don't worry, pet. No one will keep me from you."

I look over to find Tristan's heated gaze watching me with intensity as I dress.

"In fact, I think I'll shower with you," he says.

My heart catapults in my throat as he walks over toward me and captures my lips. The kiss is torturously slow at first, but it increases each moment with a renewed intensity. I feel his hands running through my hair and then down my ass. It isn't long before we're both crashing back onto the bed. My head spins with thoughts of Tristan taking me once again.

"I need you," he says, breaking the kiss.

I bite back a moan as his lips graze down my neck.

"I need you, too."

Tristan's erection digs into my stomach as he grinds his hips, leaving me breathless and gasping for him. I've never been so turned on without even taking off my clothes.

"Fuck, I want to spank you again and bury my cock inside you."

Despite the deep tenor of Tristan's voice, I don't blush at his words. Instead, I swivel my hips into his as he grinds his erection against me again. Last night was the first time anyone has ever spanked me, and I can't help but hope it won't be the last. It's strange to admit, but I loved the explosive sensation that rippled through me when Tristan did it. I'm not even sure why that is, but it doesn't stop me from wanting more. I slide up my nightie at the feeling of his erection rubbing against my thigh. He moans in approval.

"Why are you so fucking beautiful?"

Tristan's words both shock and amaze me. I watch with anticipation as he takes charge and pushes me back against his bed. My heart swells as he looks down at me with a blinding smile. The sight of it renders me speechless, and it only widens at my silence. There's a wild look about Tristan as his hair sits ruffled back on his head. His light bronze skin blends perfectly with his hazel eyes.

"I wish we were back at my studio," he says with a growl. "I have some chains that you would look lovely in."

Whoa, chains?

Tristan smiles as if reading my racing thoughts. I wish we could stay here. I'm afraid the moment we walk out of this room, everything will change. Reality sinks in even further as each minute passes. Unfortunately, we can't stay in here forever.

"What are you thinking about?" Tristan asks, pulling back.

I hesitate at first to answer him, but after several seconds, I give myself permission to touch him. His eyes widen as I reach out and trace my hand from his neck, over his chest, and down to his abs. Me being here with him feels so surreal. It's difficult to even wrap my head around the idea. Tristan's ragged breathing turns heavier.

"I keep thinking about how much I wish you would've never left."

Tristan stops touching me and pulls back. He sits on his heels and watches me from the edge of the bed. The pensive look on his face immediately makes me regret bringing up the topic. It takes him several seconds before he finally answers me.

"I can't take the past back, but I can tell you there wasn't a day I didn't think about you."

I want to believe his words. I want to know they're true, but I was the only one he pushed away.

"Why did you stay away from me?" I blurt. "Nick still had you, but you completely cut me off."

A sea of emotions washes over Tristan's face.

"I couldn't have you…"

"What's different now? I ask.

His face suddenly grows serious.

"There's a lot you don't know about."

My chest aches as Tristan reaches out and brushes back a blonde strand of my hair. He's all I've ever wanted. I tried to forget him over the years, but trying to forget him only made me think about him more. You exhaust more energy attempting to forget someone than letting it occur naturally. I've only managed to etch him further into my heart.

"So tell me…" I plead.

A loud rapping on the door interrupts us. My gaze goes flying to it as I stumble backward on the bed.

"Morning, sunshine!"

Ceci's bright voice calls to me through the door. My heart skips a beat as the doorknob jiggles. Did we lock it? A streak of panic goes off like a flare gun as we both scramble to gather our clothes. *Oh, God.* I nearly fall off of the bed as I scramble for my clothes. Tristan wrangles on a pair of black jeans and a tight black t-shirt. After a few seconds, he helps me slip my nightie back on.

"Emily, why is your door locked?" Ceci calls.

"I'm getting dressed," I blurt.

I turn my gaze to Tristan as he watches me frantically pace the room.

"What are we going to do? If Ceci finds out, she'll tell Nicholas," I say.

"I'll go out the window," he chuckles.

I hurry to get Tristan out of my room, practically pushing him out the bedroom window. The irritated look on his face is almost comical, but I'm willing to bet he'll find a way to make me pay for it later. A grin appears on his face before he leans toward me and smashes his lips against mine. He's gone by the time I open my eyes, but the butterflies that fill my stomach linger.

CHAPTER 2

EMILY

My head is still reeling from Tristan's kiss as my best friend comes crashing into my room. Ceci's eyes light up with a look of mischief as she watches me flipping through the latest issue of *Stars*. I self-consciously brush my face, weary that I've left some kind of trace of Tristan's lips on me. My cheeks warm just thinking about Tristan's touch on my skin. I'm not sure how I've gone without it for so long. I clear my throat, but that only makes her stare at me more intently.

"So how was it?" she asks, jumping on my bed with a handful of black licorice. A streak of anxiety fills me. *Shit*. Does Ceci know something? Did she see Tristan leaving my room? I close my magazine and turn my full attention to her. She smiles as her eyes gleam with interest while a million thoughts float through my mind as she waits with baited breath. What if she does know? Hell, I don't even know what's going on between Tristan and me. How am I going to explain it to someone else?

"Dang, that good?" Ceci says, chewing on the several strands of black licorice in her hand. I haven't seen her look this excited since

I announced I was going to try online dating. It seems like her short-term relationships aren't excitement enough.

"I don't know what you're talking about," I say.

She stares at me with a look of disbelief.

"Um, a hot bartender with tattoos sound familiar?"

Relief washes over me. For a second there, I thought she might have seen Tristan leaving my room.

"Oh, Tyler?" I ask. "No, I left Oasis alone."

Ceci's eyebrows quirk up at me in surprise. I'm sure she doesn't believe me, albeit I'm telling the truth.

"I'm not buying it."

I laugh. "I guess you were too busy flirting to even really notice."

A strange look crosses her face as she turns to me.

"No, to be honest, the only guy I wanted to flirt with was Tristan," she admits. "Unfortunately, he seemed a little preoccupied."

My heart sinks at her confession. I really didn't think Ceci's interest in Tristan would last so long. She has the attention span of a squirrel when it comes to men. Thank God she didn't see what happened between Tristan and me at the club.

"Emily, you're not saying anything."

I blush. What can I say without hurting her feelings? I've never laid claim to Tristan. She doesn't even know the history between us. The only soul I've told is Augie and that's because if I didn't tell someone, I would've exploded.

"Um..."

Ceci rolls her eyes at me as she paces back and forth across my bedroom.

"Um? That's all you're going to say? Look, I know you don't look at him like that, but I think he's sex on a stick."

I've never felt so weird hearing Ceci objectify any guy except Tristan. He's more than just sex to me, although I would be an idiot to say that isn't important. I've always felt a connection to him. Maybe that's why I couldn't help but imagine myself as the woman he was sleeping with whenever he would bring someone home. I couldn't be her, so I lived vicariously through each one.

"It's not that. I just..."

"You think he's too good for me?" Ceci asks.

The words hang in the air for what seems like minutes. A look of annoyance crosses her face as she waits for my reply. *Yes.* My heart squeezes at the thought. Before I can summon up the strength to say something, Ceci leaves the room in an angry huff and slamming the door behind her. I watch with a heavy heart as my best friend walks out.

A sense of dread fills me as I mull over Ceci's words. The last thing I wanted was to hurt my best friend, but I don't want to see her anywhere near Tristan. Just the thought of them together is enough to make me sick.

My cellphone vibrates on my lap.

I look down to find my roommates broad grin staring back at me as his name flashes across the screen. I swipe my phone open, desperate to talk to him.

"Augie, thanks for calling me back."

"Of course, what's wrong? You sounded upset on the voicemail."

A small sense of relief fills me with the sound of my roommate's voice. Although nothing seems to make sense right now, I take comfort in the fact that he's always been there for me. I laugh at the thought of how ridiculous I must've sounded leaving him my message. Deciphering my babble should be part of our college course electives.

"I slept with him," I blurt.

"...Tristan?"

My eyes begin to water. Within forty-eight hours, the world seems to be running upside down on its axis. I'm not even sure how to function throughout the day. Am I supposed to pretend like nothing is happening between Tristan and me? What does this mean when we go back to the city? Was I just a distraction for him?

"Yes, Tristan."

"Why does it sound like you're crying? Did he do something wrong? Tell me. I have no problem kicking his ass. Even if he does have a lot more muscle mass than me…God, I'm so jealous of his six-pack. I—"

"Augie!"

I bite my thumb as I wait for him to continue his questioning. My eyes scan the doorway for any sign of Ceci or my brother standing nearby.

"Right, fuck, sorry. Did he mess up?"

"No. At least not yet."

Augie sighs on the other end of the phone.

"Well, then, what is it?"

"I'm afraid he's going to leave, and I won't be able to walk away from this in one piece."

My hands begin to shake at the thought of watching Tristan walk out of my life again.

"Who says he'll leave?"

"He will."

The last time Tristan left, he did it at the worse possible moment. I needed him. More than anyone, I needed him.

"I know why you're saying that, but try not to over think things."

Easier said than done.

"Okay, I'll try."

"I'll see you Tuesday?"

"Yes, I'll see you then."

CHAPTER 3

TRISTAN

The taste of Emily's lips stains my soul.

A light feeling fills my chest as I run across the wet sand. Sweat pools at the back of my neck, but the wind quickly offers relief as it whips around me. My lungs take in the cool mist as heavy waves crash only a few feet away. A million thoughts race through my mind as my lungs burn from the cold air.

This morning I woke with a start that felt like a shot of adrenaline coursing through my veins. My head is still swimming with flashes of her in the sheets beneath me. Last night, I crossed the line between Emily and me again. As much as I know I shouldn't have, I wanted to. I still want to.

I'm not the type of man she needs in her life. I've been with more women than I'm comfortable admitting, and while I'm not living the BDSM lifestyle twenty-four-hours a day, I can't hide that I like things most guys her age wouldn't be into. She should be focused on finishing school and getting her first job. And much as I hate to admit it, she should be doing other normal college age things like dating other men. I can't steal that learning process from her. She might hate me for it years down the line.

And yet, I don't want her to be with anyone else. Maybe that's selfish... No, it is selfish. What am I doing? Why do I keep doing this?

One thing's for certain—the spanking I gave Emily last night ignited something wicked inside of her. Each rapid inhale of air that came from her only turned me on more. If my cock hadn't been so needy, I would've taken my time exploring every curve and dip of her body.

Fortunately for me, there's still time for all of that.

CHAPTER 4

EMILY

I'm drawn to the kitchen by the sound of a deep tenor singing. It isn't until I'm standing in the doorway of the kitchen I realize it's Tristan's voice. As I enter, I spot him shirtless, standing in front of the stove as he flips what looks to be a pancake. My eyes trail down the well-defined muscles of his back to the indents just above the waist of his black jeans. Taunting me, his jeans sit low, bringing back the delicious memories of him on top of me.

I'm not sure how I managed to shower and dress myself without replaying every intimate detail over and over again, but I did. My body is drawn forward toward him. I'm halfway through the door when I realize Ceci is sitting a few feet away. Her figure pops into my view as she takes a seat at the breakfast bar. Her position gives her the best view of Tristan's body. She doesn't bother looking up at me as I approach. My heart aches at her indifference toward me. From behind, I can barely make out the outline of her smile as she continues to stare at Tristan. Something about the look on her face makes me curious to know what's spinning through her head.

"Good morning," I say, sliding next to her.

DRAWN TO YOU

A tight-lipped smile appears on her face, but it vanishes just as quickly. Despite my best attempt at getting her to acknowledge me, her gaze never wavers from Tristan's lean body. I reach next to her for the pitcher of orange juice hoping she'll turn toward me, but she keeps her intense gaze on Tristan. To my surprise, Tristan turns and places a plate of fresh eggs and waffles in front of me. On top, is a pile of sliced strawberries waiting to be eaten. It's as if he's been anticipating my appearance.

"Eat," Tristan commands.

Ceci's eyes shift over at me with curiosity. Did she catch the same deep tenor in his voice when he gave me his order? My cheeks flame bright as I feel both of their gazes on me. There's an uncomfortable shift between us.

"Would you like some eggs & waffles, Ceci?"

"I would love that. I bet yours are incredible." Ceci's seductive tone rolls off her like velvet to the ear. A streak of jealousy runs up my spine as she adjusts her breasts in her shirt. I'm not going to lie and say Ceci's breasts aren't bigger than mine are—because they are. I was graced with the body of a dancer, but the tits of a pubescent twelve-year-old.

"Emily, aren't you hungry? You need to eat," Tristan says.

I shovel a fork full of waffle into my mouth to keep myself from saying anything stupid. Tristan watches me with a slight smile of approval as he slides over a cup of orange juice and maple syrup for my waffles. Despite the animosity in the room between Ceci and me, I'm still enjoying the silent conversation between Tristan and myself. I smile as he pops a strawberry into his mouth without taking his eyes off me.

Tristan avoids crossing me and instead, takes a seat next to Ceci. I watch him as he pours himself a cup of coffee. My best friend leans into him as he grabs a packet of sugar off the counter forcing Tristan to subtly shift missing her boob grazing his hand. His eyes meet mine for a brief moment before he draws his attention back to the cup in front of him. I have a feeling we'll be having a conversation about this later. Ceci isn't detoured from her seduction so I busy myself by reading the Sunday paper, allowing me to only catch snippets of Ceci's words, but the parts that I do turn my stomach.

"So, Tristan, are you seeing anyone?"

My heart stills as Ceci's question hangs in the air between us. I try my best not to look up at Tristan, but I feel his eyes wash over me. He goes silent for a few seconds before eventually answering my best friend.

"No, I'm not seeing anyone. My work schedule doesn't really give me much free time."

"Oh, that's a shame," Ceci says.

She isn't sad about it. In fact, I can almost see her smiling at her newfound information as the wheels turn realizing there's no competition for his affection. If it weren't for the fact I love Ceci, I wouldn't hesitate tackling her to the ground right now. I can't blame her for her infatuation because I can't seem to get over mine. Unable to stand the open flirting directed at Tristan any longer, I leap up from the table, causing them to briefly direct their attention to me while I place my dishes in the sink. I'm halfway out of the kitchen when I feel Tristan behind me. His fingertips are almost touching me, but they fall back at the sight of my brother entering the room.

"Good morning," he says with a devilish grin.

"Where have you been?" I ask

His eyes light up with mischief.

"I stayed out late last night."

Apparently, with the blonde he left with. No surprise there.

"You look like you had fun." Tristan laughs.

Nicholas's grin widens. I'm not sure how so many women fall into Nicholas's trap, but they do. No one seems to be able to resist his charm. I can't wait for the day some woman puts him in his place. I don't want my brother to be a manwhore forever.

"So, I was thinking we should go sailing today," Nicholas says, stepping around us.

"Oh, my gosh. That sounds like so much fun!" Ceci squeals, jumping up from the breakfast counter and grabbing Tristan's arm.

Her eyes briefly turn back to me.

"Oh! We should totally invite the sexy bartender you met last night. I can't believe you didn't go home with him."

I catch sight of a smirk on Tristan's face as Ceci goes on recalling how I had left the Oasis without Tyler, the bartender. I wish Augie were here. He would know what to do about this whole ridiculous situation. Why isn't Tristan pushing Ceci away? Instead, I watch as he sits enraptured by the words spewing from her mouth.

"What do you think, Em?" Ceci asks.

Half an hour ago, she was pissed at me, but now she wants to set me up on another date. I silently watch her with Tristan as they both stare at me waiting for me to speak. I'm not even sure how to act around the man I slept with last night and the friend who seems to think he's hers.

I smile through my gritted teeth.

"Sounds great."

"He was totally a hottie," she says. "And he was totally ogling your ass."

Tristan clears his throat, and the sound reverberates across the kitchen's open air straight to my clit. I avoid his pointed stare, but it's no use. My eyes flicker up quickly and then back down as his hazel eyes tug at my heart.

"I'm going to go get ready," I offer.

"Make sure you pack some extra clothes because I think we're going to stay over night on the yacht."

I gulp. Overnight?

Sleeping in the same place as Tristan and Tyler doesn't sound like a good idea. Even if it's a yacht. It's still not enough room to handle that much testosterone. God help me.

CHAPTER 5

EMILY

Tristan's hot gaze scorches me.

I feel it trickle down my neck like sweat, covering me, overwhelming my senses with its intensity. Despite the breeze and never ending ocean that surrounds us, I feel stifled. The sun beats down on me as we sit sunbathing on the deck of Nicholas's luxury yacht. I'm going to need more sunblock if he keeps staring at me like that.

Tristan hasn't said anything to me since we left the beach house. The whole drive to the marina he kept up the small talk with Ceci and Nicholas, but he didn't even bother trying to talk to me. His silence is a reminder of the hurt I felt the years he spent avoiding me. I look up from my glass of champagne to find him staring intently at something on the deck. As I turn, Tyler's muscular form pops into view. Tristan's glare extends to Tyler, but it never quite reaches me. *I shouldn't care.* I'm fooling myself if I think Tristan could ever be serious about me. It was evident from his response in the kitchen. *Wasn't it?*

"No, I'm not seeing anyone."

His words taunt me. What was I expecting him to say? He never asked me to be his girlfriend. I was stupid to think we'd ride off into the sunset after last night. The past four years we've spent apart changed both of us. My ears strain to hear the private conversation that my brother shares with Tristan. His grin brightens his brooding look, but it quickly vanishes as Nicholas walks away. I'm starting to wonder if his feelings for me are as much a facade as the emotions he portrays.

"Hey, Emily."

My eyes widen at the ripples of Tyler's chest. I wasn't expecting his body to be so lean underneath his t-shirt and board shorts. His grin widens as he catches me staring at the artwork on his skin. A sleeve of tattoos runs up his forearm wrapping around his chest, accentuating the outline of his muscles as his bronze skin is illuminated against the ocean backdrop.

I'm not blind when it comes to men, so it's not hard to figure out Tyler is definitely a guy who could date almost any woman he wanted. He's easy on the eyes, and for some reason, he's interested in me, despite ditching him the other night.

"Wow, when your friend and you called me today, I wasn't expecting to be spending the day on a yacht."

I smile, and I'm embarrassed at the awe in his voice. When I first met my roommate Augie, he was a bit star struck at my family's wealth, too. It's not something I've ever gotten used to. Most of the time, I'm too embarrassed to invite new friends out because they're either caught up in making eyes at my brother or mesmerized by my family's lavish living arrangements.

"I'm glad you came." I smile.

"Are you?"

A strange sensation fills my chest as Tyler leans into me. His blue eyes quietly assess me as I stare out at the ocean waves that break against the yacht. My gaze is distracted by the sight of Ceci walking up from the lower deck of the boat wearing a bright pink halter. The middle of it dips and hangs tightly over her breasts leaving little to the imagination. Her smile widens as she spots Tristan standing near Nicholas. My heart clenches as she sways her hips and flips her hair over her shoulder. Ceci turns more heads than I care to admit. It's never been a problem until now.

Tristan offers her a smile and the sight of it guts me. *She's trying too hard.* Her laughter is vivacious and over the top as she pushes her chest up toward Tristan. Who wouldn't be attracted to my best friend? She's a lot more outgoing than I am. Maybe she's the type of women Tristan likes.

I'm so caught up in my own thoughts I barely hear Tyler trying to talk to me. It isn't until I feel his hand grazing my shoulder that I turn. My cheeks flame as soon as I realize he's called my name about two or three times. He steps forward closing the space between us, trapping me between him and the railing allowing him to lean forward and grab the necklace Tristan gave me between his thumb and forefinger. His eyes quietly assess it with interest. A slight jab hits me in the chest as I watch him. I've been wearing this necklace since Tristan gave it to me, a silent truth my heart is still claimed.

The small charm lands softly against my chest as he lets go. Tyler's face tilts as his gaze washes over me.

"Thanks for inviting me. I kind of thought you weren't into me after you left last night."

A shy grin lights up his face as he brushes his fingers through his hair. Tyler's black rebellious hair sort of makes him look like Tom Cruise in *Top Gun* and his sleeve of tattoos only add to his outward bad boy persona.

"Well, I'm glad you decided to join us today," I say, avoiding his underlying question.

A throaty chuckle fills the air as I catch Tristan playfully punching Nicholas in the shoulder. If he's too busy to notice me, then I might as well enjoy my time with Tyler.

"Do you want something to drink?" I ask.

"That would be great."

I smile. "I think my brother brought a bottle of Dom Pérignon. I'll go get it."

I can feel Tyler's eyes trained on my backside as I leave. My heart is conflicted. Part of me is happy Tyler seems so interested in me and the other half wishes it was Tristan. I'm halfway to the kitchen on the lower deck of the yacht when I hear Ceci calling to me. Surprise fills me as a bright smile flashes across her face. *I thought she was pissed at me.*

"Hey, how is it going with the cute bartender?"

"Fine."

Despite my curt tone, Ceci continues babbling on about how dreamy Tyler is and how we would look so good together. Uneasiness fills me as she continues her sales pitch. I'm not sure why, but I get the feeling she really wants me to hook up with Tyler.

"So, do you like him?" she asks.

"He's nice."

"Just nice?"

"I don't really know him."

She huffs at my answer with annoyance as she combs a manicured finger through her long brown hair. I nearly yelp as she impatiently pulls me to the ice chest across the deck. She pours herself a glass of champagne and tips it back, swallowing it in one gulp. Her peculiar attitude has my head spinning as I try to figure out what's really going on in her head.

"I think you should give him a chance. It's not like you're involved with anyone else, right?"

It's a loaded question.

Ceci's gaze lingers over me as she waits for my response. I briefly look up at Tristan, and to my surprise, he's staring right back at me.

"No, I'm not involved with anyone," I lie.

CHAPTER 6

EMILY

Sandwiched between two men might sound like every girl's dream, but the tension that vibrates off of Tristan is enough to shake my whole world.

The day sped by a lot faster than I had anticipated, but I guess it helped having Tyler to talk to—even if it meant constantly having to deal with Tristan's strange mood. It was manageable up until the point that Tristan decided to sit on the other side of me.

I stab a marshmallow into the fire pit in front of me as I try to distract myself. It sizzles and pops. I smile as I pull it out of the fire. It's burned to hell. Just the way I like it. Before I have a chance to grab it off my stick, Tyler grabs it.

"Here you go." He smiles.

He holds the burned marshmallow to my mouth. It feels strange having him hand feed me. His eyes are fixed on me as I force my mouth to open and take a bite. Warm sweetness fills my mouth as its sticky texture clings to my lips.

I turn my head at the sound of a low growl coming from Tristan's lips. His eyes connect with mine with a furious heat. My heart palpitates in my chest as the awkwardness of the situation grows. Fortunately, Nick, Ceci, and Tyler seem too oblivious to notice the silent conversation that passes between us. This morning jealousy got the best of me after watching Ceci parade herself around Tristan. The worst part is he didn't even push her away. It's like watching them openly flirt at the beach all over again. I can't help but feel everything he's told me this morning isn't true.

I smile at the thought of Tristan feeling jealous over Tyler feeding me a marshmallow. A simple, but effective way to even the playing field.

"Hey, Tristan. Nick said a few of your paintings are being auctioned off for charity." He smiles.

"They are! I'm really excited about it."

"That's amazing! You should show them to me sometime," Ceci says, tipping back a shot of tequila before giggling and groping his arm.

The yacht sways as it breaks across bigger waves. A sickening feeling spreads across my stomach. I'm not sure if it's being on the ocean that's making me sick or watching my best friend throw herself at Tristan.

"Are you okay?" Tyler asks, rubbing his tattooed thumb over my wrist. "You seem a little tense, and you're looking a little green."

I flinch involuntarily and look away as my best friend exchanges a secret conversation with Tristan. The sound of waves crashing against the side of the boat drowns out their words. The only other sound is Ceci's nauseating giggle.

"Did you hear me?"

I look up to find Tyler's curious gray eyes watching me. The sympathetic smile he wears gives him a boyish appearance.

"I'm fine." I smile.

Tristan's voice breaks across a gust of wind as the yacht starts to sway harder.

"You should all come to the fundraiser a colleague of mine is hosting. You remember Sebastian, right, Emily? Sebastian Wolfe."

The image of Selena, the slave I met at Tristan's studio creeps into my mind. My cheeks burn. Of course, I remember the mysterious Dom. How could I forget the man who walked a woman on a leash in front of me like she was a pet? A flicker of amusement flashes across Tristan's face as he watches me from the rim of his beer. He's bringing up that day to rile me up? Or is it to distract me from Tyler's conversation?

Ceci stares up at Tristan with a curious gaze as she glances from him to me. I can only imagine the look on her face if she knew the kind of paintings Tristan does. Then again, she might like it. I have her to thank for ending up at the Pleasure Chest.

I lean into Tyler's embrace, closing the space between us. Despite the awkwardness that I feel doing so, I push away any thoughts of guilt. The scowl on Tristan's face haunts me briefly, but he quickly recovers and makes his way over to the helm of the yacht where Nick stands. I'm grateful for the small opportunity to breathe. Every time Tristan comes near me, I feel my whole body tense. I'm not sure how to act around him anymore. I'm too afraid someone else will notice.

"So is he your brother, too?" Tyler asks.

My eyes zip back to him. I can tell from my startled expression that Tyler isn't enjoying the idea of competition. A look of annoyance crosses his face as he examines Tristan from head to toe. If I didn't know any better, I would say he's sizing him up.

"He's a family friend," I say.

"Are you sure? He's been staring at you this whole time."

I force myself not to look in the direction of Nick and Tristan. Tyler pushes a wisp of hair from my face as he studies the freckles on my cheeks.

"I'm positive. He's known me since I was a little girl."

He smiles. "I bet you were cute as a little girl."

His hand wraps around the same wild strand as he tugs it lightly.

"Now, you're just sexy."

"Uh, thank you." I smile in embarrassment.

He's trying hard to win me over, and if it weren't for the man standing only a few feet away, I would let him. His gray eyes scan my face as he slowly leans toward me. A gust of wind whips my hair, sending it flying over my eyes, but he quickly tames it with his hand. He leans in closer, barely within inches of my lips.

A raspy voice cuts the air and Tyler freezes, quickly sitting back. A shadow cascades over us, and as I look up, I spot the reflection of Tristan's anger shining back down on me.

"Emily, I need to talk to you."

I gulp as he pulls me up to my feet without bothering to excuse us from Tyler. His rude attitude goes unnoticed by everyone else except my date. We're halfway across to the other side of the yacht when I feel him tug on my arm and spin me toward him.

Shit.

Tristan's anger vibrates off of him as he pushes me against the railing of the boat where prying eyes can't see us. I'm stunned to silence as I watch the world spin around me. Is he fucking jealous?

"What the hell is going on?" he seethes.

His icy tone sends me crashing to a halt. It pierces me with a bitter vengeance. I turn to him, ready to face his wrath head on. How can he be pissed off at me? He was the one letting my best friend flirt with him earlier. I'm the one who should be pissed.

His hazel eyes gleam despite the darkness that surrounds us. My heart flutters at the sight of his fingers running through his black hair in frustration. I'm honestly glad to see he seems bothered. I was starting to think I imagined things when it came to his feelings for me. Even last night is starting to feel more like a dream than reality.

"Nothing is going on," I reply.

"You like him?"

Tristan's tone is almost threatening as he gazes down at me. His hands fall to his waist as he waits for my reply. I bite back a smile as fingers pensively tap against his hip. I know my reluctance to answer is only irritating him more.

"What if I do?" I taunt. If he only knew how much I hate seeing Ceci draped all over him.

Tristan scoffs at me as if liking Tyler is inconceivable.

"You deserve better," he says.

Deserve better? What the hell does that mean? Better apparently doesn't seem to include him. My thoughts slip from my mouth before I have a chance to think about them. A look of unease passes over his grim expression.

"Do I deserve you?" I press.

The air is silent with only the waves crashing behind us to cut the tension. Several droplets of water spray on top of me sliding down my face. Tristan's eyes watch me, drinking up each salty drop—especially the ones that touch my lips.

"You deserve better than me."

The words come out in a pained gasp.

Perplexed, I watch as Tristan turns to pace back and forth across the deck of the ship. In my mind, there's no one better than he is. I don't understand why he thinks he's so bad for me. Is there something he's not telling me?

"What if I said I don't want anyone else? Just you," I blurt.

He looks up at me, and for a moment, I can almost see a sliver of hope in his eyes.

I hesitate before stepping forward toward him. Tristan's breath grows shallow as I close the space between us. He reaches out to touch me but stops as if he thinks better of it. Disappointment fills me. It seems I won't be feeling his hands on me anytime soon.

"You're too young. You don't know what you want," he says writing me off.

His words leave flesh wounds across my soul. Tristan's age isn't something I thought of as a hindrance to us. Four years doesn't seem like that much older. Does my inexperience turn him off? I may be more shy and reserved than I want to be, but that doesn't mean I'm clueless. Or maybe it's the lack of lifestyle that's making Tristan hold back. I'm not sure how to be a proper submissive and maybe that's what he really wants. Although if that's true, why is he paying any attention to Ceci?

"Why? Is it because you think I can't tell the difference

between wanting you to make love to me or tying me up and fucking me?"

A smile emerges from Tristan's lips. I step back as a dark look crosses his face. He advances toward me with a predatory smile.

"Watch your mouth, pet. Or do I have to teach you a lesson right here?"

His hand cups my face.

The heat sears me as his thumb traces my lips. I open my mouth and suck. A strangled noise comes from Tristan as I open my eyes. His thumb leaves my mouth with a pop.

"Fuck, I want my cock inside those velvet lips."

I melt at his words.

There's no denying I want him, too.

"I thought you saw me as your sister?" I tease.

For a moment, his eyes leave me as he stares over my shoulder. A slight tint spreads across his cheeks. *Is he blushing?* The realization hits me that I don't think I've ever seen Tristan blush. Not even once. My sex grows wet with desire.

"That's the last way I think about you," he growls.

My heart skips as Tristan pushes me up against the yacht railing, not once letting go. His lips make contact with mine in a mind-blowing kiss as his hand massages my breast. My nails tear into his hair, desperate to show him how much he turns me on. Tristan yanks my hands behind me and sinks his teeth into my neck. I gasp at the sensation as it leaves me on the tip of an orgasm. His warmth recedes as he pulls away from me. Our ragged breaths reach a fevered pitch. I pant trying to wrap my head around what just happened as Tristan steps back putting space between us. He lifts my chin up, forcing me to look into his eyes.

"Most of the time, I think about you in chains with your sweet pussy soaking wet for me. I think about fucking you with my paintbrush and then my mouth until you're bursting and until you're begging me to come inside you. To own you. To devour you. I think about fucking that sweet little ass. Does that make you feel better? To know that anytime I'm near you, I'm fighting to keep my desire under control?"

I blush, unable to vocalize just how much I need him to want me that exact way.

A low chuckle escapes him as I bite my bottom lip.

"You'll be the end of me."

Or the beginning of our infinity.

> "she is my dark lady, my MUSE."

CHAPTER 7

TRISTAN

My desire overtakes all rational thoughts.

It takes all of my strength to break away from Emily as a familiar voice calls for her. My insides heat at the sound of her name on his lips. It's that little asshole, Tyler. I could beat the shit out of him for trying to kiss her. Who the fuck does he think he is?

"Emily!"

My chest constricts at the look of disappointment that plagues her face. She wants me just as much as I need her. Emily reaches out for me as I step back. Our bodies are always entangled in a never-ending dance. *I need to go.* My fingertips itch to touch her again, but there's an invisible restraint that keeps me immobile. I watch as she smooths her hair and straightens out the sundress that she's wearing. The yellow color pops against her skin, giving her a youthful glow. Even in the darkness, she's like a light that beckons me.

"Tristan?"

Her voice is small and needy. It pulls at me with an irresistible force.

"Emily, if you don't leave now…" I warn.

My cock is begging to break free from the hold of my jeans.

Begging to be buried in between Emily's sweet folds. Her eyes widen as her eyes lower to the bulge in my jeans. *Fucking hell.*

"Go," I command. "And if I see that bartender with his paws all over you, I'm going to throw him overboard."

A smile breaks across her flushed face. I'm tempted to throw him overboard now, but I force myself to forget the anger I felt when he touched her. I inhale the smell of her sweet lavender scent, and it only seems to make my cock stiffen more.

"Can we talk later?" she begs.

"Yes, but, dammit woman, if you don't go in the next five seconds, I'm going to do something idiotic like fucking you in front of him."

Her jaw drops in surprise.

"You would like that, wouldn't you," I chuckle.

The thought has crossed my mind more than once today. As much as I'd like to say I'm a gentleman, Emily causes feelings inside me that make me feel more like a feral animal. I grab her by the waist and smash my lips against hers for one last kiss. I can only hope the taste is enough to satisfy my desires until we get back to the city. Her arms wrap around my neck, and it takes all of my strength to untangle myself from her.

Her cheeks somehow redden even more. God, I love that blush. It's enough to push me over the edge. I'm stunned how this sweet vixen bewitches me.

"Good night, Tristan," floats from her lips like an open invitation.

"Goodnight, Lily Pad."

I plant a kiss in the middle of her palm before disappearing to find Nicholas. Each step I take away from Emily sends an electric shock to my heart. A part of me wonders if there will ever be a day where I don't have to walk away from her...

I lean back against the railing of the yacht as Nicholas babbles on about traveling to Europe this winter. We drive past the miles of rolling sea so dark it seems neverending. The view in front of us is just one black abyss. I'm easily lost in thoughts of Emily. My mind wanders to images of her soft curves lying next to me. Curves that quickly draw me in. My cock stirs at the thought of binding her delicate wrists, and the beauty of watching her skin grow pink with each stroke of my leather paddle. There are many things I can imagine doing to her. Even now, my hands ache to feel her skin again. My Lily Pad. It seems we've come a long way from what we used to be. *I've had all of this time to forget you and I haven't.* Maybe I'm a sadist, just torturing myself over her, dreaming of someone I can't have.

Leaving her room this morning is definitely at the top of things I hate the most in my life. I know it was for the best, but it seems like there's nothing but obstacles between us. Emily is young and sweet, but much too naive for her own good. If she knew all of the women I've been with at the Pleasure Chest, she wouldn't want anything to do with me. My knuckles curl at the thought of any man touching her. How many men has she been with? I refuse to accept the fact that someone else has touched her. No, that would gut me in the worst possible way.

I wanted to punish her the night she came to the Pleasure Chest looking for some random Dom because of Ceci. Emily was like bait just hanging there waiting for someone to bite. I wish I could be the knight in shining armor I know she needs, but I can't. She needs someone her own age. Someone who doesn't hate her father. Someone who doesn't feel guilt every time he touches her…

" she is my dark lady, my MUSE. "

CHAPTER 8

EMILY

My head is still swimming with the heat of Tristan's words as I rush across the deck of the ship to find my place back at the fire pit. Anxiety gnaws at me with the possibility that my absence hasn't gone unnoticed. Disappearing off with Tristan probably wasn't the best idea, but then again, it's not like I had much of a choice. I couldn't have stopped him even if I wanted to.

I'm half way across the deck when I run into a set of broad, muscular shoulders. The impact nearly knocks me off my feet, but a set of warm hands capture me as I stumble. The darkness of the night around us shields his body, but against the moonlight, I can just make out Tyler's smile.

"Whoa, there you are!" he exclaims.

It takes me several minutes to untangle myself from his grip. He reluctantly lets go after what seems like an eternity. Shit. If Tristan sees us now, he's really going to throw him overboard. I bite back a laugh at the memory of Tristan's face when I said I might like Tyler.

"What are you smiling at?" Tyler asks.

"Oh, nothing."

He looks down at me with curiosity as I take a step back several inches away from him. I watch him as he buries his hands in his pockets and awkwardly smiles at me. I haven't known Tyler for very long, but his expression tells me there's definitely something on his mind.

"So, do you want to go somewhere we can talk… privately."

Privately? The word screams SEX. Being on a yacht in the middle of the ocean is just as private as you can get. No, I get the feeling Tyler's idea of privacy is a lot different from mine.

"I'm going to bed," I announce.

I feign tiredness, but his expression tells me he isn't buying it.

"So soon?"

Disappointment shows in his eyes as he studies my face. Only minutes ago, we were sitting so close he could kiss me without even trying. Now, I'm all too anxious to leave and put as much distance as I can between us. I don't want to mess things up with Tristan since getting him to agree to talk was probably the biggest step for us.

"Do you want company?" he smiles.

This is definitely not the impression I meant to give Tyler when I invited him out today.

"I'm exhausted. I think I soaked up too much sun," I lie.

Waves break on the side of the boat as an awkward silence falls between us. There's a strange look of anger behind his expression. The easy smile he once had is replaced with a tight-lipped frown.

"Goodnight, I guess." He waits several seconds for me to say something before turning and walking away. I watch as his figure slowly fades into the night.

Ceci's bright blue eyes pop into view as she steps in front of my bedroom quarters. I watch her pensive face as she watches me unpack my toothbrush from my overnight bag. God, I hope she brought her own toothbrush and isn't looking to borrow mine. Gross.

"What are you doing?" Ceci asks.

"Getting ready to go to bed."

She strides over and pulls me to the side like she's my mother ready to discipline me. She tosses her thick brown hair as she stares at me with an impatient look. I know that look. It's the '*you fucked up big time*' look. The only difference is—it's extra bitchy because she's been drinking, the alcohol permeating the air around us.

"Why are you going to bed so early?" she asks.

"I'm tired."

"Seriously? You have a hot tattooed bartender who wants to fuck your brains out across the hall. For the past thirty minutes, he's been blabbing on and on about how stunning you are."

I blush at the compliment.

"He's really nice, but I'm just not into him."

"Liar. I totally saw you with him earlier. You were leading him on."

A sliver of guilt makes its way into my chest. She's right. I was definitely leading Tyler on, something I would normally never do. In fact, I was using him to piss off Tristan, which to my surprise, worked perfectly.

"He's really nice, but there's no chemistry there."

She snorts in amusement as she rolls her eyes at me. It doesn't take her long to get distracted by another subject entirely.

"What were you talking to Tristan about?"

My nerves jump at her question. She stares at me with a curious look as I begin to brush my teeth over the bathroom sink.

"Nothing. We were just talking about a new piece he's working on," I mumble.

The lie easily rolls off of me.

Whether she believes me or not, I'll never know as her face gives nothing away. She grabs my hairbrush from the sink and combs it through her hair. A streak of irritation runs through me as I watch her tackle her split ends realizing Ceci is always taking things that don't belong to her. Maybe she's always been like this, and I've never noticed until now.

"Hey, can I borrow your phone?" she asks, before grabbing my cell.

"Uh, sure, what for?"

"I think I'm going to call Augie and see how he's doing."

A strange sensation filters through my chest as she grabs my cell and scans through my contacts. Despite my better judgment, I leave her with it and head to bed. Sleep comes easily as I lay back and dream of Tristan. My thoughts float to the hungry look on his face as he cornered me on the deck. I replay the image over in my head until the last thing I see are his hazel eyes reaching out to me.

CHAPTER 9

TRISTAN

I'm pissed drunk by the time I get back to my bedroom.

After drinking nearly ten beers with Nicholas, I'm surprised I was even able to make it all the way downstairs to the lower compartment of the yacht. I stumble into my room, acutely aware of how close Emily's bedroom is to mine. My cock stirs at the possibilities that run through my mind. I could sneak into her room and wrap her around me.

No, I'm far too wasted.

My cock disagrees, but my mind is far too fuzzy to fight it.

To my satisfaction, Tyler's room is on the other end of the hall. Far enough that he would have to pass my room to see her. There's no way in hell I'm letting him sneak into her room. I prop open my door giving me the perfect view of Emily's door. If anyone is trying to sneak by, I'll know. I switch off my bedroom light and then fall back on my bed. I'm exhausted, and my muscles feel strained as I soak in the warmth of the bed covers.

I pull out my phone and scan for Emily's number. In the

darkness, her picture pops up next to her number. Without thinking, I open a new text and type in a message.

Me: Come to my room.

It takes her what feels like an eternity to answer, but eventually, she does. I smile as her name pops onto my screen.

Emily: Now?

Me: Yes, I promise to behave. I just want you here.

Emily: And if I don't behave?

I grin like a fool at her text message. Who am I kidding? I would be lying if I said I hated when she misbehaved. She makes me angry as hell, but I've never wanted her so much in my life.

Me: I don't like breaking promises. But I'm willing to break them for you.

Emily: Be right there.

I leave my phone on silent, and then turn, allowing myself to sink deeper into the satin sheets. After several minutes, I feel the bed move and a soft body pressing against my back. My hands itch to touch her skin, but the alcohol I drank earlier makes me sluggish. After clumsily trying to turn over, I give up. To my surprise, I feel her cool lips sliding across my shoulder and down my arm. She doesn't say a word, but from her ragged breathing, I know she's just as turned on as I am.

My cock stirs against the bed. I moan as I grind my hips into the mattress wishing to God it was her. Exhausted from the weekend, I decide to keep my promise and behave.

Her hands never seem to stop touching me, but after a while, the sensation fades into a general warmth that covers me.

I lift my head to whisper goodnight and spot a strand of Emily's hair. I blink through the darkness as my eyes try to adjust.

The strand looks darker than I remember, but it only deters my sleep for a second before I'm sucked back into unconsciousness. Somewhere between falling and dreaming, I feel her soft flesh wrap herself in my arms and press against me. The last thing I hear is her whispering.

"I'm so glad you knew it was me."

> she is my dark lady, my MUSE.

CHAPTER 10

EMILY

I wake with Tristan's name on my lips.

My night was restless. Twice, I rolled to see if Ceci had finally come to bed, but both times, I found her side empty and her bed sheets untouched. Where the hell did she sleep? Oh, God. I really hope she didn't drink more and fall overboard. That would be her luck. I can just imagine the newspaper headlines. *New York Socialite Drowns After Party on Yacht.*

I reach out for my phone to glance at the time, but to my dismay it's nowhere in sight. The last time I saw it was in Ceci's hand. Where the hell did she put it? I search underneath my pillows and on the nightstand next to my bed where I usually keep it, but it's not there. The only trace of its existence is the power cord plugged into the wall. After tearing about the bed, I finally give up and begin to get ready for the day ahead of me. Today we leave paradise and head back to the city.

I'm secretly dreading it.

It's not every day I get to spend twenty-four hours with Tristan.

DRAWN TO YOU

I was just getting used to seeing him every day. It also doesn't help that we've spent a good majority of this trip fighting.

After brushing my teeth and combing my bed hair, I sneak out of my room in my pajamas in search of Ceci. I'm only halfway down the hallway when I spot Tristan's bedroom door ajar. A shiver runs up my spine as a million naughty possibilities run through my head. Last night's goodbye was not only frustrating, but it left me with a lady boner. I'm tempted to sneak into his room and show him just how frustrated he made me feel after kissing me the way he did.

I glance down the hallway toward my brother's room and listen for any type of movement. The lower deck is completely silent. I turn and hurry toward Tristan's bedroom. Excitement filters through me as I go. I feel like a little kid ditching school to stay home and read.

I'm halfway through the door when something brown catches my eye. Deep beneath the covers, a messy head of brown hairs rises up just as I enter. My stomach sinks at the sight of Ceci lying there. Her thin arms lay draped over Tristan's naked form, but they break free as soon as she sees me. A small smile plagues her lips as she looks over toward Tristan. I gasp so loudly that I wake him with a start. He bolts up in bed just in time to see me staring at him with a torn look. His eyes grow wide as he spots me—and then he sees Ceci in her bra and panties next to him.

My heart catapults into my throat as a sob threatens to break free. *I fucking hate you.*

"How could you?"
The broken words fall from my lips. My knees grow weak as I suddenly lose my balance. Tristan's arms are there to catch me as I stumble and nearly take him down with me. His fingers quickly firmly wrap behind my back like he pulls me up straight.

The man I love fucked my best friend. I can't think of anything worse. The pain that seeps through my chest threatens to disintegrate me.

"You invited me to your room, Tristan. Don't you remember?" Ceci's face breaks into a smile.

"You fucking bitch!"

My fist hits Ceci across the mouth with a furious vengeance. Despite my petite frame, I have one hell of a punch, and I have my brothers to thank for it. Ceci yelps like an injured dog as she goes flying onto the bed. I straddle her as blind rage consumes me.

"How could you?" I scream.

Ceci pushes my hands off her, but it doesn't stop me from slapping her hard across the cheek.

"Get her off of me," she screams.

"Emily, that's enough," Tristan pulls me off her.

I push out of his arms as his touch sears me. The pain is blinding.

"Don't you ever fucking touch me again."

Tristan's eyes immediately darken.

"Emily. Wait."

Ceci stands as she wipes her mouth. A small gash adorns her lip.

"I knew it. I knew something was going on between you guys, but I never guessed you were in love with him."

I may have physically struck Ceci, but the cruelty of her words knocks the wind out of me. Tristan looks at me with pleading eyes. He steps toward me with open arms, but I immediately retreat. I can't stand to look at him. The sight of his bare form sends a wave of nausea through me. The feeling of betrayal is enough to suffocate me.

"I hope you guys are happy together," I blurt.

My body is moving before my mind can catch up. I walk out of the room and head back to my bedroom. Tears flow down my face as a shooting pain hits me in the chest. The sensation sends me swaying against the hallway. I gasp to catch my breath just as my brother walks out of his bedroom. I can only imagine how I look with puffy eyes and a red nose. I'm a mess.

"Emily, what's going on?"

He heads straight toward me. As he reaches me, his gaze shifts in confusion. I feel my cheeks warm in embarrassment as he stares down at me in surprise.

"What's going on?" he asks again.

"Nothing."

"It doesn't look like nothing."

Nicholas pulls me into his arms and holds me. I sob into his shoulder as his warmth surrounds me. I've never needed my brother more than I do now.

"I heard shouting. I almost fell trying to get dressed to see what the hell was going on."

"It was nothing."

"Then who the fuck made you cry? Is it that bartender?"

On cue, the guest bedroom where Tyler had been sleeping opens. His half-naked form pops into view. Before Nicholas has the chance to stride over and kick his ass, I stop him.

"It wasn't him," I say tugging on his arm.

"Then who? Ceci? Tristan?"

His eyes grow wide.

"NO."

Without another word, I run to my room and slam the door closed behind me. Nicholas's voice carries across the hall as he approaches Tristan's room. For a moment, all hell seems like it's going to break loose, but the voices in the hall eventually dissipate. The only noise left is the sound of my heart drumming against my chest. I lay there, broken. Too hurt to move and too alive not to feel.

CHAPTER 11

TRISTAN

Pain radiates through my chest as I watch Emily walk—no, run away from me.

I'm just about to chase after her when I hear Ceci behind me. I turn on my heel to confront the little monster who had ruined everything. Ceci's eyes widen as she looks up at me. Her lip is still bleeding from the shot Emily took to her face. If it were any other situation, I would be proud of Emily for sticking up for herself, but this isn't any other situation. This is a goddamn disaster.

I hate myself for not knowing the petite frame sliding in bed with me last night wasn't Emily. I should've known when I didn't smell Emily's lavender shampoo. God, why would Ceci even do this? I've never had a moment of interest in her. She's only been a means of distraction with mind numbing conversation, especially when I have to watch Emily talking to that bartender from Oasis.

I can't count how many times I wished I could just punch him in the face. I never thought Ceci would take my interest in her conversations as an interest in her. That fucking shows me.

DRAWN TO YOU

"What were you thinking when you climbed in my bed?" I growl.

Embarrassment washes over her face as she presses her hand to her lips. A trail of blood trickles down the gash on her bottom lip. I almost feel sorry for her, but not after the way she reacted when I woke. She did this on purpose, and it befuddles me why she would purposely hurt Emily if she knew she had feelings for me.

"I was thinking of how much I like you," she admits.

Ceci steps forward to place her arms around me, but I immediately stop her. She's the last person I want to touch me right now. She just ruined any chance Emily and I might have had. Now, Emily will never trust me. The loss of her trust isn't something I take lightly, either.

"While that's flattering, I can't say I feel the same."

Her face falls at the coldness of my words.

She steps back slowly lowering her head in defeat. I know what Ceci wants. She's starved for attention. A product of her wealthy parents ignoring her over the years. I've met plenty of women like her, but I'm not here to soothe her. That's someone else's job. I grab the pink halter and shorts that are scattered on the floor in front of my bed and throw them to her. Her lips quickly form a scowl as she looks at them and then up at me.

"I thought you liked me," she blurts.

"I did, but not the way you think. You're Emily's friend and that's the only way I look at you."

She brushes a stray cluster of hair from her face. She won't admit it, but I know from her watery eyes that she's hurt by my words.

Ceci has some serious growing up to do.

"Do you like her?" Ceci asks.

"I love her."

It feels strange saying it to someone else. I've never even allowed myself the pleasure of saying this to myself.

Ceci looks up at me in shock. I'm sure she wasn't expecting

that confession. She takes several seconds to wrap her head around the idea of us before continuing her interrogation.

"I didn't know it was so serious."

I grit my teeth as I grab my shirt off of the floor and slip it over my head.

"We have a history together."

Her eyes widen with understanding.

"You're the guy she lost her virginity to? She mentioned it to me soon after her brother died. I thought she was joking because we were drunk."

I wince at the memory of the night on the stairs. It's not my proudest moment, but it led us down this twisted road. I've often wondered how different things would've turned out if I had never crossed that line between us.

"she is my dark lady, my MUSE."

CHAPTER 12

EMILY

"Emily!"

It's the desperation in Tristan's voice that gets me. He's outside my door calling for me at the top of his lungs. The knocking on the door continues despite my refusal to answer him. He's persistent, but I've never known him to be anything but. The minutes click by and the knocking only grows. God help me if Nicholas can hear him. The door shakes from the pressure of Tristan's hand. It vibrates the whole right side of the wall.

"I know you're in there."

Tristan's words are fueled by anger.

I shove my clothes in my small suitcase and begin pushing my toiletries in a plastic zip lock. I'm getting the hell out of here. I can't spend another minute on this boat with Tristan or Ceci. The sting of Tristan's betrayal festers inside of me as I watch his shadow beneath the door. I don't know how I'll ever be able to look at Ceci again. My heart hurts just thinking about her and Tristan together. The sight of her half-naked in his bed sears its way into my mind. I don't think I'll ever be able to scrub it out of my memory.

DRAWN TO YOU

"Emily, open up," he commands. "I need to explain to you what happened."

I never thought Tristan would sleep with me, and then move on to my best friend, but I guess I was naive. This was why he didn't push her away every time she threw herself at him. How could he say all of those things to me and then sleep with my friend? Women have always surrounded him, so I guess I should've known it wouldn't be any different with me. I fooled myself thinking he cared about me this whole time. I believed every beautiful word he said to me. A bitter taste fills my mouth at the thought of all of the lies he's spewed.

After several seconds, Tristan's pounding stops. I cross the room and press my ear against the door. Tristan's breathing is ragged like he's been running. The door creaks as his frame presses against it.

"Emily, open the door... I didn't sleep with her."

"Fuck you."

The words fly out of my mouth without a second thought. I hear an exasperated sigh as something slags against the door. There might be several inches of a door between us, but I can still feel his disappointment.

"Pet, open the door."

"No."

"Hey, what the hell are you doing?" Someone else calls out.

The strangely familiar voice calls out again, but this time, it sounds like it's right outside my door. Is that Tyler?

Tristan's voice booms throughout the hallway.

"What the fuck do you want?" Tristan growls.

Shit. I push open the door to find Tyler standing right outside. His familiar boyish smile is set in a thin-lipped scowl as he watches Tristan. His eyes disconnect from him as he looks over to me.

"Is he bothering you?"

"Yes."

"No," Tristan argues.

Tyler glances back at me as if trying to decipher the emotions on my face. I can only imagine I'm not sending off very positive vibes toward Tristan. In fact, I'm glaring at him now. Tyler steps back and puts up his hands to surrender.

"Look, I don't want to fight, but you need to leave her the hell alone. If she doesn't want to talk to you, then she shouldn't have to."

Tristan crosses his arms over his chest and lets out a hostile laugh. He finally stops laughing after he notices me just outside my bedroom door.

"I'm only going to tell you this once. Get the fuck out of my way."

A sliver of anxiety runs through me as I watch Tristan advance on him. Tyler might be younger, but he's nowhere near as built as Tristan. The menacing look on his face is enough to make me fear for Tyler's safety. I have no doubt Tristan could do a lot of damage.

"I'm not afraid of you," Tyler says, puffing his chest.

"You should be."

I step between them before Tristan has a chance to get any closer. He looks down at me in surprise. I'm sure he wasn't expecting me to get in the middle of this fight, but there's no way in hell I'm letting him hit Tyler over me. I push my hands against Tristan's chest as I force him to step back.

"Stop this."

"Let's talk inside the room," Tristan says, grabbing my wrist.

I pull myself out of his grasp with a force that nearly sends me flying back.

"I'm not going anywhere with you."

Tyler steps to my right as he waits for me to slip back into his room. Tristan doesn't let up as he tries again to pull me to the side to listen to him.

"Tristan, please, just leave."

"Emily, you're not listening to me."

"Please, I can't take this anymore."

"I need you."

I know what I'm about to say is going to hurt him, but I shouldn't care. I don't. I don't care. Maybe if I keep saying it, it will finally come true.

DRAWN TO YOU

"I don't need you," I lie.

The surprised look on his face hurts my heart. The man I've fallen in love with slowly backs away in defeat. He presses his fist against the hallway wall as if he's ready to knock it down before slowly backing away.

Tristan turns and begins to walk away. He's only a few feet away when I see him turn and look up.

"I know you're saying you don't need me now, but I will always be here if you decide one day you do," he says.

Hot tears come crashing down my cheeks as I watch him disappear out of view. Tyler grabs my shoulders as I sway against my door. I want to run after him, but my pride tells me to stop. I'm tired of being on his yo-yo string. One day, he needs me. The next day, he's sleeping with my best friend. My heart can't take it anymore. No amount of poetry could wash away the pain he's caused. I'm done with Tristan Knight.

CHAPTER 13

EMILY

The car ride from the marina back to the beach house is painful to say the least, but I'm fortunate enough to get a small reprieve when Tyler sits next to me. It takes all of my strength not to break down and cry in the car with Tristan sitting only a few feet away. Even my brother seems to look at me strange during the trip back. I'm sure he's noticed my strange mood since I got in the car. Thankfully, I found out from Tyler that Nicholas was up on the deck talking to another yacht owner back at the marina.

A sigh of relief escapes me as we pull up to the beach house. Tristan exits the car without so much as looking back at me. I fight the need to run after him as I watch him enter the house. Nicholas and Ceci trail not too far off behind him, leaving me with my thoughts.

"Hey, you okay?"

I turn to find Tyler watching me with a sympathetic expression.

"Yes, sorry."

I blush as his curious eyes watch me.

DRAWN TO YOU

"Well, thank you for inviting me this weekend. It was… interesting," he says.

I laugh despite the suffocating feeling in my chest. I like Tyler despite the fact that he's nothing like Tristan. I'm almost certain that maybe in another life we could've been together.

"I'm sorry, for all of that earlier."

He smiles.

"Hey, if I thought I had any chance of making you like me more than *him*…I would pounce on it."

Tyler steps forward and plants a chaste kiss on my lips.

"If you ever come back to Oasis, text me. I would love to take you out."

I wave weakly as I watch him step inside his white Mustang and peel away. I wish I could more than like him, but someone else has stolen my heart.

Several hours later, I find myself staring at the endless rolling sea. I keep telling myself if I just keep breathing, eventually, the pain inside my soul will dissipate. Ocean waves crash on the sand sending a cold ocean spray against me. I inhale with every receding wave and exhale as each one breaks across the sand.

I look down at the necklace in my hand that Tristan gave me years ago. The sterling metal is cool against my skin as I tighten my grip on it. Tears slide down my cheeks as a sickening feeling in my chest grows. The memory of naked skin flashes through my mind. My heart thrums against my chest at the memory of Ceci's hands draped over Tristan. Their betrayal stings more than anything I've ever felt.

The chain of the necklace slips from my grip and I almost lose it in the water. I stare at it dangling from my hand. The small flower glistens.

I need to let you go.

It slowly begins to slip from my grip even more, but at the last minute, I catch it with both hands. The expression 'my heart in my hands' never rang so true. Tears freely flow down my face as I slip the wretched necklace in the pocket of my jeans. I feel defeated by my inability to even detach myself from one of Tristan's things. How am I supposed to separate myself from him?

The more I move, the sicker I find myself. I'm practically on my knees when Ceci's figure pops into view. She couldn't have picked a worse possible moment to talk to me, but here she is. Pity stains her face as she approaches me. The sight of it boils my blood. I can't bring myself to even look at her. God, we've never been in a fight this long. Most of our arguments end with us making up within the hour.

"What are you doing?"

"Nothing," I answer annoyed. "You should go."

"I came to check on you."

"If Tristan asked you to check up on me, you can tell him to go fuck himself—or fuck you."

Ceci's bored expression only makes it clearer that checking in on me is the last thing she wants to do. I don't blame her. I just seem to be getting in the way of her end goal.

"Tristan just left back to the city. I wanted to check up on you."

My eyes look up to find her gaze trained on me. I try to look away, but she steps closer and in my line of sight. Her expression is laced tight. It gives away nothing, and it's hardly a look to make me think she's worried about me.

"I'm sorry," she finally says.

"You don't understand, Ceci. You can't just say I'm sorry and hope everything will be better."

"I have to start somewhere. Unless you want to hit me in the face again."

I laugh despite the pain that swells in my chest.

"Actually, that's quite tempting."

"Emily, I didn't sleep with him," she says, pulling out my phone from her pocket.

I was wondering where the hell it was, but I figured she probably chucked it overboard after I punched her. I scroll through the text messages she sent back and forth with Tristan. It pains me to think that his original intent was to ask me to his room, but somehow, he didn't say a word when Ceci showed up.

"Even if I believed you, the damage is already done."

"I know," she says. "I just wanted to try to fix this."

"I don't know if you can, Ceci. If you knew I had feelings for Tristan, and that he had feelings for me, then why did you get in the middle?"

"I guess I was jealous. Tyler likes you. Tristan loves you. I suppose I wanted someone to care about me, too."

My heart squeezes at her words.

Tristan loves you.

"He doesn't love me."

She laughs, bitterly.

"He does. He told me."

I scan Ceci's face to see if she's bullshitting me, but her face remains stoic. She's either getting really good at lying to me, or she's telling the truth.

"I'm not going to say anything to Nicholas."

"You're not?" I ask surprised.

"No."

Before I can ask her why, Ceci walks away and heads back to the beach house. A slow burn lights in my stomach and travels its way up my body at the memory of her words. Love is not a word I've ever heard Tristan say to me.

CHAPTER 14

EMILY

It's been two weeks since the trip to the beach house, and I haven't been able to stop thinking about Ceci's words.

"He does. He told me."

I've thrown myself into getting ready for my first semester back at school, but that only provides a temporary distraction. Even Augie has tried to break me from my never-ending bitch cycle, but I'm not sure how many more nights I can stomach being dragged to bars and parties with him and Harvey. I know they're trying to help me get over Tristan, but every guy I meet only succeeds in pushing him higher in my mind. I've even avoided talking to my brother because I know he'll ask why I was acting so strange the day we left the Hamptons.

My phone vibrates as I arrive at The Grind near NYU. My favorite morning macchiato is calling my name as I step in line behind a dozen other students. I fish for my phone in my pocket as I step up to place my order. I know I shouldn't be expecting Tristan to call me, but a part of me misses hearing from him. The paintings that hang in the coffee house only manage to remind me of his art. Deep down inside, I know it's one of the main reasons why I come to this coffee shop. Sitting among the bright colors has a homier feel. The Grind even has bookshelves where you can borrow books and return them when you want. It all works on an honor system, but lately I find myself more often taking books of poetry home to hoard.

Disappointment fills me at the sight of Augie's number flashing across my screen. I'm surprised he's calling me when he's supposed to be meeting up with Harvey for lunch. The two have been getting pretty serious lately. It's been less than a month and they're already saying 'I love you' to each other.

My heart squeezes at the thought of those words. While I'm happy for Augie, I can't help but feel a strange sense of jealousy. I honestly wish I could have their relationship. They make falling in love look easy. I reluctantly pick up his call.

"Emily?"

He sounds almost confused as if he was expecting my phone to go to voicemail.

"Hey, what's up?"

"Where are you?"

I look around the coffee shop with curiosity. Is Augie here? The shop is packed with students taking summer classes. Half of them are either grabbing coffee or sitting to write papers.

"I'm heading back to the apartment in a few minutes."

"Oh, okay…"

"What's wrong?" I ask.

"…I saw him."

"Who are you talking about," I ask.

"Tristan Knight."

My heart stills at the sound of his name. Just hearing it brings back the memory of Tristan's face as I told him I didn't need him. I feel my knees growing weaker by the second as I still myself on a rack of coffee mugs for sale.

"He was walking down the opposite side of the street as us in the Meat Packing District. I swear I almost spit out my coke when I saw him. Harvey kept asking me if I was okay because I nearly choked," Augie says.

"Why are you telling me this," I ask, trying my best to sound unaffected by his revelation.

He chuckles softly into the phone. "Damn, you are still pissed. Don't get me wrong, I would be, too…"

I step outside the line of students waiting to fill up on caffeine and head to the restroom. My cheeks warm as hot tears form at the corner of my eyes. I push my way past a cluster of sorority girls and lock the bathroom door behind me. Tightness fills my chest as I stare into the bathroom mirror. My once vibrant skin is now pale looking. Even my hair seems to have a mind of its own. The strands fall flatly on my face giving my hair a dead appearance.

"He asked for you."

I curse to myself as I accidentally ram my knee into the sink countertop. I was so stupid to think the night we slept together would somehow fix what was broken between us. The only thing it's accomplished is to cause me to feel like an idiot when he slept with Ceci. Sadly, I can't even muster the energy to hate him when I know I should. I still carry the necklace on me that I almost lost at the beach.

"Augie, what are you doing?"

"Trying to tell you that I recognize pain and regret when I see it."

For the past week, he's been attempting to get me to entertain the notion that Tristan didn't sleep with Ceci. I have a feeling he had a long talk with her and that's the reason he's been pushing it so hard. I can't say I'm on good terms with Ceci. She's trying, but I'm not ready to forgive her for jumping in bed with Tristan.

"He only regrets sleeping with her because he got caught."

Augie laughs.

"Babe, he didn't sleep with Ceci. How many times do you need to hear it?"

"Until my ears bleed, I guess."

"You're torturing yourself over nothing… By the way, I gave him your cell phone number again."

"He has it," I say, rolling my eyes.

"I think he needed a little encouragement to actually call you."

I roll my eyes at Augie's need to meddle in everything. I swear he's worse than my father is. I can't even get him to stop butting his nose into what classes I'm going to take this semester at NYU. I thought he was only over controlling with Nicholas, but it extends to all his children. A loud knock sounds on the door of the bathroom as an impatient voice calls. *Are you finished already? There's a line for the bathroom!*

"I have to go, Augie. I'll see you tonight."

"Fine, but before you hang up, Harvey and I got invited to this badass party. You have to come. It's in Greenwich."

"When is it?"

"Saturday."

I roll my eyes at Augie's excited squeal.

"I'll go," I finally say. "But don't ditch me to make out in the closet again."

"Okay." He sighs. "And you should really call Tristan."

You should! Harvey's voice calls over the line. I laugh despite the pain that radiates in my chest.

I leave The Grind with the gnawing sensation that maybe Ceci wasn't lying when she told me she didn't sleep with Tristan.

CHAPTER 15

TRISTAN

Today is one hell of a day.

Seeing Emily's friend Augie was like a knife to the chest. I've been avoiding even the mention of her name. I've tested my limits of pain and realized that right now, Emily is a hard limit for me. All of my paintings are starting to take on a macabre feel. Even Sebastian Wolfe says I'm going a little too dark, and he's one of my biggest clients.

I lean back into the seat of my car as I weigh the pros and cons of walking into the Pleasure Chest. This morning, a text message was waiting for me from Francesca, the sub I was spending time with before Emily walked back into my life. It's not the temptation that led me all the way out here. No, it's the need to forget. To feel in control after letting the woman I love slip through my fingers.

Felicity's neon pink smile greets me as I enter the Pleasure Chest. Her eyebrows quirk up at me as I silently hand her my jacket and phone to store in coat check. Memories of Emily drift into my mind. The last time I was here was the night she came to the club. I haven't been back since.

DRAWN TO YOU

The club is thriving with an abnormal amount of guests as I step inside. To my dismay, *Love Will Tear Us Apart* by Joy Division is playing on the speakers. Fucking perfect.

I watch Felicity with irritation as she turns and places my belongings in the room behind her. She doesn't say a word despite my silence, but I know something is on the tip of her tongue.

"What is it?" I growl.

"You look like shit."

"I'm fine," I lie.

Felicity brushes a hand through her long red hair as she rounds the corner. She crosses her arms over her chest and proceeds to stare at me with a critical look waiting for me to unravel.

"Are you here to see Francesca?"

There's the million-dollar question.

"Yes."

A look of disappointment crosses Felicity's heart shaped face. She lets out a long sigh before handing me a key to room 23. A wave of anxiety passes through me. What if I feel worse after I do this?

"What happened to the blonde?" Felicity asks with curious eyes.

"Nothing."

"Is that the problem?"

"This isn't a gab session."

She laughs and then points me in the direction of the individual playrooms.

"I hope you know you're acting like an idiot," she calls.

I ignore her and turn down the hallway to find room number 23. It's set off to the side with a door painted red. My heart races as I turn the knob and walk inside. Despite the cool temperatures of the room, I feel my palms begin to sweat. I loosen my tie as I enter, hoping to stop the stifling rise of heat that I feel spreading across my skin.

Francesca waits for me inside on her knees. The dark-haired beauty looks up at me as I walk toward her. Her eyes are filled with primal hunger. She quickly tilts her head down letting me know that she's ready and willing to surrender to me. I begin by rolling up my sleeves to my elbows. My dress shirt isn't my regular clothing of preference when I do a scene, but today it will have to do. A smile of encouragement spreads across Francesca's lips as I slowly pull a paddle from the display rack in the room. I'll start slow. Maybe if I start slow, I'll be fine.

Emily's face pops into my mind as I walk over to the sub. The spanking that I gave Emily in bed left me itching for more. I shake my head to clear my thoughts, but the torn look on Emily's face that day on the yacht plagues me. I can't get her out of my fucking head. I slam my fist against the wall rattling the rack of floggers, leashes, and whips.

"What's wrong, Tristan?"

Fuck, what am I doing? I quickly back away from Francesca and let the paddle fall to the floor.

Everything.

I leave the Pleasure Chest in a whirlwind. I don't even bother grabbing my jacket from Felicity as she hands me my wallet, keys, and cell phone. It isn't long before I'm near my apartment again trying to maneuver through traffic. The thought of being back at my studio gives me some peace, but it doesn't drown the gnawing feeling of guilt in my stomach. I lift my phone from my pants and scroll through my list of contacts. Emily's face pops on my screen. I stare at the picture that I secretly snapped of her at the beach. She wasn't even aware of the candid I took as she swam in the water with her friend Augie. I click on her name as my phone dials her number. With each ring, my body begins to shake. Beads of sweat form on my forehead and on the back of my neck.

After several minutes, Emily's phone finally goes to voicemail.

"Emily, I love you. Please don't delete this message."

> "she is my dark lady, my MUSE."

CHAPTER 16

EMILY

It's funny how three little words can make or break you.
I love you.
His words feel like a kick to the chest. A wave of anxiety hits me as I listen to the voicemail Tristan left me on my cell. Most of his sentences come in and out, but those three words I'm certain I heard right. My chest squeezes in an all too familiar way, leaving me gasping for air. I never expected to hear him say those words ever, let alone over a voicemail. I've said them in my mind a million times over, but never out loud. I set down my book of poetry and replay the voicemail over again. Each time I hear Tristan's voice, I feel my heart break just a little more. He sounds upset. His pitch matches the same desperation I feel whenever I hear his name.

It's almost been three weeks now since I've spoken to Tristan. I thought his absence in my life would get easier, but it hasn't been easy. I don't feel like myself anymore. Every day seems a little less bright.

I've filled my days with reading to escape the reality outside my apartment. I get lost in pieces of literature where the hero and heroine always find their happy ending. Unfortunately, fiction doesn't seem to translate well in real life. I'm starting to feel like happy endings were made for fools. Although Jane Austen would say, *we are all fools in love*. I'm just feeling a bit extra foolish today.

"Emily?"

A voice calls from behind me. I turn to find Augie dressed in a pair of plaid pajamas. Not too far off behind him is Harvey. My heart squeezes at the sight of them.

"Hey," I say weakly.

"Are you okay?" he asks.

"No."

Tears rush forward as I bite back a sob.

"What's wrong?"

Augie steps forward pulling me into his arms as he tries to soothe me. Shame overwhelms me as Harvey stands in the background unsure of what to say. This is so embarrassing. I'm making the worst impression with Harvey. The thought of it unleashes a flurry of tears. God, he must think I'm the most emotional person ever. Since he's been here, all he's seen me do is cry, watch RomComs, read, stuff my face with potato chips and then cry some more. I'm a walking hot mess.

Augie rubs my back as I try to regain my composure. I straighten out my shirt although it doesn't help with the dripping mess on my face.

"Tristan finally called."

The words stumble out of my mouth. A sharp gasp releases from Augie's chest. He stares over at me with wide, concerned eyes.

"What did he do? Do I need to kick his ass?"

I laugh through my tears.

"No…it's not like that."

"Then don't keep me in suspense, woman. What did he say?"

"He left a message. He said he loved me."

A bright smile appears on his face. He glances to the side at Harvey and their eyes connect. Somehow, I know they're having a secret conversation right now. Augie grabs my phone and replays the message Tristan left. He bites his lip as if something wicked is going through his mind. He walks over to the kitchen, grabs a paper towel, and then hands me it.

"Dry your tears. Tonight we're going to that party."

"Augie, I think I changed my mind."

"You have to go," Harvey says.

Augie and I both look up at him. His face lights up with a smile.

"Yes, you have to go. And you're going to invite Tristan."

"What? No. I don't think a party is a good place."

"It's perfect," Augie says.

"Now, get ready." Harvey smiles.

> "she is my dark lady, my MUSE."

CHAPTER 17

EMILY

I'm floating, suspended in mid-air.

Or at least that's what it feels like as my head spins after way too many tequila shots.

Patron does that to you.

Electronic dance music pumps from the party speakers as I make my way through the crowd of university students watching the beer pong tournament in the dorm hallway. Augie and Harvey disappear as they head toward the makeshift dance floor near the stairs. I take a sip of the semi-warm beer in my hand. It's finally starting to taste less like piss and more like alcohol.

As I make my way to the back of the party, my phone buzzes with a text.

Tristan: I'm here. Where are you?

My heart skips as I re-read the text message at least five times. I begin to text him back when I sense someone standing behind me.

Me: I'm near the dance floor.

I turn just as I send the text. Tristan stands behind me wearing dark wash jeans, a white V-neck, and a leather jacket. He looks like he just stepped out of the movie *The Outsiders*. I'm digging the whole Matt Dillon vibe. A smirk graces his face as his eyes scan me. I'm wearing fewer clothes than I would like to be, but Augie convinced me to wear the smuttiest dress I own. It just so happens to be a black latex dress that I stole from Ceci when she slept over one night. Tit for tat. She took the love of my life and I stole one of her best dresses.

"Hi." I smile.

My head is starting to feel fuzzy.

"Hey, sweetheart."

The words roll off his tongue like black velvet. Even my ears are turned on by the sound. He steps forward just as I do. Our bodies meet and the magnetic pull I feel is enough to almost make me forget I'm supposed to be mad at him. He smiles, and for the first time in a long time, it reaches his eyes. My heart constricts as he places his hand on my hip and leads me to the dance floor just a few feet ahead of us.

My eyes search the room, and in my drunken haze, I spot Augie and Harvey throwing me the thumbs up. I wave at them making a cut it out motion. Tristan twirls me just as they start playing *Ink* by Coldplay. He pulls me to him and begins to mouth the words to me. I've never seen him so relaxed. It's like he finally took a chill pill.

"I didn't know you liked Coldplay."

"I do."

We sway together as the room around us starts to shout-sing the song. A static shift happens in the atmosphere as Tristan leans in. I feel my body reacting to his as it mimics each move. Before I know it, my lips are centimeters away from his. Tristan waits for me to make the first move. My heart beats in my ears as the world slows around me. For the first time in a long time, my mind clears of all of my misconceptions. I want to do something for myself. Even if it's wrong.

Tonight I don't feel like being a good girl. Tonight I feel like being bad.

My lips crash into his as I leap into his arms. He grunts as he lifts me. The crowd around us disperses as he wraps his hands around my bottom and carries me into a nearby bedroom. We collapse on a bed with bedding that looks like they came right off of the merchandise rack of a New York Yankees memorabilia shop. I burst into laughter as I spot a poster of a beer babe hanging on the ceiling of the room.

Tristan looks up and grins.

Frantic hands unzip the front of my dress as I begin to unbuckle Tristan's belt on his jeans. My eyes look up as a sharp intake comes from Tristan. His eyes widen as he spots the hot pink bra and panties that I'm wearing beneath my black latex dress. His mouth immediately comes down on my bra biting my nipple through the flimsy fabric. My hips jut in reaction as he grinds his still covered erection into my thigh.

"Tristan?" I moan. "Will you fuck me from behind?"

I blush as a slow chuckle erupts from his chest. He finishes unzipping my dress and then flips me over on my knees. I feel his grip tighten on my ponytail. His hands nearly rip off the pink lace covering my intimate area.

"I like this," he says, nipping my ear.

"Me, too," I moan. "Are you going to punish me?"

I can almost hear him smiling.

"No, I'm not going to punish you. At least not right now."

"No?"

"No. Right now, I'm going to fuck you until your knees collapse underneath you."

Oh. Fuck.

"You don't come until I say so," he growls.

I moan, thrusting my bottom into his pelvis. I hear his pants fall and then the sound of a condom ripping open. I hadn't even thought of protection. I was too preoccupied with the thought of his cock inside me. My thoughts are cut short by the pressure of Tristan thrusting inside me. I grunt as he pulls my ponytail and bottoms out inside me. My fingers grip the sheets as he pushes and holds. I can feel my insides tightening around him. He stops and for a moment, I think I might cry. My torture is short lived as his motions speed up. My head spins as euphoria sets in.

"*I fucking love you,*" he whispers next to my ear as he lets my ponytail go and opts for a handful of my ass.

I'm just about to come when I hear him calling me. "Little one, are you close?" he moans.

"Yes," I pant.

"Good."

Tristan pulls out and then lies on the bed next to me.

"Come ride me, baby."

Hearing those words are all I need. In my tipsy stupor, I climb on top of him. His hands reach up as he rolls my nipples between his index finger and his thumb. I lean back as I swivel my hips. He groans each time I lift myself and then slam back down on top of him. I smile at the shift in power. His hands grab my hips pushing me to go faster, but I stop him. He chuckles as I look down at him with a mischievous smile. I'm almost done with my teasing when I feel him lift his hips and me along with it. The sensation is nothing like I've ever felt before. As his finger finds my clit, I realize that, in a way, this moment is my punishment. My body is pushed to extremes, but the outcome is pure bliss.

"Tristan?" I shudder. My release is so close.

"Come for me, sweetheart."

That's all it takes. His words are the final piece to push me over the edge. I feel his hips meet mine in one last thrust. Beads of sweat run down my breast and to my neck. I lean forward, pressing against his chest, my pink bra still intact. Our hearts pound in unison as the two of us silently kiss. My mind races back to all of the stupid things I said to Tristan that day on the yacht. I was wrong to tell him I didn't need him. I do.

"I love you," I say against his lips.

"I love you too, little one."

CHAPTER 18

EMILY

After several more shots of tequila with Tristan, I barely feel his hand wrapped around my waist as we exit the dorm building. A gust of wind hits me like an ice cold shower as we make our way down the sidewalk. We don't make it very far before Tristan pulls me to the side and asks me to wait for him to pull up the car. I'm reluctant to let him out of my grasp. Tristan leans in and kisses me before running to get his car down the street. My eyelids slip closed as I lean back against the brick wall behind me and let a heavy feeling of sleep wash over me. My limbs are warm and yet numb all at once.

God, I drank too much.

I tug the bottom of my dress just as the sound of a camera shutter clicks away. *Click. Click. Click.* My eyes jolt open as I spot a paparazzo hiding behind a line of cars. My vision might be blurry, but I know he's capturing every second of me leaning against this brownstone drunk. Of course, I'm standing in perfect view for his lens. My father is going to kill me if this ends up in the tabloids.

Click. Click. Click.

DRAWN TO YOU

"Fuck," I say, boiling with anger as I shove my dress down and then shield my face.

Not that it matters. I know the paparazzi all too well. Privacy isn't a concept they seem to understand. Over the years, I've grown to avoid them like the plague, but it doesn't matter where I am, they always find me. Tonight isn't any different. I make a beeline straight for the paparazzo. My stomach turns from the amount of alcohol filtering through my system. I turn and speed walk down the sidewalk nearly twisting my ankle as I pull off my shoes.

"Nice one, princess. Someone's going to pay a pretty penny for this," the paparazzo says.

The balding man looks ever so familiar. He crudely stares at me over his camera lens.

"What's wrong, princess? Is life too hard on Millionaire's Row?"

"Fuck you," I yell.

I'm all too tempted to throw my shoes at the paparazzo. He laughs coldly as I try in vain to walk past him.

"Seems like you're just as much trouble as your brother."

His words trigger my memory of the night Augie and I drove to The Somerset to pick up Nicholas. *Fuck.* This is the same asshole who was taunting my brother.

"Get out of my way."

"Why, princess? The world loves to hate you," he says, snapping a shot of my face. "They're sure going to love when they see photos of you and that tall bastard you were with."

A blur of black walks past me and slams into the paparazzo sending him flying across the sidewalk. A surprised yelp echoes throughout the city streets as I watch the paparazzo land hard on the sidewalk. His camera skids across the cement only a few inches from my feet. To my surprise, I spot Tristan leaning over the balding man in a huff of anger. His chest rises and falls with each ragged breath. Did he run here? Good God, he looks good. My eyes trace him in appreciation. Tristan's hazel eyes quickly assess me before returning to the troll on the ground.

"Get your filthy camera away from her before I end you," Tristan seethes.

"Fucking asshole. This is the second time I've had to replace my camera."

Tristan laughs.

"Maybe stop acting like an asshole and people will quit smashing your things."

The paparazzo angrily mutters under his breath as he looks up at me with rage. He spits a pool of blood on the ground and wipes off his clothes as he stands.

"Go ahead and break my camera, but I already have plenty of pictures to sell of your little princess. I'm sure her daddy will love to see her acting like a whore with you."

"You fucking dick," Tristan punches him across the jaw.

The paparazzo looks up as he spews blood from his mouth. He smiles with bloody teeth.

"You're going to pay for that."

"Leave," Tristan commands.

"This is a public sidewalk."

"I'm not asking."

The paparazzo reluctantly leaves, but not without muttering a slew of curse words under his breath. My head spins as I watch him hobble down the street toward his car. I almost feel bad for him. Almost. Until I realize he still has a wide selection of photos of Tristan and me. Photos that could end everything before it begins.

"My father is going to have a heart attack when he sees those photos."

Hot tears slip down my cheeks at the sinking embarrassment that overwhelms me.

"Come here," Tristan says.

He steps forward pulling me into his arms. His warmth surrounds me in a calm embrace.

"Let me take you home."

"Tristan, what am I going to tell my father about the photos?"

"Nothing. I'll take care of it," he says, walking me to his car. "No one is finding out about us until we want them to."

CHAPTER 19

TRISTAN

Anger ripples through me as I grip the steering wheel of my car. That little prick paparazzo is going to sell the photos to the highest bidder, and I won't have a chance in hell to stop him. Guilt plagues me as I make my way back to the Meat Packing District. I should've never left Emily alone. I glance over to the petite figure sleeping on my right. She sits fast asleep against the car door frame. Her clothes and hair are in sorted disarray, along with her red high heels. Somehow, she managed to break them. I reach out and brush back golden strands from Emily's face. She looks like an angel resting. Any man would be foolish not to see her as a great beauty.

She stirs as I caress her face in my hand. *I would move hell and earth for you.*

I bring Emily back to my studio. She hardly moves as I carry her inside. After a heavy night of drinking and sex, I'm sure I've exhausted her. I grin to myself. At least one can hope. My heart aches as she wraps her arms around me, hugging me closer to her chest. For the first time in a very long time, I feel like the knight in shining armor I know she deserves. Emily sprawls out across my bed leaving little room to lie down. She moans as she rubs her cheek against the cool satin sheets that I cover her with. I wish I could stay and watch her fall asleep, but I have business to attend to.

Still reeling from anger, I find myself back in Greenwich scouring the streets for the paparazzo from earlier. To my surprise, he isn't far off from where he was first taking photos of Emily. I park my car down the street to avoid his detection.

"Hey, asshole!" I yell.

The smug old man turns toward me as he sits inside his yellow sports car. I'm sure the asshole thinks he's going to make a fortune from Emily's photos. I know all too well how the paparazzi ruin lives. Watching them as they did it to Nicholas and Emily was enough pain to last me a lifetime. The man turns to me and flings his cigarette on the pavement. A look of irritation crosses his face as he recognizes me. I'm sure I was the last person he thought he would be seeing.

"You again? What do you want?" he spits.

"I want the photos you took tonight."

He laughs at me in a condescending manner. Fury burns through me as he gives me a look that clearly says 'fuck you.'

"It's all fair and legal. I took those photos on a public sidewalk," he says.

I watch as he slowly steps out of his car and onto the pavement. If I didn't know any better, I'd think he was getting ready to fight me. Sadly, I don't think I'm going to get that opportunity.

"You did and I'm willing to pay you for them."

The paparazzo sneers at me.

"You couldn't afford it."

Prick. I'm willing to bet that my fists can wipe that smile off of his face.

"I can," I challenge.

His skeptical look tells me he isn't buying what I'm saying. I pull a paper with an offer from my pocket and hand it to him. Several years ago, I never would've thought I would be standing here offering a paparazzo a small fortune for pictures. While I would love to see Stefan's face when he finds out about Emily and me, I also know I would be hurting two other people I genuinely care for. Emily and Nicholas.

"She's worth that much to you?"

More. So much more.

"Take it and hand over the digital copies. All of them. Don't even think about synching them somewhere else." I pull a copy of the contract Sebastian Wolfe drew up and emailed to me. It pays to have a friend who practices law. It took Sebastian less than five minutes to send me it. I hate the thought of owing someone a favor, but if I had to choose someone to owe something to, it would be Sebastian Wolfe.

I watch as the paparazzo purses his lips as if considering my offer. A streak of anxiety filters through me at the thought that he might not sell me the photos.

"I want more," he says.

"Look, you greedy little prick, the offer is more than generous…"

A look of boredom encompasses his face as he looks up at me. He slowly swipes his phone and pulls up an album with a dozen or so pictures of Emily. I cringe as he zooms in on a shot of her in her ripped dress. She looks like a wild animal mauled her. The tabloids are going to eat this up. As he swipes through the screen of shots, a hopeless feeling fills my stomach. I could beat the shit out of him and take the photos, but there's no guaranteeing he didn't already upload them somewhere else.

"You were saying?" he smiles.

"How much?" I grimace.

"Eighty grand."

There it is. Something I thought I would never hear.

"You're insane," I growl.

Last week, I sold a painting for twice that amount to a kinkster, but it wasn't long ago that I barely had enough money to buy my bus fare. The paparazzo waits for my response with a shark-like smile. He's more than happy to gouge me for the money. This is definitely payback for punching him in the face.

"Sign the contract, and the money is yours."

He snaps the document from my hand and quickly signs it over without bothering to read any of the fine print Sebastian included. Wolfe would be so disappointed. He loves his fucking contracts.

CHAPTER 20

EMILY

Tristan.

I wake to find myself alone in the bed and Tristan nowhere in sight. My head throbs at the sunlight that cascades in from the windows on the second floor of his studio. God, I drank too much last night.

Embarrassment overwhelms me as memories of my run-in with the paparazzi fill my thoughts. I couldn't admit it to myself last night, but I'm so glad he showed up. I slip the bed covers off me to find myself in nothing but my underwear and pink bra. Somehow, Tristan undressed me and slipped me into bed.

My cheeks flame.

I feel strangely disappointed that it didn't turn into more.

The rest of my clothes from yesterday sit carefully folded in a pile on top of his dresser. I get up to grab them, but to my surprise, my legs are shackled to the bed.

What the hell?

I pull on the metal restraints, but they don't budge. I'm fixed to several inches of cold steel. I'm dumbfounded as to how I got here.

DRAWN TO YOU

Did I sleep like this all night? I scoot on my bottom and then bend my knees to get a closer look at my restraints. After several minutes of trying to pick them open, I give up. Why the hell would Tristan do this?

One word pops into my mind.

Punishment.

A strange electric excitement filters through me as I lay back on the bed in exhaustion. The smell of Tristan lingers over my skin and to my pleasure, his bed sheets as well. Butterflies fill my stomach at the thought of him watching me from another room. My eyes trace his apartment, but Tristan's nowhere to be seen. As I scan the nightstand near the bed, I spot a serving tray and a single card sitting on top of it. At a closer glance, I can just make out Tristan's handwriting...

I told you if I had the chance, I would chain you to my bed. Eat up. You'll need your strength.

P.S. I took care of the photos.

Oh, thank God.

I can't help but wonder what Tristan had to do to get the photos from the paparazzo...

I smile as I re-read the note. Shivers run down my spine at the promise in his words. *You'll need your strength?* My strength for what? An endless amount of possibilities filter through my mind. After last night, I can't help but feel a shiver of excitement run through me. I set down Tristan's card and uncover the silver tray next to me.

What's under here?

I smile at the perfectly crafted omelet that sits at the center of the tray. Even the colors seem to create an artful masterpiece. He cooked for me? I search the nightstand for a fork, but there's none. My stomach growls at the sight of the omelet. You'd think after a night of drinking, my stomach wouldn't want anything. I grab the food with my fingers like a small child and then shovel the delicious breakfast into my mouth without a second thought. A moan escapes me as I take in the taste of bell peppers and pepper jack cheese.

This is one of the best omelets I've ever had.

Thirty minutes later, I'm staring up at the ceiling of Tristan's studio singing to myself as I slowly drift back to sleep.

"Good evening, little one."

My eyes flicker open as a set of hazel eyes looks down at me with a smile. It feels like I haven't seen Tristan in days, but I know it's only been a few hours. *Where was he this whole time?* I sit up as he walks over and sits on the side of the bed next to me. I try to move, but the chains around my ankles restrain me from stepping off the bed. Tristan's eyes look down at my feet and then back at me. He chuckles with vigor.

"What are these for?" I ask annoyed.

"You didn't read the note?"

"Oh, I read it. I also ate that amazing omelet you left me, but I still don't understand why you chained me to your bed."

His gaze darkens with a liquid heat as he grabs my chin and kisses me hard. The taste of mint swirls in his mouth. I open my lips welcoming the taste. He pulls back with an embarrassed look on his face.

"I wanted to make sure you were here when I got back. I couldn't have you changing your mind about us."

I laugh as a slow smile erupts from his lips. I've never seen Tristan this vulnerable. He always seems so sure of himself.

"You didn't even leave me a fork to eat with," I say, hoping to lighten the mood.

"Forks are earned."

He moves, placing his hands on the bed as he leans toward me. I inch back letting him hover over me with his delicious frame. It's only been a few hours, but I'm already needy to be his again. Tristan grabs my wrist and places it over his heart. Beneath all the muscle, it beats in a chaotic rhythm. He leans in and presses his lips to mine. A surge of confidence shoots through me as I tease his lips with my tongue. It only takes a second for Tristan to match my force. He grinds against me as we meld further into the bed. Tristan breaks the kiss and hovers above me watching me with a renewed intensity. His eyes darken as he trails one hand between my breasts and down my pelvis. I arch as his fingers slip over my sex. My thoughts escape me as they concentrate on Tristan's fingers. He sends me in a tizzy as he pinches my clit.

"You're getting wet just thinking about me, aren't you?"

"Yes," I shiver.

His eyes glow with a honey glaze that only seems to intensify his stare. I could melt in those eyes. Wrap myself within them and never look back.

"Do you think about me when you touch yourself?"

My cheeks flame at the bluntness of his question. I can't lie to him. Somehow, I'm convinced he'd know.

"I think about you all the time."

Having sex with Tristan has been one of my recurring fantasies. It always started the same. I'm in my old bedroom, and I can hear him fucking another woman downstairs, but when I get to his room, he's waiting for me, alone. The other woman is gone, or perhaps she never existed. Instead, it's just him and me, and suddenly, I'm the woman he's devouring on top of his bed.

"Good," he says, before crashing his lips against mine again.

Tristan's hand snakes up my neck as he grabs a fistful of my hair. The hairs on the back of my neck rise in excitement as he tugs on my blonde strands. I moan in response and it only encourages him to pull a little harder.

"Tristan?" I ask, breaking the kiss.

"What is it, angel?"

His lips don't stop kissing me even as I gasp for breath. I feel them trail over the side of my face and down my neck. The feeling leaves me in a state of ecstasy. I'm paralyzed as a wave of pleasure washes over me. Each kiss leaves me reeling. Tristan's lips pause just above the top of my breast. I bite back a moan at the loss of his scorching touch. To my surprise, he leans back and loosens the tie around his neck.

"Give me your hands," he commands.

I comply without a second thought. I watch as Tristan wraps his red silk tie around my wrists and then pushes my hands above my head. A hungry look flashes across his face as he sits back, admiring his work.

"Don't move."

A tremor of excitement pulses through me as he leans back. I clench in anticipation as his lips hover over my sex.

"I can't wait to taste you, pet, but I have a feeling once I start, I won't be able to stop."

I blush and then smile as a wicked grin flashes on his handsome face. I close my eyes savoring each time his tongue runs over my sex. At this moment, I feel my most naked. My most vulnerable. And for the first time, I know it'll be okay.

> she is my dark lady, my MUSE.

CHAPTER 21

TRISTAN

"You're going with me to the fundraiser tonight."

Emily turns and smiles as she stands on her tiptoes in the restroom across from my room. She brushes her long blonde hair as she stares at me with a beautiful smile. Her skin glows brightly against the sunshine that filters through the studio. We've spent the last two weeks on a staycation. I convinced her to stay with me despite the need she felt to at least go home and grab clothes. Fortunately, I convinced her that clothing would be optional for this trip.

Every morning, we spend the first hour fucking, then eating, reading, painting, showering, and then in the final hours of sunlight we dance. Despite being good at it, I used to hate dancing, but somehow, it feels natural with her. The last time we danced together, it didn't end so well, but now things are different. Emotions are unrestrained.

"I don't know if I'm going to the fundraiser tonight. I was kind of thinking I would stay here. Maybe watch some RomCom and eat popcorn," she teases.

"And leave me all alone? Whom will I dance with?"

"I'm sure Nicholas has plenty of slots open on his card."

I laugh. "Are you kidding me? He probably won't even make it through dinner without taking someone home."

"He's such a rogue."

"He is."

"Do I detect a sliver of envy?"

"Never," I say, winking at her. "Hey, stay right there."

She smiles as I walk over to my easel and place a blank canvas on it. I sit and begin etching the lines of her silhouette. She stands on her tiptoes likes a dancer as she applies a layer of foundation and mascara. After half an hour, I finish a rough sketch of a new painting. As I stare at the raw sketch, I realize something I hadn't noticed before. Around Emily's neck sits the necklace I gave her all those years ago.

Emily sets down her makeup and then picks up a pair of dangling earrings. She's completely unaware of the emotions running through me as I watch her slowly place each hook into her earlobes. When she's finally done, she turns to me with a broad smile.

"You're still wearing it?" I choke, staring at the necklace.

Her eyes travel down to the top of her chest. She picks up the sterling necklace with her palm.

"It stays with me wherever I go," she admits

Her words hit me like a steel train. I never expected her to keep the necklace on after she had thought I slept with Ceci. I was almost sure I would never see it again, but it's been too painful to even think of asking about it.

The fog clouding my mind lifts as Emily walks over to me and sits on my lap. I've watched the woman I love slip from my fingers over and over again, but I'm not going to make that mistake anymore. I'm going to do the one thing I thought I would never do—chain her to me. I'm going to make this beautiful angel my wife.

Now, if only I can convince her to do it before she changes her mind about us. And about me.

CHAPTER 22

TRISTAN

"Tristan? Aren't we going to the fundraiser?"

I smile at the puzzled look on her face. She really has no idea where I'm taking her. Her eyes peer out the side of the car to the city around us. My heart swells at the breathtaking sight of Emily in her Vera Wang dress. The sheer champagne fabric pops against her aquamarine eyes. She looks like a princess on her way to the ball. God, I hope she feels like a princess tonight.

"We're on our way. Do you have your driver's license on you?"

"Uh, yes. Of course," she says, eyeing me.

"Good."

Emily checks her lipstick as we hit a snag of traffic just outside of the courthouse. The sight of the building is enough to send my body into a fit of sweat. I loosen my bow tie as it sits strangling my neck. My nerves are starting to get the better of me. Where the hell is Augie? I told him to be here at four-thirty p.m. I can only pull so many strings to get the courthouse to stay open later. My heart palpitates as I feel Emily's eyes staring at me. I know she senses something's wrong.

"Tristan, why are we sitting in front of the courthouse? I thought the fundraiser was in Midtown?"

I gulp trying to swallow the lump crawling its way from my chest to my throat. Emily's hands grab my face as she forces me to look at her. Her eyes search mine as if trying to decipher the disaster going on in my mind. God, what if she says no. This is not the way I pictured first doing this, but it just feels so right.

"Are you regretting taking me tonight?" she asks.

Her eyes grow deadly serious. Regret is the last thing I feel when it comes to us.

"No!"

"Then what?"

I struggle to say the words. In my head, this seemed so much easier.

"I want you to marry me."

Her eyes widen as she looks at me and then at the courthouse a few yards in front of her. My heart thumps against my chest as I wait for her to refuse me. This is crazy. She won't ever say yes. She's probably biding her time until she gets tired of me.

"We have to do it quick before the courthouse closes. We need to apply for the certificate and then tomorrow we'll have to—"

"Yes," she says, cutting me off. A rush of tears slips down her face as she looks at me.

"Wait. What?"

"I said, yes!"

Her lips crash into mine as she kisses me like it's my dying wish. She only breaks away from me at the sound of a tap on the window. Augie's face pops into view just before slamming her birth certificate against the tinted window. Perfect! The last piece. Behind Augie, his boyfriend Harvey stands holding a bouquet of lilies.

"Oh, my God. Augie knew before me?"

"Not much more."

She laughs, kneeling to open the door, but I quickly stop her. Her gaze grows serious as she waits for me to speak. It takes what feels like an eternity for me to say the words. My heart catapults as she leans toward me with a smile.

"What is it, Mr. Knight?"

For the first time, I realize Emily won't be the beautiful blonde angel I've known since she was little. She's going to be my wife.

"We won't be able to tell Nicholas or your father. At least not until I open my gallery and get things moving. Not until I know I can provide for you without fearing that your father will ruin everything."

"As long as I have you, I don't care," she says.

"You will. It'll be hard keeping secrets from the ones we love most."

"But I'll keep them."

"Are you sure?" I ask.

My heart hammers against my chest as fear seeps into it. This is a lot to ask.

She laughs. "Why are we still in the car?"

I pull her onto my lap for one last kiss before stepping outside. Emily leans in as she wraps her petite arms around my neck.

"Tristan?"

"Yes, sweetheart?"

Her gaze snaps up at me. A pensive look graces her face before breaking into a mesmerizing smile.

"Do you mind if we say our vows here... I know it's just the application, but—"

"Emily StoneHaven... I promise to protect, honor, and most of all love you."

Her eyes water as she squeezes my hand.

"Tristan Knight...I promise to love you. Honor you. And obey you."

A grin slides up my face.

We both know the obeying part won't be so easy, but she has time to learn.

ALSO BY VANESSA BOOKE

Millionaire's Row Series

Bound to You: Volume 1
Bound to You: Volume 2
Bound to You: Volume 3

Bound to You: The Boxed Set (Volumes 1-3)

Drawn to You: Volume 1
Drawn to You: Volume 2
Drawn to You: Volume 3

MEET THE AUTHOR

Vanessa Booke is a lover of poetry, Rom-Coms, the combination of peanut butter and chocolate, and all things Jane Austen. She is an avid reader and graduate from Cal State University, San Bernardino where she received her Bachelor's degree in English Literature. Vanessa lives in beautiful Southern California with her husband Ryan and their three dachshunds Zer0, Zoey, and Zelda. When she isn't working on her novels, Vanessa spends most of her time window shopping and taking grand adventures with her partner in crime.

Vanessa loves getting emails from her readers.
You can contact her at VanessaBooke@gmail.com.

Connect with Vanessa online:

AuthorVanessaBooke.com
Facebook.com/V.M.Boeke
Twitter.com/VanessaBooke

Printed in Great Britain
by Amazon